Praise for *The Marrying Kind*:

"With its timely, provocative premise, fabulous characters, and a wonderfully wry, sly narrative, *The Marrying Kind* is bound to launch debut novelist Ken O'Neill on a stellar career path!"—Wendy Markham, *New York Times* bestselling author

"*The Marrying Kind* is that rare novel that both prods and applauds our most valuable resource: love. Ken O'Neill makes you laugh, think, and get mad as hell—all within just a few pages. If you believe in hard-won, human romance, this is the book that levels the playing field."—Doug Crandell, author of *The Flawless Skin of Ugly People* and *The Peculiar Boars of Malloy*

"Pleasurable, sophisticated, moving and thought-provoking… and on top of all that I laughed out loud throughout."—Michael Tonello, author of *Bringing Home the Birkin*

"A boisterously funny novel that's topical and political without ever being preachy, *The Marrying Kind* skewers both overt hypocrisy and 'benign neglect' with razor-sharp humor."—Rob Byrnes, Lambda Literary Award–winning author of *When the Stars Come Out*

THE MARRYING KIND

by

Ken O'Neill

A Division of Bold Strokes Books

2012

THIS TRADE PAPERBACK ORIGINAL IS PUBLISHED BY
BOLD STROKES BOOKS, INC.
P.O. BOX 249
VALLEY FALLS, NY 12185

FIRST EDITION: JUNE 2012

CREDITS

EDITORS: GREG HERREN AND STACIA SEAMAN
PRODUCTION DESIGN: STACIA SEAMAN
COVER DESIGN BY SHERI (GRAPHICARTIST2020@HOTMAIL.COM)

Acknowledgments

Writing a novel seems like a solitary enterprise until you begin remembering everyone who has helped you. I am grateful to so many people for making writing feel almost like a team sport.

My agent Katherine Fausset manages to make me feel like I am her only client, which I hope for her sake is not the case. I am filled with gratitude to be represented by her, and to be her friend. She fought tirelessly for this book. It is because of Katherine's perseverance that *The Marrying Kind* found a home. And what a spectacular home. Thank you to everyone at Bold Strokes Books, especially my publisher Len Barot and my editor Greg Herren.

I must thank a few of the early readers whose comments and support helped shape this book: Diane Meier, Aaron Krach, Helen Rogers, and Jennifer Westfeldt. I send love to Diane Domenici for leaving me a tearful message of praise on my answering machine. I listen to it whenever I'm having a bad day. And most especially, I am indebted to Medi Ford. Her thoughts and suggestions made this a much better book.

I thank my parents for their love, and for encouraging me to always say something funny. I appreciate my entire family for their wit and humor, and for providing me with such wonderful source material. I am especially grateful to Sophie Pittu and Carrie Pittu for their assistance with all things Romanian. Alison Russo gives me friendship, love, and makes me funnier. She believed this book would find a home when I did not. Thank you.

I am beholden to the thousands of strangers/friends who have embraced this book, and its message of equality, on Facebook. I'm beholden to many real friends too, especially Ping Fang , Billy Cunningham, Neil Dennehy, and Eric Rayman.

The idea for this novel came to me while watching Oprah. I thank Ms. Winfrey for providing me with my "Aha!" moment.

And finally, I never would have written this book without the love and encouragement of Marcus Edward. For him, thank you does not suffice.

For Marcus

Author's Note

The Marrying Kind was written, and the story is set, in the year 2007. Since that time, there have been several victories in the fight for marriage equality, including the legalization of same-sex marriage in the state of New York. But full equality for all LGBT Americans is still a long way from being achieved. More than thirty states have laws on their books banning the unions. And even in New York, and in the other states that recognize same-sex marriage, the Defense of Marriage Act (DOMA) makes those weddings illegal in the eyes of the United States federal government.

Sadly, Steven and Adam, and all same-sex couples, continue to be denied the 1,138 federal rights and responsibilities of marriage that are afforded straight couples.

Ken O'Neill
October 3, 2011

CHAPTER ONE: MY NAME IS STEVEN WORTH, BUT I AM NOT A WASP

On Monday, the first of September, 1980, Raggedy Andy and I were tucked into my bed, spooning and sleeping. The ever-smiling Andy was dressed in his classic attire: sailor's cap atop his flaming-red curls, red and white checkerboard shirt, and blue khaki pants cropped at a very sporty capri-length. I was coordinated in red, white, and blue flannel pajamas. Mine, however, were standard trouser length. I was hatless.

Without warning, a sudden intrusion fell upon our delicious slumber. Something warm and moist crept across my face. I startled, gasped, smelled the familiar blend of coffee, olive oil, oregano, and Jean Naté.

My mother, Onda, was waking me with kisses to my cheeks and forehead.

"Honey, it's five thirty in the morning. You know what that means?"

What that meant was that it was time for me to get up and join her in watching the last twelve hours of the Jerry Lewis Labor Day Telethon. Being only six, I'd been allowed to sleep during the evening hours of the show. My mother, however, had kept vigil with Jerry, not missing a moment of the spectacle. Now, raring to go, she wanted company.

"Steven, hurry!" Onda shouted as she tickled me. For a woman who'd been awake for close to twenty-four hours, my mother was surprisingly animated.

Then, in less time than it took me to rub the sleep from my eyes, my mother's energy abandoned her. I watched as she shrank in front of me. Her chest caved, her shoulders slumped. She bit her top lip and grimaced. With voice quavering, she spoke. "Honey, I'm very sorry to have to be the one to tell you this: She...she's already performed. You missed Lola Falana." She trailed off at the end of Ms. Falana's name in an effort to defuse the sting.

Then Onda inhaled mournfully, clutched me to her chest, and awaited the arrival of my disappointment. It never came. Not surprising, really, as I had no idea who Lola Falana was.

"Cheer up!" she said, loosening her grip. Somehow she mistook my look of bewilderment for one of bereavement. My mother's stature and voice were now fully restored. She was ecstatic once again. "There are still a lot of good people left. Charo's up next!"

With that, my mother snatched Andy from my grip and tossed him aside. He crashed against my hippity hop, which I was no longer allowed to play with as a result of my mother's recent dream featuring me with my arm in a sling. Andy sailed across the room, Wallenda style, finally coming to rest against my Easy-Bake Oven. Throughout his perilous flight, Andy remained placid. Never once did his smile waver.

With one quick tug, the covers were pulled from me. My mother, in a never-to-be-repeated moment of abandon, left the blankets in a heap, neglecting to make the bed. She whisked me into her arms. Clenching me tightly, she rushed through the hallway. When we passed my baby brother's room, I peered in. His bed was empty.

"Where's Peter?" I asked, still distracted by concerns for Andy's welfare.

"Honey, remember? Maia and Papu are babysitting. It's just you and me! We're having a special mother-son weekend." My mother picked up her pace as she raced down the two flights of stairs to our finished basement. We arrived just as Charo delivered her first *Cuchi-Cuchi*.

I tried to wiggle from my mother's hold so I could sprawl across the lush goldenrod and olive green shag carpet. But Onda had a different idea. She placed me right beside her on the sofa. And there I sat—except for a few brief timeouts for snacks and the bathroom, all timed to coincide with the Love Network's station breaks—until Ed McMahon announced the fund-raiser's final tally.

At some point, late in the proceedings, I'd grown restless and had begun fidgeting. My legs were starting to cramp from the hours of immobility. I wanted to get off the couch.

My mother, in what would develop into an ongoing routine, looked at me and sobbed. "Sit still, Steven. Do you know how lucky *I* am? *I'm* so lucky. You could be one of Jerry's kids." Then she paused.

Her tearing eyes widened. "Oh. My. God." She began making the sign of the cross. "God. Forbid. What have I said?" She spat in my face.

I wiped the spittle away and fidgeted once again.

My mother's tears vanished; she began giggling at the men on screen. "Honey, you're going to love this. Don't move. Please, sit. Watch the Smothers Brothers."

I sat. I watched. I didn't understand their humor.

For a woman whose greatest fear was having a crippled child, my mother really seemed to enjoy having me glued to a chair.

❖

This past Labor Day, that memory came rushing back to me, from whatever lobe of the brain is responsible for repressing childhood miseries, when my boyfriend Adam innocently flipped on the telethon.

We had been together for six years, but in previous years we'd always visited our friends Malcolm and Jack at their Fire Island beach house over the holiday weekend. They refuse to own a television, arguing that it's a poison that destroys our reason, imagination, and creative souls. Maybe. But my counter is *Desperate Housewives* really is a hoot.

With Malcolm and Jack away on their honeymoon, Adam and I found ourselves at home in our mid-century-modern, Upper West Side two-bedroom, equipped with a flat screen and 249 channels.

I was in the kitchen making a tequila, lime, and chili marinade for the pork tenderloin I was grilling that night, when I heard Adam shouting.

"Honey, hurry. Come out here!"

I rushed into the living room still holding the bottle of Cuervo and found Adam sitting on the couch, staring at the TV.

"Honey, sit. It's the telethon. Charo's up next."

The bottle slipped from my grip and smashed against the oak floor that we paid a fortune to have refinished last year. "Please, God! No!" I cried at the sight of Jerry welcoming an eerily unchanged Charo to the stage.

Melodramatic, even for me.

Adam dropped the TV remote and shook his head. "Am I to assume from your response that, unlike the French, you do not consider Mr. Lewis a comic genius?"

He helped clean up the mess, picking up shards of glass that had sprayed across the room, as I shared with him some of my past telethon experiences. Adam seemed especially keen to hear me describe how my mother would join Jerry in performing Rodgers and Hammerstein's heart-wrenching "You'll Never Walk Alone." My mother's voice, a nuanced, earthy alto, would remain strong when Jerry's emotions got the best of him. Jerry, live from the Sahara Hotel in Las Vegas, faltered and wept. But my mother, live from the Finished Basement in Bridgeport, single-handedly carried the number to its rousing conclusion.

By breakfast the next morning, my "Please, God! No!" had become another in a long line of shared inside jokes. A repeated response to any question either Adam or I asked.

"Want some oatmeal, sweetheart?" I asked as Adam entered the kitchen.

"Please, God! No!" Followed by several minutes of Adam's infectious giggling.

Later I would realize that morning was the last time I heard his laughter for a very long time. On that Tuesday after Labor Day things started to change for Adam. A melancholy washed over him that I didn't understand.

During our breakfast of steel-cut oats with bananas, dried cherries, and walnuts, I was still blissfully unaware of Adam's burgeoning discontent. He must not have been showing any signs of the unhappiness he was feeling. Had he been, I feel certain I would have seen them. Growing up around my mother's undulating moods, I've become a divining rod of despair. Sussing it out before the first lip has quivered or Xanax prescription's been filled.

We ate. We managed to sneak in "Please, God! No!" three or four more times. Adam gave the kids kisses on the tops of their heads. I got one on the lips. He grabbed his portfolio and was off to another busy workday as a wedding planner. He was scheduled to meet with a couple that had decided on throwing a barn-raising in lieu of a more traditional reception. Adam was thrilled by the novelty of it and had planned a totally over-the-top Amish-inspired event. Think *Witness*. Just add electricity and shrimp remoulade, and remove Harrison Ford and those unflattering hats.

I cleared the dishes, cleaned up the kitchen, and got ready for work.

As far as I could tell, everything was fine with Adam.

And everything was fine with me. I'm sure of that because I left our apartment that morning wearing a pair of Lucky Brand Jeans. Obviously, I could not have been feeling too insecure if I made the choice to pull on a pair of low-rise pants.

I stood on the sidewalk in front of our building. The air, by Manhattan standards, was clear. The temperature was in the upper eighties, but it wasn't particularly humid. It felt and smelled much more like July than September. Loving the heat, I found this weather extremely pleasant for a second or two until *An Inconvenient Truth* started rerunning through my brain.

Panic began setting in as I recalled each and every time I'd failed to recycle or turn off a light switch when I walked out of a room. It was hot today because I alone was responsible for destroying the ozone layer. For me, these sorts of thoughts are typical.

And are generally followed by a wave of crippling despair.

But, miraculously, gloom did not come crashing down on me.

Uncharacteristically, I decided to remain focused on the present. Today it was beautiful. The warm breeze, blowing east from the Hudson, energized me. Its current sparked along my spine and sent tingles deep into my limbs. It was a sort of full-body excitement I've experienced only a few times before: the day I met Adam, the blustery February morning we brought the kids home, and the time I found myself standing first in line at the Prada sample sale.

With spirits high, and humidity low, and not being particularly eager to get to work, I decided to forgo the subway and walk from our apartment on West End Ave. and Seventy-eighth to the newsroom on Eleventh and Thirty-sixth. I tracked the journey by landmarks I passed along the way. There was Lincoln Center, Starbucks, Roosevelt Hospital, another Starbucks, the Amish Market, two more Starbucks, and hundreds of little shops, cafés, delis, and more Starbuckses, which lined the streets from the Upper West Side down through Hell's Kitchen.

When all signs of life, any vestige of anything that could remotely be considered part of a neighborhood, disappeared, I knew I had arrived. Such is the lot for those of us working in the far west thirties. It's a place so vacant no one's ever bothered to give it a name. A land beyond the borders of Chelsea; Hell's Kitchen will have no part of it. When I tell lifelong New Yorkers where I work, they pause a moment, thinking, trying to conjure up an association that refuses to come. Sometimes, in the process, a forehead is scratched. Eventually they give up, an unspoken *huh?* forms on their lips. Then they look past me with muddled stares that seem to say *I don't believe I've ever been there.*

I scanned the façade of the tenement building housing the newspaper where I work. It's undistinguished. There are no moldings or carvings; no gargoyles or griffins fly from the side. There is only filthy brick, which once, long ago, was presumably brown. Now it's soot black, so dark and evenly stained that it takes a moment for me to realize that a Goth decorator has not recently painted the place.

Inside, through a front door that hasn't locked since the last time INS broke it down, I began my five-flight climb. Floor one: Fine Time Apparel—Men, Floor two: Fine Time Apparel—Women. These establishments would loosely be described as *fashion houses*, and were, I guess, Immigration's destination when they came calling, unannounced, through our front door. The third floor is the studio of a sculptor named Thomas Brian James-Allen, whose works are made out of deer fencing, papier-mâché, and his own sloughed-off skin. The fourth floor is vacant and available for rent.

Previously, it housed a private investigator by the name of Vic Spiegel. Alas, while in pursuit of a philandering husband, the PI tracked said philanderer back to the Spiegel household—whereupon Vic's wife opened the door and greeted the philanderer wrapped only in Saran. Mr. Spiegel took this as a sign that it was time to change professions, and spouses, and is now doing chakra rebalancing in Santa Fe. I heard this story from Thomas Brian James-Allen, one afternoon while he was busy exfoliating, so I'm not sure if it's true or not.

Finally, slightly winded, I arrived on the fifth floor and stared at the paper's logo on the front door: An enormous "G" followed by a miniscule "n y t."

I could put it off no longer; it was time for work.

I'm a columnist for *The Gay New York Times*—I beg of you, do not get me started on that name. It's a free weekly and I'm responsible for the mindless, fluffy human-interest pieces. I'm kind of like Dave Barry except I'm queer and no one's ever heard of me. I'm blessed with the freedom to write about anything I want, and since the world is filled with enough bad news, I choose to keep my articles very "light," reporting (if you can call it that) on fashion trends, food, life at the gym, and of course, my favorite and most frequent topic, the idiosyncrasies of myself and my family members.

As the regular readers of my column—at last count there were seventeen of you—already know, I am always with my family and therefore have plenty to write about. My family is my constant source of—oh, there are so many ways I could end this sentence, but I'll play it safe and say—inspiration.

For those of you who don't count yourself among my seventeen loyal fans, perhaps now would be a good time to highlight some of the columns I've written over the years that I am most proud of. Don't worry; it's a rather short list.

My debut column was titled: "My Name Is Steven Worth, But I Am Not A WASP."

In it, I described what it's like going through life with an Anglican last name when you are in fact a second-generation Macedonian-Romanian American, raised in the Orthodox Church. If you're trying to solve that riddle, Worth was the last name of my English paternal grandfather. However, my other three grandparents—last names Batsu, Nastu, and Nastu (don't ask)—were all Romanians.

I have probably written fifty columns about my boyfriend, Adam More—an actual WASP, a very successful wedding planner and the owner of More Weddings. My favorite piece about him was called: "Adam More, Son of a Daughter of the American Revolution." It chronicled the day I discovered Madras pants hanging in his closet. He claimed they were only worn in the country; I had my doubts.

Without question, the story that garnered the greatest number of responses (I printed and saved all six e-mails) had to do with Adam and me fixing up our straight siblings. For those of you who've been patiently waiting for an update: Yes, my brother Peter and Adam's sister Amanda are still very happily cohabitating. Suggesting—if we can draw conclusions from just the four of us—that the English/Romanian, More/Worth, combination is a good one.

And that concludes the highlights of over four years of work.

It is somewhat sobering to discover that I've been able to summarize my entire journalistic career in fewer words than I generally devote to a single column—but there you have it.

And there I found myself, standing in the newsroom. A slight hint of tobacco lingered in the air, left over from some past decade when people still smoked indoors. I surveyed the room. Even the full-spectrum lightbulbs could not manage to raise the illumination beyond the level of murky. It might come as a surprise to learn that the office has three walls of floor-to-ceiling windows. Unfortunately, the windows all face the airshafts of neighboring, taller structures, offering a constant reminder of both the possibility and impossibility of ever seeing natural light. If there's a special hell for the sufferers of Seasonal Affective Disorder, I work there.

Adding to the darkness, the main office area is crammed with a half dozen ancient, massive, solid mahogany desks, so cumbrous that I can't imagine anyone carrying them up five flights of stairs. Two of the desks are used solely for storage; a third holds the coffeemaker— which is practical, as we rarely have more than three people in at any one time. Everything in the room is thick, solid and musty. Whoever was responsible for the décor obviously missed the key word in the name of our publication.

I glanced at my desk; it seemed larger somehow than the others. Perhaps because there was virtually nothing on it—not a scrap of paper, no pens, nothing, except for a computer. This, I must confess, is not an indication of my organizational skills. But rather, my complete lack of productivity.

But today would be different; today I would finish a column. I stopped by the coffee desk and poured a mug. I then made my way over to my pristine, slightly warped desk. I started my computer and sipped the black coffee, hoping in vain that I'd be able to string together the few hundred words required of me so that I could end my torment and complete my assignment.

Fortunately for me, I remembered that while I was still in the civilization of Hell's Kitchen, I'd stopped off at a bakery and was therefore in possession of what I like to call my creative muse. I placed the bakery bag gently on my desk. Opened it, peered inside. It contained the key to my divine inspiration: the carrot muffin. I could smell it; I could almost taste it.

But I closed the bag quickly because I heard footsteps coming toward me.

Brad Barrett, my boss and the editor of *The Gay New York Times*, was standing right behind me casting his hunky shadow across my blank computer screen. "Take a look at *this*, Gail," he said.

As if by magic, Gail seemed to instantly appear next to Brad. Gail, an ardent feminist, would kill me for beginning a description of her this way: She's a bombshell. She's got Lauren Bacall's husky voice purring within Jane Russell's body. Should you care to look up the word "hourglass" in your Webster's you will notice that it says: See Gail. Her astonishing curves alone could almost make me straight. Which wouldn't do me any good, since she's a lesbian. In the '50s, with her voluptuous frame, Gail could have been a movie star. She would, however, have decked Mr. Mayer if he tried showing her his casting couch.

I consider Gail one of my closest friends. In addition to her obvious sex appeal, she's funny, smart, opinionated, and loyal. But she can also be a bit of a bully. Those aggressive tendencies were on display today.

"Steven, I see that once again you haven't written anything."

"Good morning, Gail."

She ignored my salutation. "We've talked about this," Gail said, making a big show of studying her watch and tapping at it with her crooked finger, as if she was my tormentor-slash-supervisor instead of my pal-slash-colleague.

Gail thrust her watch in front of my eyes and asked, "Are you aware of the time?"

"Are you aware that I just arrived?" Considering it was 10:45, this did not exactly help my case.

She proceeded to deliver a tough-love motivational speech designed to get me to write.

It didn't work.

Instead, I pulled my carrot muffin out of the bag and began eating. Forget Gail's quasi-inspirational lecture, I needed the kind of encouragement one can only receive from a bread product.

"What is that?"

"*Please*, Brad."

"Don't *please Brad* me. What is that?"

This is a pattern with us. We bicker like an old married couple. Perhaps that's because Brad was my first boyfriend. We met at the University of Connecticut. I was a freshman undergraduate and Brad was in the master's program. He was the teaching assistant in my contemporary fiction class. He was dashing and sophisticated and he had about him a sense of calm that only comes from having vast amounts of inherited wealth. But we were not meant to be. Our relationship was doomed to failure because I couldn't cope with the difference in our ages, which at eighteen and twenty-five seemed enormous and insurmountable to me. Now that we are thirty-three and forty, the seven-year age difference seems like such a silly reason for a breakup, especially with so many better—*far better*—reasons to leave Brad.

"What are you eating, Steven?" He just refused to let it drop.

"I am eating a muffin, Brad."

"You are not! You are eating the Big Lie."

"Excuse me?"

"The muffin," Brad explained, "is the Big Lie. It was invented by a man—"

"Or woman," Gail said in her biggest, loudest Gail voice.

"Or woman, who was—"

"Or transgender person." Gail loves messing with Brad's head.

"May I?" Brad directed this question to Gail. She nodded; he continued: "The muffin was invented by a *person* who was looking for a socially acceptable way to eat cake for breakfast.*"*

I sank my teeth into the Big Lie. Even under Brad's scornful glance it was tasty.

"Want a bite?" I asked after swallowing.

"Do you know what's in that?"

"I don't want to know, Brad."

He didn't care. He told me anyway.

"Sugar, white flour, and saturated fat."

Brad and all eight-packs of his flawless torso choked on the word "fat," as if even uttering the word might have some negative effect upon his body, or as he prefers calling it, his "temple."

Brad walked away, having given up on me.

Gail also considered me a lost cause. She returned to her behemoth desk, every inch of it stacked with papers and files, and instantly her fingers began flying across her keypad in a style more reminiscent of channeling than writing. I assumed this was another attempt to shame me into productivity. As I gawked at her two-hundred-word-per-minute typing, she tossed me a quick glance, shook her head, and raised her eyeballs heavenward. "You're not writing, Steven!"

More tough love.

Gail was being combative. Regrettably, I responded by instantly feeling like my eleven-year-old self again. I was fat and on the playground. Any second the kids would be yelling and taunting me with, "Hey! It's Steven Worth-*Less*."

I sensed I was about to start traveling down the dysfunctional memory lane of my husky-pants-wearing youth. I couldn't let that happen. I shut down my computer; I hadn't written a word, so there was no need to hit Save.

"Gail, I'll be working from home today."

"I'll believe it when I see it."

"I will."

"Promise," her voice pleaded.

Gail's not prone to begging, but I understood why she was doing it now. My column was my only responsibility. She managed everything else. Despite the fact that Brad was the editor, and that it was his trust fund that kept us afloat, Gail was the one who really ran the show. She had a hand in virtually every story that went to print. *The Gail New York Times* is what we should be called.

"Promise," I assured her.

❖

Not that I was looking for diversions, but one must eat. I decided to stop off at Citarella for groceries on my way home. Writing was my top priority, though, so I planned to make something quick and simple for dinner: grilled grouper with my homemade tapenade, sautéed Swiss chard, and roasted fingerling potatoes with shallots and garlic. Yum! One of Adam's favorite suppers.

Being Protestant, Adam never actually ate before we met. I mean he ate hors d'oeuvres and Welsh rarebit, but not anything I'd consider a meal. Now that I've been cooking for him all these years, that's changed. He appreciates good food as much as I do.

Over the six years of our relationship, I've seen how we've affected and changed each other in all sorts of little ways, not just culinary. Fortunately we haven't become one of those couples who start resembling each other physically—well, we are both lean and muscular. But all gay guys are lean and muscular. I suppose, with the exception of Adam's inexplicable fondness for resort casual, that we also dress similarly. But all gay guys dress similarly. Aside from the bodies and the shared fashion sense, Adam and I look nothing alike. He's tall with dirty blond hair, blue, bordering-on-Elizabeth Taylor–violet eyes, and a chest and back that are hairless. I'm of average height, black hair, brown eyes, and... Well, I'm hairless, too.

But I've spent a fortune achieving that effect.

In matters of personality we're quite different. He's very hard working and driven to succeed. I believe I've already demonstrated that I'm not. I'm anxious and moody in a charming sort of way. Adam is calm and generally optimistic.

I was thinking about Adam and his sweet, even-keeled personality, when I entered our apartment that afternoon, Citarella bags in hand, and discovered him sitting on the sofa, looking forlorn and weeping silently. I was shocked.

I dropped the bags and ran to him. "Honey?" I asked, speaking in a shorthand that I thought would prompt him to explain what was wrong.

It didn't. His tears continued.

Perhaps a different endearment might elicit a response. "Sweetheart?"

Nothing.

I tried an actual question. "Are you sick?"

"No," Adam whispered as he dried his eyes.

"What happened?"

"Nothing. I just needed a break. I'm so tired."

That didn't explain the tears, but it was certainly understandable. Adam was reaching the end of his busiest season. He'd worked non-stop since May, planning at least twenty weddings.

"Once you're through this month things will quiet down a little."

"I just need some rest."

"Of course you do," I said, wrapping him in my arms. It occurred to me that maybe something beyond fatigue was troubling him. But I had no idea what it might be. And then, since I was raised to believe nothing is more comforting then food, I added, "I'm grilling grouper tonight."

He brightened slightly. "With tapenade?"

"With tapenade."

Adam's lips curled up at the corners, hinting at a smile. "Maybe I'll go take a nap with the kids."

"Excellent idea."

I kissed him and watched as he slowly began shuffling out of the room. He stopped, turned to look at me. "I don't suppose you're tired?"

I wasn't. Not any more than usual. "As a matter of fact, I am," I responded.

"Care to join me?"

I nodded.

I could always write later.

❖

Even with a two-hour nap, Adam had no problem falling asleep that night. This was not really surprising, as he's the soundest sleeper in the world. From our first night together, he has fallen asleep within thirty seconds of hitting the pillow. And I, to say the least, have not.

On my worst nights, I toss and turn, envious of his effortless rest. Nine hours later, he awakes refreshed; I awake desperate for coffee. At least on this night, I wasn't fretting about my insomnia. I was taking great pleasure in the sight of my beautiful family enjoying deep, peaceful slumber. The kids were in bed with us, too. Curled up, side by side, between Adam's thighs. Before you consider contacting Child Services, I should probably let you know that our kids are cats.

There's an old, sentimental Irving Berlin song called "Count Your Blessings (Instead of Sheep)." I've loved the song since the first time I heard Bing Crosby sing it in *White Christmas*. As I gazed at Adam, I found the song running through my mind. I began making my own list of blessings. At some point during my counting, just like Adam and the kids, I was sleeping, too.

And there we stayed, until Adam had the nightmare.

CHAPTER TWO:
TELL ME WHAT YOU DREAMT

I was roused from my slumber by the sound of Adam's screams.

They were bloodcurdling. I never understood that expression before, as I thought curdling was something only dairy products did. But when you've heard a sound like that, had it rip you from your own sweet dream—a dream featuring not only Nate Berkus but Anderson Cooper, too—you understand how a sound, a scream, can literally sour your blood. Okay, not literally. But I *was* terrified.

I was not half as terrified as my poor distressed and disoriented partner. He was bolt up in bed, crying and shaking. I'd never witnessed such a thing. He sat, staring at me, drenched in sweat, looking as if he'd been privy to a guided tour of the apocalypse.

I held Adam tightly in my arms, felt his smooth, hard flesh. Gazed at the sinuous ripples of his biceps—perhaps not the appropriate time to focus on such things, but I had just been dreaming of Nate and Anderson. I pushed those boys out of my head and focused solely on Adam. "Sweetheart, it was just a bad dream. You're here with me and Vincent and Theo."

Actually, Vincent and Theo, our kids, had scurried under the bed when Adam started wailing. I was sure they were with us in spirit, though. Vincent was born with only one ear, which makes him devastatingly handsome; I can't explain why, perhaps it's the asymmetry. Theo's a looker, too, of course. I don't play favorites.

"Adam, can you remember the dream?" I asked.

He nodded, sobbed bitterly.

"Tell me what you dreamt. We'll figure it out."

"I was at the office. Vanessa and Max were there, too. We were planning a wedding." He stopped, unable to say more.

"Honey, that makes sense, doesn't it? You are a wedding planner, after all."

"That's not the bad part. The phone started ringing. We were all moving in slow motion, desperate to get to it in time. It seemed to take forever to reach it. Vanessa and I got there at the same instant, but I wrestled the receiver from her hand."

"That's so butch."

"I know. Right?"

Vincent and Theo jumped back on the bed; they didn't want to be left out of the 3:00 A.M. story hour. Vincent, my sweet boy (I really don't play favorites), climbed into my lap. Adam scooped up Theo and continued his tale: "I clutched the receiver and I said…hello." Adam paused here, as if saying "hello" when answering a phone was some novel expression that he'd just coined. His tears returned. "Do you know who was on the other end of the line?"

I shook my head. We weren't going to be playing twenty questions on that one.

"It was Laura Bush. Can you believe that? She asked *me* to plan Jenna's wedding."

"And you woke up screaming." It made perfect sense to me.

"No. I was really excited. I mean, I was ecstatic. It felt like my moment had arrived. You know? All this time, I've been so close to it—to becoming a famous celebrity-wedding planner. It's all I've ever wanted. But I never quite get the A-list jobs. I'm always B+. Gosh! I thought when I did *The View*—"

I pulled Adam even closer to me, pecked him on the mouth. If he started analyzing why his appearance on *The View* had not been his ticket to fame, we'd be up all night. It was a tender kiss; it seemed to calm him, and it brought us back to the subject at hand.

"A lot of stuff happened in the dream that I can't remember, but I know Vanessa, Max, and I did an amazing job. We created a spectacular event."

"Then when did it turn into a nightmare?"

Adam thought. Already the dream was vanishing. "I guess…Well, at some point Barbara Bush came in. And just as I began helping her with her pearls, I woke up screaming."

That would do it.

I began asking questions, hoping I could help Adam remember the missing parts of the dream.

Adam had a flash: "I can see myself. I'm alone with Jenna, and… I'm lacing her corset. She's got a tight grip on one of the posts of her bed."

I sensed that this might be beyond my skills of dream interpretation, but I persevered. "Can you remember anything else?"

"Like what?"

"I don't know. What about the clothes?"

Adam thought, petted Theo; she purred. "Jenna has a crinoline on. No. No, it's the frame of a hoop skirt."

The image was familiar to me, but I wasn't quite placing it. "What about you? What are you wearing?"

"I'm in my gray Prada suit."

"The pin stripe?"

"Honey, the pin stripe is Dolce and Gabbana," Adam said, aghast at my sartorial slip. "The Prada's gray flannel."

"I love that flannel on you."

"It's the way it drapes. The line is sensational."

And we were off, talking fashion for at least five minutes. Finally, I pulled us back to the mystery we were trying to solve. "We should go back to the dream. Remember anything else?"

"No," Adam said decisively. But then another flash: "That's funny…I have a red *schmata* tied on my head."

I saw it clearly then: saw the whole scene as if I'd dreamt it myself. When was the last time we saw that movie?

I wanted to tell Adam the origin of his dream, but I lost my chance. He'd fallen back to sleep, Theo still cradled in his arms. Vincent climbed out of my lap and pressed himself along Adam's back. What a tender picture, my three angels spooned tightly together. Two purrs. One snore.

I was wide-awake wondering what on earth had caused Adam to dream that he was Hattie McDaniel in *Gone With the Wind*. And why on earth had he cast Jenna Bush as Miss Scarlett O'Hara?

Insomnia had once again set in, so I began scanning my memory, going over recent events, looking for clues. And then I remembered Malcolm and Jack.

❖

Because of Adam's profession, I spent most of my weekends alone while he worked around the clock. I'd gotten used to his schedule and had even grown to appreciate the perks of having date night on a Tuesday. Even without booking a month in advance, there was always a table available at a nice restaurant. If we had a whim, at the very last minute, we could easily find a pair of tickets to a Broadway show. And after the show, it was never a problem hailing a cab.

Still, I was excited that on a Saturday, *the official date night*, Adam and I would be going out together like normal people. It was the Saturday of Labor Day weekend and Adam's schedule was completely free. He'd actually turned down a few jobs for that day. Our friends, Malcolm and Jack, had decided to make their decade-long relationship official by tying the knot. We had no intention of missing the event.

I can't remember anything out of the ordinary during the service. We sat with our siblings, Peter and Amanda—our lives are so intertwined that we have huge overlap in our friendships. I don't even recall how they came to know Malcolm and Jack, but it must have been through us.

It may have been nearly autumn, but the temperature, even with my preference for tropical conditions, was beyond oppressive. It had passed ninety degrees by eleven in the morning; I could hear Al Gore whispering in my ear that it was all my fault. The four of us sat in a pew in St. Luke's Episcopal, about a third of the way back from the altar. The quaint, charming old church relied on windows and ceiling fans for cooling, creating a Sahara-like breeze so intensely hot that the bouquets had shriveled and the unlit beeswax altar candles began melting, bending until they snapped in two.

Amanda and my brother fell instantly into heatstroke-induced sleep. Only the rise in their chests assured me they were still alive.

I looked at Adam. He was dripping sweat; I was, too. We dripped through the readings, the hymns, the sermon and the vows. The ink from the programs we were using as fans bled onto our sweltering palms. It was an endless service.

When it was finally over, we roused our siblings and escaped to the sidewalk. I asked only Adam what he thought of the ceremony, since obviously Peter and Amanda had seen none of it. Adam paused a moment. "I didn't think it would be so…"

"Hot?" Amanda panted, oblivious to the fact that she was in a spaghetti-strap sundress while the three of us were being boiled alive in worsted-wool suits.

"No," Adam said.
"Long?" I asked.
Adam thought a moment. "Traditional."

❖

The air-conditioning was running on high at the University Club. The room was beautiful, as were many of the guests. Jack had spent years in the Netherlands working in international finance, and the room was swarming with gorgeous, gay Dutchmen.

At our table, Peter, Amanda, Adam, and I were joined by six of them—each one taller, blonder, and more fair-skinned than the next. Even Adam and Amanda—who between them own the entire Lilly Pulitzer collection—looked vaguely ethnic in comparison.

You know how Emilio Estevez and Charlie Sheen look nothing alike, and yet they both manage to look exactly like their father, Martin? It's the same with Adam and Amanda—I don't mean to suggest they look like Martin Sheen. (Well, you could make a case that their ears are reminiscent.) What I mean is Adam and Amanda don't resemble each other. Yet, when you compare them with photos of their late father, Prescott, you can instantly connect the dots and see the similarities.

Looking at Adam from the nose up, he's the spitting image of his dad. Adam has the same sharp, hawk nose, Wilhelmina Agency cheekbones, billboard-height forehead and, most strikingly, Adam's you-must be-wearing-colored-contact eyes are an exact duplicate of Prescott's.

Amanda received the lower half of her face from her father. The jaw and chin, which were too small, curved and soft on Prescott, are, on Amanda, simultaneously strong and feminine. Without a doubt, it's the dazzling lips that were Amanda's richest inheritance from her father. They're so full and large that it seems incomprehensible that the effect was achieved without the aid of injectables. Beneath the movie star lips hide perfectly straight, oversized teeth, which are constantly being revealed in easy, effortless smiles.

I watched Amanda offer her gregarious grin as she elegantly extended her hand in greeting to the Dutchman named Joop, who was seated to her left. She immediately announced that she was on the faculty at Columbia in the woman's studies program, and that she taught a course on the history of marriage—an institution she disapproved of. And then the smile dropped and the lecture began. She went as far as saying she couldn't understand why anyone would enter into this antiquated institution designed to enslave women. "Did you know that there are cultures that force widows—*force them!*—to have sex with the relatives of their deceased husbands?"

"I didn't know that," Joop said with a mix of politeness and distress.

I found Amanda's comments completely inappropriate, in light of where we were; I considered kicking her under the table, but she's not *my* sister. Adam finally shut her up by pointing out to the Netherlanders that the magnificent wedding cake on display in the center of the room had been designed and baked by my brother, Peter. My brother remained quiet; he gets a little shy when praise is being heaped upon him, which is becoming more and more common. He's the owner of the bakery Great Cakes. Recently, Barry Diller and Diane Von Furstenberg ordered one of Peter's creations, and suddenly Great Cakes has become *the* cake of *the* moment.

The talk at the table turned to sweets, which, unless you're surrounded by a bunch of hypoglycemics, is always a safe topic.

I don't believe any of us had ever attended a reception as grand as this one—not even Adam, who attends weddings about forty-five weeks a year. The dinner was seven courses with French service. The swing band had eighteen pieces and two singers. That way, the entire band never had to stop performing. Individual musicians would step out for breaks, leaving the rest playing. The Venetian table held forty-six different desserts. I tried nine of them and regretted it later.

It was a wedding like none I had ever attended before. Malcolm and Jack had worked very hard to make everything "the best," and—depending on how you define it—everything was.

They each had their own best man; Malcolm's friend Paul was his. Paul spoke first and gave a completely acceptable, if totally unmemorable I-wish-you-a-life-of-happiness speech.

Jack had a Dutch friend named Joop as his best man. All of the men from our table, including the other guy named Joop, seemed to know him; they cheered when he stood. He was considerably older than the hotties at our table (I guessed mid-fifties) but he was just as striking as all the other Dutchmen in the room.

He stood a minute or two before saying anything. Just as restlessness was about to overtake the crowd, he spoke:

"I'm very happy to be here for Jack and Malcolm. I'm from

Amsterdam, and it's delightful to come and be with my friends in New York. Four years ago, after twenty-one years together, Rijk and I got married, and Malcolm and Jack, you both were there. Thank you. It was different, of course, from today: no band, definitely not so much food."

At this, the crowd began laughing and Joop waited a moment before he began speaking again. "The other big difference, of course, is that we actually got married. We waited many years, but now we're really, *legally* married." Joop raised his glass as many of the guests began squirming awkwardly in their seats. "My promise to Malcolm and Jack," he continued, "is that I will begin and end every day of my life praying to God that someday you will be able to get married, too."

An uncomfortable silence fell over the room. Joop had said what no one else would. What most of the rest of us had not even thought of.

Finally, someone started a bit of polite applause for Joop as he sat.

The band quickly started playing "It's Raining Men." It was an obvious and stereotypical choice, but it did get the crowd to the dance floor.

I glanced at Adam, who was in no mood for dancing. "As soon as they cut the cake, we're out of here," he whispered.

❖

Could Joop's toast have been the catalyst for Adam's traumatic dream? It didn't seem possible. It's not as if Joop said anything we didn't already know. Of course it was true that Malcolm and Jack didn't have a legally binding marriage. But the reason we'd all come together was to celebrate their spiritual union. That's what I found so moving. They made a decision to commit to each other before God and their families. As far as I was concerned, it was as real a ceremony as I'd ever witnessed.

❖

I sat up in bed, quietly watching my number-one angel (the snorer, not one of the two purrers). He was sleeping soundly now. No sign of that earlier disturbance. I'd have to keep close watch on Adam. Something was wrong—I felt it. I wanted to curl up behind him, comfort him, but little Vince wasn't having it. I curled up behind him instead, blew his fur out of my mouth.

Four spoons.

Snug.

CHAPTER THREE:
AND YOU HATE ME WHY?

Each morning that I awoke after an uninterrupted night's sleep, finding the four of us entwined together, I became a little more hopeful that Adam's dream had been a fluke. Neither one of us mentioned the incident again. We all have bad dreams now and then. Since the nightmare, we'd had two restful, uneventful evenings—eighteen hours of solid sleep (well, eighteen hours for Adam and the kids—I'd had about ten).

Still, I continued to feel that something was off with Adam. He was distracted, a little distant. It seemed to me he was working very hard at being his normal, cheerful, chipper self. I didn't know how to help him.

At a loss, and finding no alternative, I decided to take drastic measures: I called my mother.

Although she's in fact a first-generation American, my mother, Onda, is the most ethnic-looking woman under sixty-five in the tri-state area. She dresses only in black. And not glam, sexy, evening black— strike that image from your mind. Onda wears the kind of black that would only be featured in the Ellis Island winter collection. A shame really, because her strict adherence to the Mediterranean diet has kept her a very fit, perfect size six for the last thirty years.

Her style of dressing is more a manifestation of her depressive mood than of her glorification of the old country. In some ways, my mother is quite modern and independent. She's politically liberal, lives alone and, except on the rare occasions when she forgets to take her medication, isn't afraid to travel or meet new people. However, there is this other part of her that's very superstitious and leery. It's this part of her that clings to traditions that were dead long before she was born. What is most indicative of my mother's old-world ways is her proficiency in the ancient art of *di ocui*.

The *di ocui* is a Romanian diagnostic tool used to determine if someone has the evil eye. Not just anyone can do it. You have to have at least a modicum of clairvoyant abilities and, more importantly, you have to know the magic words. I don't know what these words are. Perhaps it's a prayer. Maybe it's a nonsensical rhyme. Whatever the words, they've been passed down from generation to generation. It doesn't always follow along bloodlines, but my mother has proudly suggested that she thinks I have the gift. What makes her think this is beyond me. I can barely interpret the present, let alone the future.

I'm not sure I'd want to receive the gift even if it was offered. Being the chosen administrant of the *di ocui* means that every day ten or fifteen ailing Romanians from all over the eastern seaboard, most of whom you've never met, call you to find out what is wrong with them. They do this instead of paying a visit to their primary care physician. Sometimes this strategy works out for them, as few Western doctors are really trained to diagnose and treat curses. However, should the cause of their malaise be more physiological in nature, this strategy can prove problematic. There've been many times when I've heard my mother, after interpreting the *di ocui*, scream into the phone at the sad, sickly Romanian she's just done a reading for, "Don't panic! Hang up right now and call 911! *Call* 911!"

To perform *di ocui* you take a glass, fill it with about two inches of water, and silently whisper the incantation as you drip olive oil (in a pinch you could use canola) into the water-filled glass. How the oil moves through the glass—and yes, I have seen oil and water mix—determines whether or not you're ill, depressed, fatigued, or actually cursed.

Onda had done several readings on Adam but she still had no clear handle on the case. "It's probably *only* depression," she said. For my mother, the words "only" and "depression" are inseparable, because who isn't depressed, so how seriously can we take it?

Romanians are funny and social but have, as you might have already guessed, an extremely dark core. Depression is just part of our personalities, and we don't pay it much mind. The evil eye, on the other hand, well, that's another story. That we take very seriously. Just to be safe, she recommended that I treat him.

"What should I do, Mom?"

"Do you remember when my cousin Mariwada's husband was diagnosed with…" My mother's voice trailed off, not daring to utter the specific ailment lest she bring bad luck upon herself.

Never before had I heard mention of a cousin named Mariwada. I'm fairly certain I'd remember the name. Still, I thought it far less complicated to simply say, "Of course I do."

"What a sweet woman, wasn't she? What a tragedy." Fortunately my mother did not pause long enough for me to opine upon Mariwada's specific misfortune.

"Okay. This is what I told her, God rest her soul. And this is what I'm telling you. Follow my instructions exactly," she warned. "First: Tell Adam he's ugly. Then don't speak to him for three days. Don't even look at him. Make him sleep with a crucifix. Spit on him morning and night."

I wondered how I was going to spit on him without actually looking at him, and just how bad his dreams would have to get before he allowed me to begin this rather drastic "treatment."

❖

It was Friday, the day of Adam's cousin Julia's wedding.

He was understandably tense. The previous day, he'd spent eleven hours at the Puck Building transforming the top-floor ballroom into an ordered, French garden.

Albeit a French garden with a dance floor and tables for two hundred.

Adam had nearly obliterated the fingerprints on his left hand, wielding his hot-glue gun. In general, he's a master with a glue gun, but of late he'd been a bit jumpy. After breakfast, I soothed his scorched fingers with aloe.

"How did this happen, sweetie?" I asked.

"I was affixing tiny crystal beads on to the mini lampshades that are covering the candles on the centerpieces. I guess I got distracted."

"You really should let Vanessa or Max do that. You have more important things to do."

"They always smear the glue." He frowned.

"Your cousin is going to be thrilled with her wedding," I said, trying to bolster his obviously flagging spirits.

"Oh, I don't care." He said this in a way that made it clear that he cared very much. Adam needed everything about tonight's event to be perfect.

Poor Adam. Working for family: so much more difficult than working for strangers.

And in Adam's case, he was working for a strained family. The Mores, who had arrived in this country via the *Mayflower*, had always appeared to be a united clan. But for seventeen years, starting on Thanksgiving 1987, Adam's mother, Margaret More (the Mayflower Mother, as I like to call her) and her sisters Grace, Virginia, and Arlene did not speak to each other. The reasons for the split vary depending on which sister you ask, but according to Margaret there had always been trouble. "Our mother wasn't a warm person, and when we arrived at the club that Thanksgiving and discovered there was no reservation, and remember, *your* great-great-grandfather was a founding member, well…things were said. Things we couldn't take back."

And they were not taken back. That is, not until they all saw each other again at their mother's funeral seventeen years later. Even after that, holidays were mostly avoided. "It's hard to go back," Margaret lamented as she sucked down one of her ever-present martinis.

Weddings, however, were attended. Most of each wedding would be spent trying to figure out who was a relative and who wasn't. That task was getting a little easier. Arlene had six daughters, and three of them were married just last year. (Arlene had converted to Catholicism when she got married.) Adam, just as he was doing this evening, had planned all of them.

Adam felt the burden of maintaining his tenuous family relationships resting solely on his shoulders—one mishap tonight, he thought, could lead to another seventeen-year feud.

As Adam was gathering supplies and heading for our front door, I thought of my mother's diagnosis and prescribed treatment. I ran to catch Adam before he left. But he must have sensed my lips beginning to purse, because he hit the ground shouting, "No spitting!"

"Would you at least sleep with a crucifix?" I pleaded.

"You're crazy. I love *you*. Please don't turn into your mother."

Adam kissed me, more intensely than I would have expected, considering I'd just tried expectorating on him. Out the door he went, shouting back, "See you in a bit."

As the door was closing I whispered, "You're ugly." I was desperate.

❖

I arrived at the Puck Building at 2:00 for a wedding that was not set to begin until 6:00. Over breakfast that morning, I casually asked

Adam if he'd like me to come early and help. I was totally surprised when he accepted my offer, and then felt that it would be shallow of me to mention the *Petticoat Junction* marathon running all afternoon on TV Land that I'd been so looking forward to watching.

I came in carrying our tuxes, hung them up, and waited for my assignment. While I waited, I surveyed the room. It was an anomaly, but a glorious and grand one. I was happy to be here *now*, while the room was still mostly empty. From my vantage point, at the edge of the faux-garden Adam had created, I had the opportunity to admire his genius. If it weren't for the central air-conditioning, which was making my teeth chatter, I would have believed I was outdoors standing in an actual garden. There were topiaries and fountains. Iron benches and marble statues. Stone footpaths, edged with boxwood boarders, linked the dining tables.

Adam always refers to himself as crafty—not as in cunning, but as in good at crafts. He certainly can decoupage with the best of them—but he's so much more than that. Adam is an artist. He works on a canvas that is not one I would choose for myself, but it is his—his medium—and he works in it with the skill and passion shared by any of the great masters.

I wasn't sure why Adam's cousin—a girl from New Jersey, with no French blood and who'd never traveled to Europe—would want a French garden–themed wedding. But glancing around this magnificent room, there was no denying she'd made an excellent choice.

"Steven, I need you." It was Vanessa, Adam's assistant, office manager, confidante, and all-around Gal Friday. She was standing next to me looking frazzled. She had not, however, allowed her rapidly rising stress level to negatively impact upon her impeccable sense of fashion. As she always was, Vanessa was completely pulled together, from the Robert Marc eyeglasses right down to the alligator mules.

"New?" I asked, eyeing the footwear.

Vanessa nodded. "Donald Pliner. Like slippers."

Vanessa once told me that while she was only fluent in English, she knew the words for "shoe" and "price" in eight languages. She could even draw the Japanese kanji.

Now she was shoving a rag in my hand. "Thanks so much for helping out. I have a million things to do and I'm standing here polishing silver. *Clearly*, a waste of my skills. I thought it would be a perfect job for you." Having given me my chore, she was off to find a more worthy endeavor.

A different person might have been insulted, but I garner such comfort in cleaning that I just grabbed the Tarnex and jumped right in. I rubbed, buffed, and polished until all two hundred place settings gleamed. I was high. I'm not sure whether that was from the sense of accomplishment or the Tarnex I'd been inhaling for two and a half hours. I was glad that I'd volunteered my services because every time I looked over at Adam, he seemed out of sorts and distracted. I wasn't sure that he was actually accomplishing anything, unless you count walking around and fretting as an accomplishment.

Having completed my job, I sat down to take a break and instantly realized that my brother would be walking into the room any moment. We are not twins. I'm three years older than my baby brother, so it's not that we have that psychic thing going on—you know, like one twin gets shot and the other one bleeds. I knew Peter was about to enter the room because I could hear his employee, Barney, singing in the hall. I recognized the tune and the voice; I'd heard it many times before.

Barney was conscientious, earnest, and completely trustworthy. He was the perfect employee in every way—but one. He suffered from a serious linguistic tic.

This tic developed following a 2005 Cinco de Mayo celebration. Barney had danced and drunk the night away with a beautiful young man named Hector. Their first dance had been "Quando Quando Quando." They requested the song over and over, dancing and singing along to its infectious melody. Barney brought Hector home and they made love softly singing in each other's ears, "Quando Quando Quando." When Barney awoke he reached for his new love, but Hector was already gone. The song, however, remained: a continuous loop etched in his brain. And he sang it aloud, constantly.

Max, a fine party planner himself and Adam's on-staff florist, had spent most of this day with his linebacker's frame hunched in two. With pruning shears in one hand and yardstick in the other, Max was making sure the garden's hedges stood exactly twenty-four inches off the ground. The maddening detail of the assignment was making his already crossed eyes move even nearer to center. When he saw, through what must have been terribly blurred vision, Peter and Barney trying to navigate—*foxtrot,* really, as Barney was still singing—their way through the maze of boxwoods, he ran over to guide them. They seemed to be in fine shape, and awfully good dancers, but I, too, jumped and ran over to help, feeling vaguely guilty for sitting while work was happening. It became quickly apparent that I was just in the way, so I took a step back and awkwardly shuffled between my right and left feet in an attempt to appear "busy."

When the cake was in position, Adam and Vanessa joined us, and we all stood admiring the feat that my brother had achieved. How had he made that meticulously detailed palace?

Peter threw off our compliments. It is true that creating a cake in the shape of Versailles was no small task, and Peter had accomplished it masterfully. But he did not believe it was an appropriate choice for a wedding cake. He was a traditionalist when it came to desserts; an American wedding cake was not meant to resemble a French palace. Especially a French palace with the inscription *Let Them Eat Cake* piped around the sides in butter cream. Peter had informed Amanda's cousin that if she wanted Louis XVI and Marie Antoinette statues in place of a bride and groom, she'd have to find them herself. He had his limits.

The cater waiters had begun arriving. Barney, Max, and Vanessa, having each completed their assignments, said their good-byes. Peter, Adam, and I stayed behind and transformed ourselves into party guests.

When I met Adam, I had never once worn a tuxedo. Despite the fact that my class of '92 had voted for the Vanessa Williams–inspired theme *Save The Best For Last*, I skipped my senior prom. Instead, I went with my girlfriend Tina Balamaci, the only girl and the only Romanian I would ever date, to see the Broadway revival of *Guys and Dolls* starring Nathan Lane. The prom would have been the sole event in my life where black tie would have been appropriate. The annual teen mixer that my mother forced me to attend, sponsored by the Romanian social club, Societatea Farsarotul, was more of a Dockers affair.

I remember the puzzled look on Adam's face when I told him early on in our relationship that I didn't own a tuxedo. I also recall his puzzled look when I tried teaching him how to pronounce Societatea Farsarotul. Say it with me. "Sue-she-ta-ta Far-sha-row-tal."

After abandoning the Romanian lesson, Adam asked: "Doesn't it get expensive renting? You should really consider buying one. It's not like they ever go out of style."

When I told him I'd never had occasion to wear a tux, he studied me like he was Margaret Mead stumbling upon the Polynesians for the first time.

"Really? So what do you do on Christmas eve, for example?" he asked, genuinely curious.

On Christmas Eve I sang in St. Dimitri's choir, came home, ate way too many pieces of *pita di lapte* (sweet milk pie), got into bed, and waited for Santa. What did Adam do, I wondered. Visions of *Brideshead Revisited* danced in my head.

Now, as the three of us used the Puck Building's gentlemen's lavatory as our dressing room, I could see that Adam's early introduction to evening wear had served him well. He was fastening himself into his monkey suit as if it was the easiest thing imaginable. I've seen him do it a hundred times before, but I always marvel at his skill. Peter and I were standing in various states of undress, incapable of accomplishing the chore and awaiting Adam's assistance.

Peter, who was under the mistaken impression that a shower would be available, had not even begun to dress yet. He was standing naked at the sink trying in vain to remove flour from parts of his body where it seemed, at least to me, unfathomable that flour could have ended up in the first place.

I had underwear on but was having a devil of a time with my button-fly pants. I was stooped over, twisting around at my crotch to no avail. Adam had long since mastered his pants and was now breezing, effortlessly, through the sea of studs required to close his shirt. I gave up trying to close my fly and waited for Adam's help.

When the men's room door flew open, Adam and I both instinctively ran over to Peter and stood by him, attempting to protect his modesty.

"I hate you, Adam!" Amanda shouted. I'm not sure what she thought her brother was doing with her naked boyfriend, but she clearly had the wrong idea.

Although perhaps her wrath had something to do with her attire.

Amanda, a bridesmaid at tonight's event, stood in the door frame, filling every inch of it with her dress. What a cruel twist of fate that Amanda, the anti-bride, had been forced to be in the wedding parties of every one of the virtual strangers known as her cousins. She'd worn several ghastly gowns in the past, suffering through nuptials and receptions decked out in an unending series of ill-conceived outfits. I remember the blinding shimmer of the rhinestones and sequins swathing Amanda as she sparked her way down the aisle at a morning wedding. She'd endured cranberry sauce red, limeade green, and bronze—those were three different dresses, all mistakes. One of her cousins did have the good sense to choose a very smart navy for the fabric for her bridesmaids' dresses. Unfortunately for Amanda, the neckline was cut so low and the leg slit so high that only Mary Magdalene (pre-retirement) would have dared to enter a church wearing it.

Today, at least, it could not be said that she was wearing an ugly dress. On the contrary, it was a dazzling silk brocade evening gown with pearl buttons. It was striking and dramatic. It was perfectly tailored. It was, however, very out of style. Two hundred and fifty years out of style, to be exact. It seemed that cousin Julia had carried her French garden theme right through to the dresses. Were it not for the BlackBerry clasped in Amanda's right hand, she could have easily passed for one of Marie Antoinette's less obsequious ladies-in-waiting.

Oddly, tucked under her left arm, Amanda seemed to be carrying an extremely docile white poodle. I was puzzled. On closer inspection, I realized it was a powdered wig, meant to complete the outfit, which Amanda was refusing to place upon her head.

Amanda, cheeks flushed either from the constricting bones of her apparel or perhaps from the humiliation of it all, was fuming. Again, she bellowed: "Sometimes I really hate you, Adam." Of course, she wasn't serious. If she had been, she never would have been so direct.

"Don't be mad at me, I didn't choose the dress."

"Not this," she said, pointing at her ensemble. She stepped into the bathroom, pushed past Adam and me, and immediately began washing flour off Peter. I didn't need to see that, but I was sort of trapped, what with my pants half off.

"I was in class today," she said, "staring out toward my mostly sleeping students, forcing myself to focus on my history of marriage speech…"

"Marriage, as in the enslavement of women?" Adam asked sarcastically.

"Correct. And I'm thinking, as I'm looking around, Amanda, nobody cares. And honestly, based on the lack of response from my students, no one did care."

Most of Amanda's students took her class because it was an easy pass and fulfilled a core requirement. It was one of those rocks-for-jocks or kiddie-lit courses students take when they're overloaded or just really lazy.

"And then I noticed Linda." Amanda inspected Peter for any last traces of flour. I'll spare telling you where she found some. Amanda continued: "Linda was different. She was perky, sitting up straight, her eyes were wide open. She was even smiling at me."

"That's great. And you hate me, why?" asked Adam.

"I'm getting there. I asked Linda what she thought. I was posing a question about the origin of the dowry. Care to hear her response?"

There was silence, so I said, "Sure!"

"She said, 'Well, I don't really know about *that*, I was wondering if you could get your brother to plan my wedding? His assistant says he's totally booked.'"

"Oh, for Linda, I'll find time." Adam goaded.

"You will not! You are constantly making me look like a fool." Adam eyed her gown. "You sure it's me?"

Peter, who by now had put on some underwear, moved to break them up before Adam and Amanda regressed further into adolescence. He just stood between them, solidly and calmly. His tall lanky presence, the vestiges of a youth spent as a track-and-field star, was enough to silence the two More kids. "Kiss," Peter said. Not a big talker, my brother. But he was effective.

Adam and Amanda obeyed. "I'm sorry, Adam, I'm just so passionate about this. Marriage does a huge disservice to women. We're expected to have a career. And be content to earn less money than our husbands for the same jobs. *Why?* Because the *men* have families to support. After working all day, at our lower-paying jobs, we go home and take care of the house, too. How is that a partnership? *We* raise the children, *we* clean the house, *we* do all the cooking—"

"I cook," Peter said, sheepishly. "I'm a baker," he muttered under his breath.

"Peter, I don't mean us. I'm speaking globally." Amanda's expression softened. She parted her glorious lips and offered my brother a big, glowing smile. Amanda had just reached out and gently placed her hands on my brother's cheeks when we heard it: The *Wedding March* was beginning.

"Shit!" Amanda shouted. "I'm on." Then, succumbing, as most of us will, to the extreme pressure of familial obligations, she thrust the towering wig upon her head. It tottered at a Pisa-like angle. "How do I look?" she asked.

It was probably best for her that she was out the door before we could respond to that question.

CHAPTER FOUR:
YOU PUT YOUR RIGHT FOOT IN

Peter and I spent the first half of the service sitting in the back row trying to look inconspicuous while Adam fastened our shirt studs and cuff links. With the reception now in full swing, we were finally pulled together.

I offered to get Adam a drink, but he was sticking with seltzer. He never drank alcohol when he was working. Besides, Adam's mother Margaret was in attendance, and considering her love of all things eighty-proof, he didn't want to give her any encouragement on the cocktail front. I stood by Adam's side and scoped out the food.

"Oh my goodness!" Adam stopped the cater waiter who was walking past carrying a large silver tray. "Are you serving pigs in blankets?"

"Want one?"

"I didn't spec out pigs in blankets!" Adam was unraveling.

"I'll take that as a no," the cater waiter said as he walked away from Adam.

But not before I could grab two.

"I will kill that caterer. I have my reputation to think about," Adam said, watching me gobble them down.

"Don't be a snob. It's sweet," I said.

"It's sweet for a Super Bowl party, not for the most important day of your life." Adam walked away from me and headed for the bar. So much for the no-drinking-on-the-job rule.

I was following behind Adam when I bumped into my boss (he's my friend, of course, too, but I always feel compelled to refer to him as my boss) Brad Barrett. What was he doing here? "How do you know Adam's cousin?" I asked.

"I don't. I know...*the groom.*" He said this in a voice so sexually provocative, I dared not ask a follow-up question.

I guess I shouldn't have been surprised to find Brad at this wedding—regardless of his relationship with the groom. Brad's invited to everything. He's beautiful and very rich, and people respond to money and looks. Also, Brad's never declined a wedding invitation in his life. It's not that he's so fond of the institution. What he's fond of are all the pretty young cater waiters that serve him during the party. All of these events are remembered not by the meal or the toasts or the music, but by the under-twenty-three-year-old he picks up and takes home. Once, when he'd met a particularly hot Swedish guy, aptly named Sven, he'd even helped break down the room so they could get back to his place faster.

I stood chatting up Brad when the object of his affections, *for today*, walked by. Another young thing carrying a large silver tray. "Hi, I'm Charlie. Shrimp puff?" Charlie was an actor, we quickly learned. "Well, you know, I'm trying to be. I'm studying Meisner."

I was the instant third wheel.

"That's exciting." Brad touched Charlie's shoulder. I bristled, flashing back to years earlier when we were together. I remembered him touching my shoulder in just that way. His signature move, I guess. Brad continued; his hand was still firmly placed on Charlie's impressive deltoid. "I bet you're *very* talented."

"I think so. Trying anyway."

I would have loved a shrimp puff, but by now Charlie's back was to me, having wedged me right out of the group.

"I have a friend in casting, I'll introduce you to him," Brad promised.

"Really? Awesome!"

Brad really does have a friend who is a casting director. When you like to sleep with very young members of the food service industry, it helps having friends in show business.

I walked away, unnoticed. Got to the bar, and found myself shut out from another conversation. Adam was talking with a middle-aged man with wild gray hair. He looked like a professor, complete with an elbow-patched, tweed jacket. (I kid you not—at an evening wedding!)

"Sigmund Freud," I heard the underdressed man say, as he extended his hand toward Adam. "My parents were practical jokers."

Adam was not sure how to respond.

"Funny part is I became a shrink."

"I'm a wedding planner," Adam said. "I guess I'm lucky my

parents didn't name me Jennifer Lopez." Adam was pleased with his little joke.

"You're a wedding planner? That must be so difficult for you."

"Not so bad. It does get a little harried in June," Adam offered.

"No, I mean emotionally." Sigmund smiled empathetically. "It must be rather conflicting."

"Not really. Why would it—?"

Sigmund Freud was distracted. "I see my wife looking for me." He waved in her direction. "It was nice chatting with you. Guess what my wife's name is."

"I don't know."

"Dr. Jung." Sigmund snorted. "How funny is that?"

❖

We had a dreadful table, and not just because it was number thirteen. I would have thought they would have skipped directly from twelve to fourteen, you know, like they do in high-rises. But I guess the bride and groom were thinking no one would notice the number thirteen, since the table was located beyond the farthest row of boxwoods, approximately three inches from the entrance to the kitchen. It was truly disgraceful. Only Brad was pleased with its placement, as it afforded him an unobstructed view of Charlie at the waiter's station.

I was joined at this outpost location by Adam, our siblings, Margaret, Brad, one empty chair, and Vickie, a woman whose name I only learned later when I began researching these events so I could chronicle them in my column.

Vickie was drunk, chatty, and holding us all captive. "I'm better off without him. Don't you think?" She was staring at us. Vickie was under the impression that we knew who she was, and a great deal about her life.

"Don't you think I'm better off without him?" She'd zeroed in on my brother, apparently not too inebriated to spot the lone straight man at the table.

Peter was understandably flustered; this wasn't his family. "Definitely."

"What do you think?" Vickie glowered at Amanda.

"Definitely," Amanda shot back with surprising conviction. "You are much better off without him."

Amanda sat squeezing Peter's hand and looking trapped. Like she'd rushed to the front door, expecting to find her lover returned home from war, and instead was greeted by a couple of Jehovah's Witnesses, pamphlets in hand.

Margaret regarded the empty chair and asked the question that I, for one, had been wondering: "Who's missing?"

Sensing calamity, Amanda furiously shook her head, hoping her mother would change the subject. Her wig came flying off and smashed into Peter's head. He grabbed his temple, presumably more from shock than pain. He sat there, face in hands, stunned and silent.

Vickie began crying. "My husband is missing. Well, no, not exactly missing. He's in the Caribbean with my sister!"

Around the table, all eyes widened, except for Brad's. His eyes were focused on Charlie, who had finagled his way into serving the table so he could be close to Brad. He was pouring wine. As he approached Vickie, she grabbed the bottle from his hand. "I'll just keep that, save you some trouble." She poured a tall glass and downed half. "I wasn't going to come, but I had this new dress and I thought, why not? I'm not the adulterer. He's the adulterer! I'll go to that wedding and hold my head up high!"

With that, Vickie's head hit the table. She was out cold.

None of us were quite sure what to do. For a moment, we just sat staring at her. Then, snapping into action, I stuck my napkin into my glass of ice water to make a cold compress and placed it at the back of Vickie's neck while Amanda, who'd retrieved her wig from the floor, began frantically fanning her with it.

Meanwhile, Margaret leaned into Adam and whispered, "Darling?" I've always been envious of the way in which Margaret addresses her children. *Darling.* I thought only characters in Noel Coward plays spoke that way.

"Darling?" Margaret looked away from Adam and focused on Vickie, eyeing the poor keeled-over-woman with disdain. "Are we related to *her*?" she asked, polishing off her third martini.

Considering Vickie's inability to hold her liquor, I was guessing she wasn't a relative of Margaret's.

❖

Tradition and ritual are what make a wedding meaningful. You can be as innovative and creative as you want, e.g., "I've never been to France, but I'm going with a Versailles theme for my special day!" But when it comes right down to it, it's the rituals everyone observes at their weddings that really matter: the toasts, the photos, the tossing of the bouquet, and of course, the couple's first dance.

You can tell a lot about a couple by the song they choose for their first dance as man and wife. Anything ever recorded by Sinatra is always a favorite, especially with folks from Jersey. After all these years, "Through the Eyes of Love," "You Light Up My Life," and "I Honestly Love You" remain extremely popular, which is regrettable for so many reasons, not the least being that these songs are impossible to dance to. Couples end up hanging on to each other for dear life and swaying back and forth like they've just ended a hunger strike and if they let go of each other they'll drop right to the floor. In any other arena, this pathetic attempt at movement would be greeted with boos and jeers. But on this solemn day, the newlywed's spastic flight across the floor is met with cheers, tears, and applause.

We watched as the newlyweds walked out onto the dance floor. I'd thought, perhaps, in keeping with the theme, that Julia would have chosen the galliard or gavotte for the first dance. But, she abandoned eighteenth-century Versailles for twentieth-century Rio. From their first step, it was immediately apparent that they'd taken lessons. They were polished and poised and moved with an ease that is generally only seen at the International Ballroom and Latin Dance Competition. They cha-cha'd with such conviction that a full verse of the song had passed before any of us realized they were dancing to a Latin arrangement of the David Soul classic, "Don't Give Up On Us." What on earth had prompted them to choose that song? I wondered if it had anything to do with the groom's alleged relationship with Brad.

I bit the inside of my mouth to keep from laughing. "What do you think?" I asked, leaning in and whispering in Adam's ear.

"Beautiful. Isn't it? Their eccentricity, their rhythm, their love. I find it all profoundly moving," he said.

I felt certain I was being Punk'd.

Adam looked past Vickie, who despite a greenish pallor was once again sitting up, and watched the newest married couple dance.

The band singer was having fun with his rendition, adding a little moan between the first and second syllable of *baby*. "Ba-ohh-by."

During the bridge, the band singer addressed the guests. "May I have all the married couples join our newest married couple?"

At table thirteen, none of us moved.

Adam and I looked at each other; I was hoping he would stand. And I guess, he was hoping I'd stand. We shifted a bit in our seats, but neither of us actually got up. As we sat, looking at each other, I noticed tears welling in Adam's eyes.

"Are you okay?"

Adam nodded.

"Are you sure?" I asked, watching a single tear roll down Adam's cheek.

"Just need some air. I'm okay, really." And with that, Adam stood from the table and excused himself.

Obviously he was not okay. So I jumped from my seat and followed him out. I caught up with him at the elevator.

"You really don't have to go outside with me. I'm fine."

"I know you are," I said, my voice betraying my concern.

We rode the elevator down to the ground level in silence. Adam's breathing was hard and rapid. I was smiling too broadly and feigning composure.

When we reached the sidewalk, Adam gasped, sucking in as much oxygen as he could. The dirty air of lower Manhattan seemed to do the trick. I could see that his breathing was returning to normal. Thankfully, whatever was going on had passed. It was just a bad moment, nothing more. I was going to suggest that we walk to the bodega on the corner and pick up a bottle of San Pellegrino when we were interrupted.

"I miss the days when it wasn't a crime to smoke." Sigmund Freud was standing beside us on the sidewalk enjoying a cigar.

We were startled. Adam introduced me to the doctor. Dr. Freud took my hand, shook it longer than was necessary, and gave me a cryptic nod.

"What made you say my work must be difficult for me?" Adam asked Sigmund.

"Isn't it?" the doctor inquired knowingly.

I was wondering what was up with Dr. Freud. Why couldn't he just answer the question?

Sigmund inhaled deeply, holding the smoke a second before exhaling it carelessly in our direction. I was not amused that the doctor was blowing smoke into the face of my recently gasping boyfriend. I was about to ask if he'd put it out when he continued speaking: "I have a cousin who's a lesbian. Guess how long she's been with her partner?"

"I don't know," Adam said.

"Twenty-two years. They've been together for twenty-two years."

Sigmund Freud returned his attention to his cigar. He took a long drag from it. "It's Cuban. I have a friend; I don't ask. They're so much better."

Sigmund pulled two more from his breast pocket and offered them to us. "Nothing like a good cigar. Please. Go ahead."

"We don't..." I trailed off. "But thank you."

Adam glanced at me, darted his eyes back toward the entrance to the Puck Building.

"Well, we'd better..." Adam started.

"Yes. Indeed you should," said the doctor emphatically.

"Very nice meeting you," I said, though I'd found the entire encounter far more disconcerting than nice.

❖

When we arrived back at the reception, I saw that most of the guests were standing in a circle on the dance floor. I'd been to more than enough weddings to know what that meant, and I was thrilled. I grabbed Adam's hand, so grateful we hadn't missed this moment. "I'm going to need you for this," I said, leading him onto the dance floor.

"What's happening?" He was digging his heels, resisting my tug.

"You'll see." I grinned as we joined the rest of the guests on the floor.

This band singer knew how to get a party started. And he understood that for many people the Hokey Pokey is a secret guilty pleasure. It's a dance that requires no skill and allows you to be silly, stupid really, without fear of judgment. It's rare that a grown-up is allowed to jut their head out and shake it in public. And that feeling, that release of inhibition, can be quite liberating.

I am, and have always been, very pro–Hokey Pokey. I pulled Adam, who had resisted each step, into a spot in the circle next to Amanda.

Vickie had managed to get to her feet and was standing next to Peter. Broad smiles and childlike giggles emanated from the guests as the band began to play. Around the circle people were putting their right hands in and shaking them all about.

Vickie was doing a particularly violent version of the dance, more left hook than simple shake. Her arm was coming dangerously close to Peter's head, and his body was tensing in response. He had, after all, already been whacked in the head by Amanda's wig, which had caused him far more distress than I, for one, would have expected. An actual fist was more than my poor brother could take.

Adam watched the group of paroxysmal partyers shaking their limbs. He stood motionless, refusing to participate. "I can't do this."

"Of course you can," I said. "Just put your right foot in and shake it all about."

Adam did not move.

CHAPTER FIVE:
ARE YOU HAVING AN AFFAIR?

What I should have done, when we left the reception, was gotten right into a cab with Adam and brought him home. But Peter suggested that we walk across town to the Westside #1 train, to avoid having to make the Times Square transfer, and Amanda was in agreement. Adam had no opinion one way or the other.

I said, "Sure, great idea." And we made our way to Houston Street.

This is what I do. I'm a go-with-the-flow guy. Something was terribly wrong with Adam. Was I addressing it? No. I was meandering across town.

I glanced over at Adam. He'd not said a single word since we'd started walking. He was staring off and shuffling. I slowed my pace so he would keep up.

As is often the case with couples, I didn't know what the problem was but I began imagining it was all my fault. Or more correctly, I imagined *he* imagined it was all my fault. I could have just asked Adam, but then I wouldn't have been able to wallow in fear and guilt. I just walked silently and let my mind run its panicked race: What did I do? What does he think I've done? And so on. Gradually, the pieces of the puzzle all came together for me: His strange behavior, his tears, his emotional distance, his refusal to dance the Hokey Pokey with me, and his...*Oh my god!* My heart sank. I trudged along the never-ending Houston Street. I said nothing.

There is something about myself I have deliberately avoided sharing. But it seems impossible to tell this story truthfully without letting you know about this quirk of mine: I don't yell. Or rather, I cannot yell. I am incapable of expressing any dark emotion with words. My only real way of showing anger is through sulks, sighs, and pouts. *Please.* Refrain from judging me. We all have our flaws.

When I am aggravated or experiencing low-level irritation, my vocal cords tighten and my voice becomes scratchy.

When I am upset or feel I'm being treated unfairly, I develop a strangled whisper.

When I'm very angry or feel betrayed, I become mute.

Since Adam wasn't talking and I was silently stewing, Peter and Amanda gave up trying to engage us and were engrossed in their own conversation. Amanda was having huge regret about our decision to walk because her get-up was causing quite a scene. She'd never realized how narrow the sidewalks were on Houston Street until she tried to negotiate them in her dress.

"Give me your jacket," she barked at Peter.

"Sure. Are you cold?"

"People are staring at me."

"Sweetheart, no one is staring at you."

Even I, distracted as I was, had noticed the stares.

At just that moment two teenage girls, who really should have known better, saw the outfit and pointed and laughed.

"I didn't choose this!" Amanda wailed with such vehemence that even Adam snapped to attention. We all watched as the terrified teenagers ran to the other side of the street.

Amanda turned to Peter. "Your jacket."

With Peter's assistance, Amanda slipped into his suit coat, her hands vanishing within the extra-long sleeves. The jacket was in no way a stylistic improvement.

She glanced down at herself, rolled up a sleeve, and took Peter's hand. "I look ridiculous. I'm so glad we're never getting married."

"Me, too," Peter said without enthusiasm. "The only good thing about that wedding was the pigs in blankets."

Amanda laughed.

"I'm serious," Peter continued. "Why are they tacky?" Peter looked at Adam and continued: "Adam, I thought you were going to have a heart attack when they started serving them."

Adam didn't respond.

"Pigs in blankets just *are* tacky. No two ways about it," Amanda said.

"They're the classic American hors d'oeuvre," Peter said, teasing her gently. "Everyone loves them."

"I don't."

"You had ten of them."

"I did not have—"

Peter grabbed Amanda and kissed her. It was a big grand kiss, made even grander by the sweep of her full skirt. It was the kind of kiss that's followed by end credits in a movie. As their mouths parted, Peter began licking his lips. "Yum," he said. "I can still taste a little mustard."

I laughed, but quietly, hoping not to interrupt their private moment. What a great couple, I thought. They complemented each other. They were respectful, considerate, made each other laugh. Of course they had differences, but they were never fraught. It seemed to me that Peter and Amanda had what it took to be together forever. As a couple, they reminded me a lot of Adam and myself.

I looked over at Adam, but he was gone.

He'd walked into the street and was trying to hail a taxi. I interrupted Peter and Amanda's private moment and offered the first excuse that popped into my mind to explain our hasty departure: "My feet are killing me. We're taking a cab. Bye." I rushed to join Adam just as the taxi approached.

❖

At home, later that evening, as we pretended all was fine, rehashed the wedding, and got ready for bed, I could feel that the tension of the day had taken its toll on me: My voice was starting to get scratchy.

"You upset about something?" Adam asked.

"No," I wheezed.

"Your voice."

"I strained it shouting over the band," I lied.

We had gotten into bed, turned out the lights, and moved into a spoon position. Vincent and Theo were having a little late-night snack, so we were alone. In less than thirty seconds Adam would be asleep. If I didn't say (or at least squeak) something right now, I'd spend the entire night wide-awake and fretting.

"Are you having an affair?" At last, I said it.

"What? Why would you think that?" he asked, turning to face me.

"You're a man."

"You're a man," Adam pointed out. "Are you having an affair?"

"No." I couldn't deny his logic.

"Okay then." There was an edge to his voice.

"You've been distant." I said. "You cried at a David Soul song tonight."

Adam was silent for a moment. He wrapped his arms around me. "I love that song. And…" He smiled a smile that I hadn't seen in a long time. "I love you. I'm thrilled by you, I'm nurtured by you…" He was touching me now, touching me like he had in the early days of our relationship, when there was still so much to discover about each other. "I'm challenged by you."

I was touching him, too. I was excited; I let my hands move right to his crotch. I looked at him, he was grinning at me.

"Steven, did I mention that I'm aroused by you?"

"I love you," I said, my voice completely restored.

What happened next, I will leave to your imagination, except to say it was nice. Very nice.

As much as I enjoy sex, love looking at and talking about men, I'm fundamentally a bit of a prude. I cherish and safeguard my personal relationship with Adam. It's private. We both love to take in the view when we stroll through Chelsea, admiring the boys in their natural habitat. But we are essentially, at least by gay standards, two very old-fashioned guys. We've even had a couple of serious conversations about having kids. By that I mean actual human children. Neither one of us has broached the subject with Vincent and Theo, as we feel it's unnecessary to alarm them prematurely.

Adam had just drifted off to sleep when my cell phone rang. It was now after midnight. Before I'd even found my phone, I was chastising myself for not owning a somber-enough-looking suit to wear to the funeral.

I grabbed the cell and darted into the bathroom so as not to awaken Adam by my anguished cries when I learned the identity of the deceased.

"Hello," I said preparing myself for the devastating news.

"It's me." It was Brad; his voice was shaky.

"What? Is it *Gail*? My God, tell me it's not Gail!"

"What are you *talking* about?"

"What are *you* talking about?"

I realized that Brad was calling for a reason other than to notify me that someone I loved had passed away. I was livid—not because all my friends were still living, but because Brad had called for some other purpose at this late hour. For better or worse, I've inherited many things from my mother. One of them is the belief that from 10:00 P.M.

until 9:00 A.M. the phone rings for one reason only: to inform you of the death of a loved one.

"Steven?"

"Do you know what time it is?"

"Since when do you sleep?"

"Tonight could have been the night, Brad."

"I'm sorry. I need to talk. I brought Charlie home after the wedding."

I suspected as much. We'd left Brad standing on the sidewalk in front of the Puck, shuffling expectantly, like a stage door Johnny awaiting a showgirl.

"Something…" Brad hesitated. He sounded upset. "Something happened."

"Are you okay?" I was truly alarmed. "Did he rob you?"

"Of course not. How could you think such a thing?"

"You're calling me on the death phone. Tell me what happened, Brad."

"Well, I invited him over to my place for a drink. And everything was going great. He really liked the apartment."

This did not come as a surprise. Brad has a coveted corner apartment at East Fifty-second and the East River. Everything in the place is expensive and an original. There are no copies anywhere. Several Warhol Brillo Boxes form a pyramid in the corner of the foyer. He has a Magritte in the half bath, and a portrait of one of Hockney's handsome young men lounging poolside graces Brad's mantel. The lines of the apartment are sleek, functional, masculine, and not at all flashy. The flash is reserved for the view. It's spectacular: the river, the United Nations. Gazing downtown, you see the Empire State Building.

"Anyway," Brad said, "things with Charlie were really escalating, if you know what I mean."

"I know what you mean, Brad."

"We kissed a little bit and it was really nice. After a while, I excused myself to use the bathroom. But when I was in there I started to panic, because I'd eaten three pigs-in-blankets at the wedding, and between the butter in the pastry and the sodium in the dogs I was sure my weight was going to be way up."

"Brad, please tell me you did not get on the scale."

"I couldn't help myself!"

Even back when we were together, Brad was addicted to weighing himself. He does it obsessively. At night, just before bed, he faces his most challenging time. Each evening, he goes into the bathroom, strips naked, and begins pinching his nonexistent waist in search of flab. He then contorts himself in front of the mirror so that he can reflect on the sorry state of his ass.

Which, for the record, is rock-hard and high.

After the visual inspection comes the dreaded pre-bed weigh-in. In the evenings after dinner, Brad weighs in at 160 pounds, 158 if he's been juicing. His morning, dehydrated, pre-breakfast weight is usually 156. But he can tolerate 157 pounds without having a complete meltdown.

I knew from the tone in his voice, his weight was up. "What did you weigh, Brad?"

"162 pounds and four ounces. Fuck! Oh God, I need to be quiet. Charlie's in bed."

"Where are you?

"I'm in the bathroom."

"Still?"

"No. Again. I got off the scale, and I somehow managed to pull myself together. It was weird. I had this moment of clarity. I guess I saw myself as others see me. And I thought: Wow, Brad, you're a stud. So I marched out into the bedroom. I didn't even bother to pull on a robe. I just strolled out naked.

"He seemed to like what he saw. Of course, like every guy I've ever been with, he made a big deal about my enormous cock and how hot he thought it was."

"I never did that."

"Yeah. Right. So anyway, he's going on and on and on about how he's never been with anybody so huge."

"Feel free to edit the story, Brad. I don't need every detail."

"I'm just trying to set the scene. So he's going down on me and he's really good at it. Rhythm. Technique. He's absolutely in the top five. No gagging, which considering my size—"

"Any chance we could jump ahead?"

"I picked him up and I carried him to the bed. And I pulled out a MagnumXL—"

"Oh, brother. I get it, Brad. Please, get to the point."

"So we're doing it. And it's really nice. I feel a real chemistry. Connection. I can't explain why. And he starts talking, which, as you know, isn't really my thing. But I figure I can play along. He's saying *fuck me.* And I'm saying, *Oh yeah? You want it? You want it?* And then..."

Just when we were getting to the good part, Brad paused.

"Oh God, Steven. I'm sorry I shouldn't have called. I'm being ridiculous. Never mind."

"Are you kidding? You can't stop now. Tell me what happened."

"Oh it's fine. It doesn't matter. It's no big deal, honestly. See you Monday. I really just wanted to check on Adam. He seemed so quiet today. Give him my love."

"Brad, tell me what—"

The phone went dead.

I turned the ringer off. If, God forbid, someone passed in the night, I'd have to learn about it in the morning. I left the bathroom and got back into bed.

Adam was still sleeping. Seeing the look of contentment on his face now, it seemed ridiculous that I'd been so paranoid about Adam's behavior at the wedding. He was fine. He'd just experienced an off moment. Who hasn't? We were pulled into a tight spoon and, as usual, the kids had joined us. I'm not sure how long I lay there enjoying the purr/snore serenade.

Finally, I fell asleep and I found myself in the middle of a very pleasant dream. Once again, Nate Berkus and Anderson Cooper had paid me a visit. We were having a delightful time. Just at the moment that Nate offered to redecorate the bedroom, I awoke to Adam's terrible screams and shouts.

"I don't know nothin' about birthin' no babies," he bellowed.

CHAPTER SIX:
ADAM MORE AND GUEST

I felt that Adam's switch from Hattie McDaniel to Butterfly McQueen in his nightmare was a sign of a worsening condition. He could not recall whose child he was supposed to be *birthin'* but I guessed from his terrified response, it wasn't a friend's.

In the morning, when Adam crawled from our bed and stumbled into the kitchen, he reminded me of my typical waking self: He was groggy and un-refreshed. I begged him to call Vanessa and tell her he was unable to come in. But it was a Saturday, they had a wedding, it was out of the question. After a long shower, a pot of coffee, and the Taleggio, porcini mushroom, and sun-dried tomato omelet I made him and insisted that he eat, he assured me he was fine and that he'd check in with me from the reception. It was an afternoon wedding, so at least he wouldn't be having a late night.

For me, I assumed it would be a typical Saturday.

Because my schedule is, to put it mildly, so much more flexible than Adam's, I do most of the household tasks. I grocery shop, I cook, and I clean. Well, we have a cleaning lady, but I usually end up cleaning after she leaves. I hate to perpetuate ethnic stereotypes, but it's been my experience that other people don't clean like Romanians do.

I fondly recall the Saturday mornings of my youth spent cleaning our bathrooms. My mother would mix a highly toxic mixture of Mr. Clean and Clorox, a combination so potentially lethal that I believe the Office of Homeland Security now officially bans it. She'd then give me the volatile concoction to scrub the grout in our tubs with. My mother would always open a window for me. "If you think you're going to pass out, run and get some air. I've pulled up the screen." She'd yell this down from the ladder where she was Endusting some mahogany moldings.

Fighting for air, keeping my head low to the ground, I'd make the bathroom sparkle. My brother usually got out of this chore because he always had an activity—first Cub Scouts, then Boy Scouts, and later track and field practice—but I didn't mind. I actually loved it. I was conquering filth. True, the skin was burning off my fingers and my tender young eyes were watering as my lungs constricted, but you could eat off the floor when I was through. My mother prided herself on the fact that we could eat off her floors. Not that she ever let us do it, but if the dining room table ever broke or was stolen, we were set.

Now I use non-toxic, organic, and safe-for-the-environment cleaning supplies. I feel good about the planet-saving choice I've made. But I must confess, the bathroom always seems a little dirty to me.

Saturday is when I do most of the chores. In addition to the bathroom, I run errands, go to the gym, and basically do anything I can think of to put off working on my column. Fortunately, I have a large desktop computer at home, which is far too heavy for me to throw out the window or hide in a closet. So eventually—usually about fifteen minutes before I know Adam will be coming in and I'll be able to stop—I sit down to write.

The sitting does not actually guarantee that writing will take place, but it's a good first step and worthy of a reward. Sit for fifteen minutes with the *thought* of writing and I allow myself a cookie; twenty minutes equals two cookies. At the other end of the reward spectrum, I get a trip to Bermuda if I *work* six hours without a break (no trip has ever been awarded). Between the two cookies and the trip to Bermuda there are hundreds of potential treats, but off the top of my head I couldn't tell you what any of them are. It's been quite a while since I've actually sat in front of the computer more than twenty continuous minutes with the intention of writing. If I also included time spent sitting and aimlessly surfing the web, I'd have been rewarded with dozens (oh, all right, hundreds) of trips.

My diversion of choice, at this moment, was sorting through the mail. This minor assignment, which I thought might take two minutes, ended up sending me into an emotional tailspin.

I like to stack the mail into three neat piles: Mine, Adam's ,and Ours. On this day, my pile included letters from People for the American Way, GLAAD, The Anti-Violence Project, and Human Rights Campaign, all groups I've done volunteer work for (although, come to think of it, it's been a while).

Adam's pile had a notice about a sale at Barneys and an ad for laser teeth whitening. The Our pile contained a copy of *Us* magazine. We both get a big kick out of the fashion police column.

There was a thick, hand calligraphied envelope that appeared to be an invitation. I was about to toss it on the Our pile when I noticed it was addressed to:

ADAM MORE & GUEST

I stared at the envelope. *Odd*, I thought. Adam and I had been together for over six years. Who knew him well enough to invite him to their wedding, but wasn't close enough to him to know about me? I tossed the invitation onto his pile. I walked away and sat at my computer.

Adam More and guest, I typed on the screen. Good start. Eleven minutes more and I'd be having a cookie. But I didn't want a cookie. I wanted to know who had the nerve to invite Adam to their wedding without me.

Certainly, I thought, *I could move the offending piece of mail to the Our pile and open it*. That would not in any way count as opening Adam's mail. I would never do such a thing.

This was a completely different situation. I mean, I *am* the *guest* in question. It's not as if he'd take someone else. So, technically the envelope was addressed to me. I'm sure you see my logic.

I ran and tore open the envelope. I glanced at the bride and groom's names, wondering who these strangers were. When I saw the bride's name, I dropped the invitation to the floor, dramatically (knees buckling, arms flailing) made my way to the sofa, and collapsed. It was probably best that only Vincent and Theo were present to witness my performance.

I was angry—not my best emotion—but mostly I was just utterly confused.

It was yet another invitation from one of Adam's cousins, one of Arlene's endless brood of daughters. She was a woman who I'd talked with, danced with, and had to our apartment for dinner. I was the one who went to Tiffany and bought the sterling sliver cheese servers for her engagement gift. Apparently, she didn't remember my name.

I began making a mental list of all the things she might have done, if in fact she had somehow forgotten it:

A) Call Adam and say: "Hey, I'm really embarrassed but…"
B) Call Margaret and ask: "What's Adam's boyfriend's name?"
C) Call either of them: "We're confirming spellings." (Only awkward if my name turned out to be John Smith.)
D) Write to Miss Manners and find out what to do.
E) Think to herself: "Screw it, they're just fags, who cares about them anyway?" and address it to "And Guest."

I myself, in a similar situation, would have gone with option C. And it's the choice she should have made because she would have lucked out. "Steven, yes. Just wasn't sure if it was a 'v' or a 'ph.'" No one would have been the wiser.

The great thing about working for a paper that no one reads is that I can write about family and friends without threat of nasty confrontations with people when they learn my true feelings about them. Even Adam doesn't read my column unless I put the paper in front of him. Not that I write anything bad about him, but he doesn't need to read about every aspect of his personality that I find odd or quirky. I am particularly fond of the series of articles I wrote on Adam's unique relationship with food. Most specifically, his view on the ideal temperature at which foods should be consumed. Aside from ice cream and watermelon, Adam doesn't believe anything should be eaten cold. For example, he loves rice pudding, but only if it's served room temperature.

"And Guest" would be a two-part story.

Week one: The invitation's arrival and the feelings of Steven Worth-lessness that it brought up for me.

Week two: My acerbic literary "regret" to the happy couple. Most of week two's column would have to be pure fiction, because I knew I would never actually confront them. I'd suck it up and attend the event as Adam's date.

I was at the computer, writing, not thinking about snacks, when Adam bounded in. He was very early. Too early. He must have forgotten something, and been forced to return home for it.

"Sweetheart, I'm Prissy!" he shouted with glee.

In my opinion, if one is presented with a setup as surefire as *I'm Prissy* it's absolutely a sin not to deliver the punch line. My mind raced through a list of pithy retorts: *No kidding, Dr. Smith* was just about to trip from my tongue when Adam barreled on.

"We have to talk," he said. He was animated, completely energized. I hadn't seen him like this in weeks. Or had it been longer?

Filled, as I was, with *And Guest* outrage, I was in no mood for upbeat. "Yes, we do," I said, barely above a whisper. "Take a look at this." I threw the offending invitation at Adam, a gesture I immediately regretted. It was a little more Joan Crawford than I'd intended. "Read it."

He did. "My cousin Jessica is getting married. You knew that."

"Yes, I knew that." Was he blind, I thought?

"So, what's the problem?" Adam said.

"Who are you taking to the wedding?"

"What?" Adam didn't have the slightest idea what was upsetting me.

"Look at the envelope," I said, but by this point I had completely lost my voice.

Adam had averted his glance when I spoke so he'd failed to read my lips. "What?"

"En-ve-lope!" I mouthed, slowly.

He turned the envelope over and read. "Adam More and…oh."

"Who's your guest going to be? Because it won't be me." My voice had returned long enough for me to make this little jab.

"That's weird," Adam said.

"I think so, too." I thought to myself that I would have chosen a stronger word than "weird"—but Adam never swears. He's told me on many occasions that the use of obscenities is a clear sign of civilization's decline. He only uses the word "fuck" when he actually feels like fucking, and even then he's more likely to opt for the phrase, "do it."

I took the invitation from him and marched into the kitchen.

I generally post invitations on the refrigerator with a set of magnets that I picked up in a shop in Vegas. It's a whole store with nothing but refrigerator magnets. I chose a series of mini Van Gogh prints— all the others were either tacky or vulgar. When I got back from the trip, I showed them to Vincent and explained that his namesake made them. He purred loudly. He definitely understood. He's surprisingly intuitive.

There was only one available magnet on the refrigerator. The three others from the set were already affixing wedding invitations to the freezer. I placed the fourth invitation using *Starry Night*. "We know way too many straight people," I muttered as I surveyed my refrigerator, now completely obscured by wedding invitations.

Adam came up behind me. He massaged my concrete shoulders and nuzzled into my ear. "I'm sorry this happened to you." He continued rubbing and caressing me. I wondered why he put up with me. He hadn't sent the invitation, his cousin had. I had acted like this was his fault. It's a pattern with me. I do this because he's the only person I trust will still love me if he sees my not-so-well-concealed dark side. Pathetic, since even with him I don't express my emotions well.

"Sorry for being a brat," I said. I should have said something more, swore that I'd reform. Be less moody and sarcastic. But I didn't. I was silent. At least I'd managed to get an apology out. I looked at Adam closely. I realized that he was excited, and had been from the moment he'd walked in the door. He was practically bursting out of his skin. "Why are you home?" I asked, aware he wasn't due for hours. "What do you mean you're prissy?"

"Not prissy," he said with a sibilant "s." "Prissy like the character in *Gone With The Wind*. And I'm home because I'm no longer a wedding planner!"

Just as the word *what?* began forming on my lips, the phone rang. I hesitated, but habit made me grab it.

"Hello."

"*Steven?*" Vanessa's voice was filled with dread. She was shouting so loudly I felt my eardrum ring. I pulled the phone several inches from my head to achieve a more sufferable volume. "I don't want to terrify you," she was still yelling. "But Adam never showed up today. Do you have any idea where he might be? Is he there?"

Adam tapped my shoulder, shook his head at me and mouthed, "No. Tell her no. I'll explain later."

I found Adam's behavior baffling. I stared at the phone; I stared back at Adam. The last time I was this confused I was watching a Fassbinder film. My eyes pleaded with Adam to take the phone, but he kept shaking his head.

"Vanessa, he's not here. I'll have him call you if I hear from him."

"Really?" She paused, sighed heavily. "He's not there?"

"No."

"Liar."

"Vanessa, I'm not—"

"I call you. *You*, the definition of alarmist, and tell *you* Adam is nowhere to be found. And your response is not gasps, sobs, or screams, I do not hear the sounds of breaking glass as you hurl yourself from the window onto the funeral pyre that I'm sure you have on hand for such occasions. No, you rather blasély respond, 'I'll have him call you if I hear from him.' Steven, I don't buy it. Put him on the phone, right now!"

I handed the phone over.

When Vanessa finally stopped yelling about the truckload of doves that instead of being perched at the ready on the rooftop of the St. Regis, awaiting their you-may-now-kiss-the-bride cue, were stuck in traffic somewhere between Stamford and Greenwich on I-95, Adam spoke: "I'm sorry. I'm really sorry. I can't explain now. Handle today, please. And I promise I'll call you tonight." He hung up the phone.

"What is going on?" I asked.

"I'm not going to plan weddings anymore." He said this with intense passion and conviction. The statement was so strong that it would have been better suited if the words "plan weddings" had been substituted with "smuggle drugs" or "overthrow governments."

"Why aren't you going to plan weddings anymore?"

"Honey, I already told you. *I'm* Prissy."

I was beginning to feel like I was playing Costello to Adam's Abbott.

"I was on the subway this morning and I was sitting there dreading going to work and not really sure why. And I looked up and noticed a print ad. A series of photos of beautiful beaches with equally beautiful couples, men and women, strolling arm in arm, kissing. The caption read: *All Your Dreams Come True in the Bahamas*.

"And suddenly it hit me. *Finally*, it hit me. I thought, where are we in those pictures? What about our dreams? That's what the nightmares have been all about. I'm a matrimony slave.

"Actually, I can't say that. That's not right. I'm not a slave. I was not forced into this. I did this, willingly. I've designed my life in such a way that nearly every waking moment I'm making dreams come true for other people. For straight people. Not that I have anything against straight people; some of my best friends are straight. But they're not the only ones who dream about getting married. It's a dream I have for myself, for *us*, I mean."

I felt tears running down my cheeks.

"I was practically at the reception; I was already over on the East Side. I got off the train and walked home through the park. And all I kept thinking was, how have I done this job, been so happy doing this job, for all these years? How could I have been so disconnected from myself? Well, I'm not doing it anymore. I absolutely refuse to spend another ounce of my energy creating events that I am *by federal law* not allowed to participate in. No more wedding planning. Not until we can get married, too."

I was stunned. I don't know why I hadn't been able to figure out that this was at the root of Adam's recent distress, but I hadn't. Maybe it had never occurred to me because Adam wasn't a particularly political person. I mean, he voted, but he'd never been a "take a strong stand on the issues" kind of guy. That was more my thing, or it used to be, I had been a bit complacent in the last few years. Don't ask me why, but I'd never once given a thought to his occupation and its obvious conflict with our lives as a gay couple.

I wept. I wept big, ugly, snot-down-the-face-and-gasping-for-breath tears.

Adam had seen this before, but it had been a while. "Why are you crying?"

"Be-cause I'm—so—pro-proud—of—you." It was messy but sincere.

I didn't want the moment to become about me. But it happened. He got me Kleenex, held me tightly, and told me everything would be fine.

"What are you going to tell Vanessa and Max?"

Adam shrugged. "Not sure. I'm thinking of changing the name from More Weddings to More Bar Mitzvahs. What do you think?"

We laughed and my tears subsided. I held Adam in my arms. As we separated, I noticed all of the wedding invitations looming large on our fridge. "Now if we could only get out of attending weddings," I joked.

One should always be careful about what they say in jest.

CHAPTER SEVEN:
HELP ME START A MOVEMENT

Lucca's is in no way our favorite Italian restaurant; it's a big, noisy family-style place with red-and-white checkered tablecloths and a line out the door. Adam and I go there very infrequently because the portions are so massive that you must order one meal and share it. Honestly, it's still way too much food. And that's trouble for me. I was raised to clean my plate. It's been years since my grandmother Maia died. But even now, when faced with more food than I can finish, I hear her voice: *What? You no like Maia's cooking? Eat. In Romania, the babies starve. Finish the pita.*

On the rare occasion that we decide to risk both gluttony and the crowds it's because we are in the mood for Lucca's rigatoni with white beans, sausage, and broccoli. This dish is so remarkable, so extraordinary with just the perfect balance of garlic, hot pepper, and onion, that I have never seen anyone taste it for the first time without exclaiming, often with food still in their mouths, "Oh my God!" I did dine with one friend who went with the expression, "Shoot me now," which I didn't really think fit the situation, but she assured me it was high praise.

We ordered a terrific Chianti and each had two bowls of the heavenly pasta. Even with all we'd eaten we hadn't finished the rigatoni. I started dishing out some more.

"Sweetie." Adam stopped me. "Let's take it home. Or, if you rather, we can FedEx it to Romania."

We were in celebration mode over Adam's decision to stop planning weddings, so we'd ordered the rice pudding, too. They make theirs with Arborio rice and figs if they're in season, dried apricots if they're not—it's heavenly. I was eating mine; Adam was going to wait until we got home to have his so it would have time to come to room temperature.

We sipped the last of our wine and I winked at him. I'd really wanted to reach across the table and take his hand—it's large and strong, and I wanted to hold it—but there was a table of ten next to us. They were teenage boys, members of a basketball team, I'd gathered from their boisterous conversation. Better not to risk holding hands, I thought. I didn't want trouble.

Invariably, this moment occurs whenever we go out. Just as I have the impulse to display any kind of slight public affection for Adam, I become paralyzed by the not completely irrational fear that someone observing us will start shouting *Faggot*. Or worse, actually try to physically harm us. I hate this about myself.

I sat there at the table overcome with a fear I knew I wouldn't be conquering tonight. I settled for the wink.

Adam winked back at me. I suspected Adam was also monitoring his behavior a bit because of the teenagers. Even when we've been in gay-friendly spots like Fire Island or Key West, we're not a big public display of affection kind of couple, but a touch of the hand would have been nice.

"You're right," he said.

The statement came out of nowhere. I had no idea what he was referring to. "Right about what?"

"*And Guest*. It's really upsetting."

"I'll get over it," I said. I didn't want to make any waves with Adam's family. His mother barely tolerated me. The last thing I wanted was to be branded as a troublemaker.

"We're not going," Adam said.

"You do know that your mother already hates me, right?"

"I don't mean just this wedding. We're not going to any weddings. Not my family's, not your family's, no one's."

"I don't know—"

"It's the best idea you've ever had." Adam toasted me with his last sip of wine.

I wanted to say, "Don't give me credit for this—you started it." But the facts were that:

I had suggested that we stop attending weddings, and—

I was delighted to skip his cousin's. I had no desire to spend another long evening seated at the right hand of Margaret, celebrating with all the Mores.

"You know what really gets me?" Adam was on a roll now. "I've never thought about this before. Why doesn't anyone ever say, 'Hey, I know this must be hard for you; we'd love to have you at our wedding. But we *totally* get it if it's too painful for you to attend.'"

What Adam said made perfect sense. But the thought that someone might actually be that PC seemed so improbable to me that I found myself chuckling lightly.

"Don't laugh, I'm serious. And then I could respond, 'Oh, that's okay, I don't want to get married, I'll just sit here and watch.'"

Again, Adam winked at me. I winked back. He gave me one more. And so on. If those jocks from the other table were watching, they might think Tourette's but they'd never guess gay.

At some point during our blink fest, Daniel, our waiter, had arrived at the table. Lucca's is one of those places where the waiters introduce themselves. "Hey, I'm Daniel, let me tell ya 'bout the specials."

I hate knowing the waiter's name. I guess it's because no matter how nice he is, I'm not interested in having dinner with my waiter. If I were, I would have made a date with him. I'm interested in having dinner with the other people who are sitting at the table with me. When I know the waiter's name, I start to feel guilty for ignoring him. Should I be including Daniel in our conversation?

This may sound shallow, and the behavior was a little too Brad-like, but I *had* cut Daniel some slack, and included him in earlier conversation, because he was so cute. Someday, he would be handsome. But at twenty-two he was still cute. Fresh. Earlier on, while we had been waiting for the rigatoni to arrive, I figured a little harmless flirting with our new pal Daniel would make for an ideal zero-calorie first course.

"Club member?" Adam asked when Daniel first left the table.

"Are you kidding?" Adam has almost no gaydar. "Of course he's a club member," I said. "Did you see the way he smiled at us as we talked?"

"He does that because he wants a tip."

"He wants something from us, but it's not a tip," I said, stealing another glance at Daniel. I really have to watch myself—I'm too young for lechery.

To prove to Adam that our waiter was gay, I shared with Daniel Adam's reason for quitting wedding planning. Daniel didn't respond in any clear way. He dropped the bread basket and walked away.

Maybe I'd been wrong about him.

"Can I get you gentlemen anything else?" Daniel was all smiles now.

Sure, now that it's tip time, he's smiling.

"Just the check," Adam said.

He pulled it from his apron and placed it on the table. "The wine's comped."

Ka-Ching! That's what we refer to as the club member's discount. Of course, it would be wrong to accept it.

"No. We can't let you——" Adam started.

Daniel crouched down next to us at the table. "We have a wedding here tomorrow night," Daniel whispered. "And we're not going to show up." He pointed toward the bar, where there were five very handsome waiters standing and raising glasses in our direction.

Adam and I stared at each other. This couldn't really be happening.

"I'm not sure how the food is going to get from the kitchen to the tables, but trust me," Daniel said. "The plates aren't going to be in this gay boy's hands."

And with that, Daniel took our credit card and sashayed away.

❖

What is it with guilt? That's what I was thinking about as Adam and I strolled home from the restaurant.

I was bloated on bread, pasta, and pudding, and I desperately wanted to unbutton the top of my pants and un-tuck my shirt so I could breathe, but I refrained. When I see someone with a shirt un-tucked, I immediately assume they're out of control and incapable of enjoying a human-size portion of food. I was wishing I wasn't so judgmental with regard to this particular issue so that I could undo my belt and get a little relief. I'd have to wait until I was home.

When I removed my clothing, I'd appear to be five months pregnant.

When we were first together, and probably still now, my food-induced hysterical pregnancies horrified Adam. "What are you doing?" he asked, the first time he witnessed it.

"What?" I said, feigning ignorance.

"Why are you sticking your stomach out like that?"

I knew that if we were to have a lasting relationship, he'd need to know about this. It couldn't be hidden. "I have the bloat," I said.

"What?"

Which word didn't he understand? "I——am——bloated," I said.

"Men don't get bloated."

I grabbed my helium-filled gut. "Romanian men do."

But on this night, Adam was far too excited to notice, or care, that I was "showing." His stroll had become more of a skip and I waddled in agony to keep up with him. "Can you believe it?" Adam said. "One conversation and we shut down a wedding!"

This is when my guilt *really* kicked in.

Adam was right to be excited. But all I could think about was the poor couple whose wedding would be ruined.

This couple had chosen to have their wedding at Lucca's, which is fun for a cheap and tasty meal, but it's kind of a dive. The couple obviously has no money, I thought. I imagined them scrimping and saving. The groom had taken on a third job digging ditches, while his bride was busy sewing buttons in a sweatshop on Canal Street.

It was hell for them, but they'd saved enough money to pay for a plate of pasta and a tiny green salad for their guests. They had hoped for shrimp cocktail as an appetizer, but just couldn't swing it; they'd settle for mini quiche.

Yes, their reception would be meager but their love, great. A sort of Italian-style Bob Cratchit family sprang into view in front of me.

"Oh my God! What have I done?"

"Did you say something, sweets?" Adam asked. He was so consumed with thoughts of the *Norma Rae* event that was to take place at Lucca's that he'd missed my outburst.

"I feel terrible for that couple," I said

Adam wrinkled his forehead—his way of indicating confusion.

"The couple," I continued, "who are getting married tomorrow."

Adam rolled his eyes in a style more mine than his.

"I do," I said. "They've made plans. Spent every cent they have." (I now believed this to be Gospel truth.) "And now, no staff is going to show up."

"Yes. Yes. Yes!" Adam leapt into the air as he shouted.

❖

At home, liberated from my pants, I sank into the tub and massaged my bloated belly while Adam sat in the kitchen eating his room-temperature rice pudding. To enhance my calming, bathing experience, I applied a thick mud mask to my face and neck. Theo stood on the edge of the tub, nuzzling the back of my head. Vincent, I guessed, was in the kitchen circling Adam's feet. Hoping some pudding would drop to the floor.

My eyes were closing and my stomach was deflating. I was enjoying the warm sensation of the water and the feeling of Theo's nose in my hair.

"Room for me?" Adam said.

I pried my lids open and saw Adam's naked torso standing next to me. I was so grateful my stomach was flat again. "Sure," I said.

Our apartment is a pretty standard two-bedroom. There is nothing exceptional about it. It's now worth a small fortune, but that has more to do with the craziness of New York real estate than with any architectural significance. The one great thing about it, though, is the master bathroom. We can take no credit for it. The former owner did the remodeling. Our bathroom features as large a tub as I've ever seen. I remember as a kid seeing a TV commercial for a honeymoon hotel in the Poconos where newlyweds drank champagne while sitting in a massive heart-shaped tub. That's how big our tub is, only it's a rectangle, not a heart. As an eleven-year-old, the risqué scene of two adults sharing a bath made me tingle a bit.

The eleven-year-old in me responded as I felt Adam slide in next to me.

"Steven," he said coyly.

"Let me just wash the mask off." Having sex with Egyptian Earth on my face was too kinky for me. I turned on the faucet and Theo jumped down. She loves the tub when it's full but she's terrified of the sight of running water. I can't figure it out.

"Sweetie, I just want to talk," Adam said.

"Oh, okay." I wondered if I should tell him I wasn't bloated anymore.

"I need to ask you a favor," he said. "Help me start a movement."

"A movement?"

"If queer folk thought about this for one minute, they'd never go to a wedding again."

"I don't know about that," I said as gently as I could.

"I really don't think they would. Certainly they'd stop working in the industry," Adam said.

"Okay, let's say you're right—"

"I *am* right, Steven."

"How do we start this movement?" I asked.

Adam had begun lightly running his fingers up and down my back. It was a surefire way to get me to do anything he wanted. I melted into his touch.

"I'll tell you how we'll start this movement: You are a writer and I am a celebrity."

"Oh, brother." I laughed. "You're not a celebrity, Adam."

He was playing with me, sort of. Deep down, he knew that he was not a celebrity. "I beg your pardon," he said. "Have I, or have I not, appeared on *The View*?"

❖

I agreed to start the movement with Adam for three reasons:

1) Adam was passionate about it, and I hadn't seen him really passionate about anything in a very long time.
2) While I didn't think it would amount to anything, I was thrilled to be handed this get-out-of-jail-free card to avoid attending the weddings of Adam's cousins, as there were still five who were single. And,
3) By doing this I felt confident that I would have at least two months' worth of material for my column.

As I sat staring at my computer, desperate for inspiration, I began to seriously doubt the soundness of reason 3.

"Can I read what you have, sweets?" Adam said as he brought me another mug of coffee.

"Not quite yet." I said, leaning in to hide the monitor. It was 2:00 A.M. and I was drinking coffee and flashing back to college all-nighters. Why exactly did Adam think we needed to stay up all night? It wasn't like I was writing anything.

"Just a peek," he said, pushing up next to me. He glanced at the screen and read aloud, "My boyfriend, Adam…"

True, only three words, but each one a gem.

"I'm totally blocked!" I cried.

"Okay, calm down. I'll help you."

"There is no help for me."

"I think maybe we've given you a little too much caffeine," Adam said as he pried the mug from my hands and pulled a chair up alongside me. "Let's hash this all out." He said it so sweetly, I was sure it would help.

"Great," I said, trying to get into the spirit, "Let's hash it out."

Neither one of us spoke.

Finally, Adam attempted to hash: "I'm a wedding planner who is not going to plan another wedding until we can get married, too."

I took a stab at it: "And tomorrow six gay waiters—"

Adam interrupted. "Now, we don't know that they're all gay, some of them might have just been sympathetic to the cause."

"Did you take a look at those boys?" I asked. His inability to spot homosexuals never ceased to amaze me. "Tomorrow six gay waiters are boycotting a wedding."

"What percentage of cater waiters would you guess are either gay or sympathetic to our cause?" Adam asked.

Suddenly things started to become clear. I smiled. Adam smiled back. I glanced toward the couch. The kids, who were just up from a nap, were smiling, too.

"Who else can we target?" I asked. I was getting into the swing now.

Adam thought a moment. "How many straight organists have you met?"

"About the same number as straight florists," I replied.

It was at that moment that it occurred to me that this thing might really work. What would happen if all the gay organists, cater waiters, and especially florists stayed home? And then I thought of more professions: hairdressers, makeup artists, and let's not forget, fashion designers. I shouted with glee.

Adam cheered me on. I felt as close to him as I ever had. "Write like the wind," he exclaimed.

And I did. Pages scrolled by on my computer. I'd need to do some serious editing to fit the story into what now seemed like my minuscule column. I was approaching page four when Adam interrupted me. "Be sure that you write that we can't give gifts either."

I pulled my fingers from my keyboard.

"Excuse me?" Which is my way of saying I'm going to pretend that I did not just hear you say that.

"I said—"

"What do you mean, no gifts?"

"We cannot in any way participate in the economy of weddings."

What he said made perfect sense, but I was focused on the shame and embarrassment attached to being, as my mother likes to say, "empty-handed."

"If we don't send gifts to people," I said, "They'll think that we're doing this because we're cheap."

"Well," Adam said with a sort of Jimmy Stewart stutter I'd never heard before, "If you really think we should buy gifts, Steven...Or, would you prefer me to call you *And Guest?*"

In my opinion, that was playing dirty. But it had the effect Adam wanted.

I began writing again.

We started chanting, "No gifts. No gifts. No gifts!"

I did it! I wrote, polished, and edited the first of what would become an entire series of columns on the subject. I was more than due a reward, but for the first time in years I actually felt that the work was reward enough. No additional treats or bribes required.

I'd experienced a shift while I was writing. I'd been swept up by Adam's fervor. Now I, too, was in the fight to obtain equal rights. I felt inspired, confident, and strong. Three words never before used in a sentence describing me.

CHAPTER EIGHT:
I'M AN ACTIVIST!

The following Monday morning at 6:30, Adam yanked me from my slumber. Resigning myself to the fact that I was never going to reach the climax of my Nate Berkus and Anderson Cooper dream, I got up. Adam had a plan, and he needed my help.

For weeks Adam had been complaining about the stainless steel nameplate outside of his office. It had a scratch, just above the second "d" in Weddings, that needed buffing out. Between his hectic schedule and the malaise he'd been suffering, he'd never managed to attend to it.

Now we were standing in the heart of Greenwich Village, on lower Fifth Avenue, at the front entrance of More Weddings. I was holding Adam's Jack Spade messenger bag for him, and watched as he polished the scratch out of his sign with a piece of extra-fine steel wool. It took about five minutes, but when Adam was through it looked good as new.

I took a step back to admire Adam's work. The sign gleamed.

"I'm ready," Adam whispered conspiratorially.

I unzipped his Jack Spade, pulled out a can of spray paint, and handed it to Adam, thus fulfilling my duty as the designated accomplice.

Adam shook the can longer than was necessary—he loves that rattling sound spray paint cans make (I wrote a column about it). He pulled the top off the can and started spraying the red paint. Again, I took a step back to fully appreciate his handiwork:

NO More Weddings!

Very nice, I thought. He'd almost purchased black spray paint but I'd suggested red. It was absolutely the right choice.

At 7:00 A.M., we had been the first customers through the doors of the hardware store around the corner from our apartment. Initially a young clerk, terribly overweight and with a face flushed from effort, helped us. The sight of the young man, so reminiscent of me at that age, broke my heart. I wanted to make it clear to him that I knew his pain and I wasn't a sizeist. I felt like holding him and saying reassuringly, *I understand and there's hope. I used to look just like you, minus the red face. Look at me now!* Of course, I said nothing; people don't change until they're ready.

Instead, I gave him an enormous warm smile and kept nodding empathetically. I couldn't help but notice that the lad was trying to discreetly move away from me. He inched himself backward until he knocked into a display case full of wrenches, sending them clanging to the ground.

We helped the embarrassed and shaken clerk restock the wrenches, and when we finished, Adam queried, "I hope you can help me. I need some paint to deface personal property."

Somehow, the overweight boy's face managed to turn an even deeper crimson. "Pardon me?"

I imagine he had been told "the customer is always right." Perhaps it was hard for him to apply that credo in this case.

"Don't worry, it's *my* personal property I'm defacing," Adam said. "I'm no law breaker," he added for clarification.

"Let me get the manager," the boy said. I guess for $7.15 an hour, he didn't feel like waiting on a nut. He dashed off with amazing speed for such a big guy.

❖

"Check me out!" Adam shouted as we entered his office. "I'm an activist!"

Considering Vanessa and Max had been informed via hasty phone calls that they were no longer in the business of planning weddings, they were in surprisingly fine spirits. They didn't actually acknowledge Adam's activist comment, but they were smiling. They were also exceedingly punctual considering they didn't really have jobs anymore. It was still quite early; I was shocked they were both in.

Apparently, Adam was as well. He glanced at his watch. "Why are you two here already?"

"I'm trying to figure out how to tell twenty-three brides that they're on their own. You have a lawyer, right? I'm just thinking, you know, when the brides start suing us, we should be prepared," Vanessa said. Max nodded in agreement.

Vanessa swung her short legs out from under her desk and pointed her shoes in my direction. "I know you always appreciate the *scarpe*. Gucci. Great. Right?"

They were great. But I couldn't focus on them. I was stopped by what she'd said about Adam needing a lawyer. I was suddenly very concerned for him. I hadn't thought about the fact that Adam had signed contracts with these couples.

Adam ignored Vanessa. He glanced toward Max as if to ask, "And why are you here?"

Max remained silent. He leaned in to block his computer screen, a maneuver I have quite a bit of familiarity with. Max was too slow for me, though. I could see what he was up to. He'd come in early to update his résumé. Hard to blame him. He had bills to pay—no reason for him to go down with this sinking ship.

Adam was too excited to pick up on any discord. He kissed me and I said my good-byes.

As I walked out the door, I heard him say: "Great. Since you're both here, shall we do some birthday party brainstorming? Everybody has one, there should be plenty of work."

"Maybe," Max said. "But just how many people spend a hundred grand on their birthday?"

He had a point.

❖

Even with the pit stop at Adam's office, I was at the paper by 8:15. Never before had I been at the paper by 8:15. Rarely have I been there by 10:15.

Gail was already working. I was surprised. Even by Gail's I-do-everything, this-is-a-one-woman-show standards, she was early. No one was due in before 9:00—we're not a breaking news kind of operation. Fortunately for me, no one was even considered late until sometime around 11:00. The trade-off for making very little money was that the whip was never cracked (except when we were covering the leather fair).

I was in early because I wanted to enjoy my carrot muffin in peace.

Gail had come in early because she needed a break from her ever-hovering girlfriend. "I think I love her, but the domination thing is wearing me down."

I put my muffin down. It could wait.

"Excuse me," I said. Gail seemed to think that she had shared with me this aspect of her relationship with Liz. She had not. "What do you mean, domination?"

"We haven't talked about this before?" Gail asked between bites of her fried egg, bacon, and cheese on a roll. "She likes me to order her around."

"You mean, sexually?"

"Well, yes," she said. "But in all arenas, she wants to be told what to do. I'm constantly making her clean my apartment. She loves it but I'm getting tired of it. I'd break it off, but honestly my bathroom has never looked so great."

"Let me ask you something. Is Liz by any chance a Romanian?"

❖

Everyone was on time for work today. I'd barely finished a fourth mug of coffee when Brad arrived. He'd undergone a makeover.

His hair was as blond as humanly possible. Any lighter, and it would have classified as white. He was wearing a Fubu hoodie. I know this because he said: "Hey, Steven, you like the hoodie? It's Fubu." Sean John jeans and enough bling around his neck to herniate a disk completed the ensemble.

He gave me a wide smile. I was relieved to discover he was not featuring any gold teeth.

A forty-year-old in hip-hop wear is a risky choice. A Caucasian forty-year-old in hip-hop wear is such a dangerous miscalculation that witnessing the sight, there is only one possible response: Gail fell from her chair in a fit of hysterical laughter.

I laughed, too, but more cautiously. I shouldn't have laughed at all, I know, but it was such an absurd sight.

Brad was hurt. He was looking at me, even though Gail was the one on the floor.

I wanted to shout, "Don't look at me, I laughed discreetly; I'm not the one on the floor." Instead, I stammered as I always do when I feel like I've been a bad boy.

"Why don't you respect me?" Brad said.

"Not sure," Gail said, finally back on her feet. "It's either that hair or those pants."

Brad was staring at me, baggy pants belted somewhere below his ass. "Steven, can I see you in my office?"

Brad turned and walked away. As he approached his office door he tripped on his oversized trousers. I was relieved, for Brad's sake, that Gail had been looking the other way and not seen him stumble.

"What do you think?" Brad was showing off his "after" look—I was really missing the "before."

"Does this have anything to do with the call you made to me the other night?"

"The call?"

Oh, I see. This is how we were going to play it.

"Does it have something to do with Charlie?"

"Oh, Charlie!" Brad beamed. "I really want the two of you to hang."

Prior to this conversation, the Brad I know would never have made that statement unless he was actually hoping that Charlie and I would be executed.

"Charlie's great. Tonight I'm meeting his peeps."

Prior to this conversation, the Brad I know would never have made that statement unless he was actually being introduced to a box of Easter candy.

"I can't wait to see his crib."

Prior to this conversation…actually in this case, considering the age difference, perhaps "crib" was the ideal word choice.

"I really like him, Steven. I'm going to do whatever it takes to make this work. I'd even consider…Um…I can't think of the word. You know what I mean."

"I don't, sorry. How about a clue?"

"You know. Like you and Adam. When you don't have sex with other people."

"I believe the word you're grasping for is 'monogamy.'"

"Exactly! I've never done that before."

"Brad, I know it was a very long time ago. But you and I were monogamous."

"We were not."

Brad's jaw slackened. He quickly glanced away from me and began fidgeting. He knocked his necklaces back and forth between his thumb and forefinger. Then, in a failed attempt at recovery: "Oh, right. That's right," he sputtered rapidly. "Of course with *you* I was monogamous. Anyway, enough about the old days. You still haven't told me what you think," he said, pointing at his ghetto-fabulous ensemble.

"It looks a little…" I just couldn't find the words.

"Go ahead, tell me."

I really wanted to say that it looked a little like a mid-life crisis, but I thought better of it. For one thing, I knew he would tell me that he was too young for a mid-life crisis and then I'd be forced to point out that he was only too young if he made it past ninety. I couldn't tell him it looked good. We were friends; I could not allow him to walk around like that. As I stood silently trying my best to figure out a delicate way to handle this situation, Brad slumped down into his chair.

"Do you have any idea what it's like to go through life with the name Brad?" he asked.

"What?" I was not seeing where he was going with this.

"Do you?"

"I can't say that I do, Brad." I said this without nearly the amount of sympathy he was looking for.

"When your name is Brad," he leaned into me now, to whisper, "people expect you to be hot and young."

"That's crazy. Besides you are hot…" I know that I shouldn't have, but I paused for a count of five before adding, "and young."

"Your name is Steven," he spat with such contempt that you would have thought my name was Satan.

"Thanks," I said. Unfortunately it came out sounding sincere instead of sarcastic.

"Steven is a neutral name," he stormed ahead. "With a name like *Steven* there are no expectations placed on you one way or the other. If you're named Walter or Norman, people are thrilled if you've managed to shower and shave."

I could see that Brad had given this issue a great deal of thought, and just as I was about to tell him his theory was nonsense, I recalled an incident years earlier when I'd canceled a blind date with a guy solely because his name was Chester. "It must be very difficult to go through life with the name Brad," I said.

Brad started crying. I realized in all the years I'd known him I'd never seen tears—not even during any of the emotionally manipulative, sappy movies we both love to watch. He didn't even cry during *Random Harvest*.

"Steven, do you think I might be having a mid-life crisis?"

"No, Brad. Not possible. You're way too young to be having a mid-life crisis."

I tried to cheer Brad up by telling him about my article and the movement, but by then he was too depressed to listen. "Let me be surprised," he said dourly. "I'll read about it along with the other four people who read this sorry excuse for a newspaper that I've devoted the best years of my life to."

It seemed like I should just allow Brad some time to wallow in self-pity. I left him in his office, pulling the skin on his neck back toward his ears.

❖

Later that afternoon my brother called. I was surprised to hear his voice, as we're not really phone people. Ours is much more of an in-person relationship. In addition to the constant couple dates, the two of us go to the movies regularly; neither Amanda nor Adam can handle scary or gory—Peter and I live for it. We also go to yoga class together, or we did. Lately, I've been going to Hot Nude Yoga. The Hot refers to the temperature of the room, but I will admit it is also kind of hot. While the class is open to all men, regardless of sexual orientation, Peter declined my invitation. "That's a little gay for me."

I was relieved; I didn't really want to take a naked yoga class with my brother.

Hearing his voice on the phone, panic set in. This is another thing I've inherited from my mother. From the moment I was old enough to pick up a phone, she told me never to bother anyone at work. She said it was rude. Calling would be disruptive. People don't have a second to spare. They're inventing gadgets, fixing cars, curing diseases, collecting tolls, painting houses, teaching toddlers, negotiating détentes, arresting criminals, or, perhaps, hunting big game. In short, they were busy—far too busy to spend a minute talking to me. My mother's lessons are etched in my brain, but I don't know why I still follow that particular rule. If my schedule is any indication of a typical workday, people have loads of time for idle chatter.

Nevertheless, I felt certain that since Peter was calling me at the paper something had to be wrong. If he had good news he'd be calling me at home, after six but before ten, of course.

Thankfully, my brother's reason for calling was not dire, as I'd feared. He merely wanted Adam and me to come over for dinner on

Friday night. *Perfect*, I thought, *the day the paper hits the stands*. We'll celebrate the start of the marriage revolution together. As I thought about weddings, I remembered the invitation to Jessica's. "Hey," I said. "Did you and Amanda get invited to Jessica's wedding?"

"Of course," Peter said, "didn't you?"

"We did. Did you by any chance open the invitation?" I asked.

"As a matter of fact, I did."

"So you saw the envelope?" I was determined to get to the bottom of this. "Was it addressed to you?"

"What are you getting at?" I could hear impatience in Peter's voice. He turned on one of the industrial-size mixers he used in his bakery—it drowned out the sound of Barney singing "Quando Quando Quando" that I'd been hearing throughout our conversation.

"Was your name on the envelope?" I spoke quickly.

"Yes. Well, mine and Amanda's."

"I have to run. I'll see you Friday." I hung up. They had managed to get Peter's name on the envelope but not mine. Peter and Amanda weren't married, they hadn't been together as long as we had—so why hadn't their invitation been addressed to *Amanda More and Guest*?

I was tense; I tried to relax, but every time I began feeling calm I thought of other things to worry about. Chief among my concerns: would any of the eight-million-plus denizens of New York be reading my column on Friday?

I found myself sitting at my desk with fingers crossed.

CHAPTER NINE: I'M MAD AS HELL
AND I'M NOT GOING TO TAKE IT ANYMORE

Here's a news flash: Crossing your fingers really works.

I was bombarded with e-mails regarding the column. Actually *bombarded*. Not my usual definition of bombarded—which is any number of responses over two. The previous record of six e-mails for a single column was wiped out by the whopping one hundred and three I received for this first wedding column. I don't really do math, so I can't tell you how that translates into an increase in percentage, but it's really big. Right?

Not every reply warmed my heart. There were a few backhanded compliments snuck in among the responses: *Wow, you're usually so self-absorbed and inane, this article was amazing. I never would have guessed you could write something of substance.*

There were two e-mails that were just completely hateful and I will not dignify them by quoting from them, but I do wonder how people with such narrow points of view find themselves in possession of a copy of *The Gay New York Times*.

I will not dwell on those few when there were a hundred positive and inspirational letters flooding my inbox. My words motivated people into action. I didn't receive mere notes of thanks (of course that would have been just fine). I received long, personal and specific stories—tales of coming out and longing, and hope and profound change.

I include the column below:

Dear Reader:

My boyfriend Adam has always been among the lucky few fortunate enough to love his job. That is, until recently. As you may know from past columns, Adam is, I mean was, a very successful wedding planner.

Without warning, Adam started changing. He was finding work more and more difficult. It became harder for him to focus. And then a wave of melancholy swept over him. So crippling was his despair that he was having unexplained bouts of tears, mood swings and interrupted sleep. In short, he started doing a terrifying and uncanny imitation of me.

Fortunately, Adam has figured out the source of his sorrow. Adam's pain grew out of injustice. It sprang from the realization that he spent the vast majority of his time working extremely hard, all in an effort to enable a segregated institution to continue.

So Adam has decided to stop planning weddings until every American, regardless of sexual orientation, can get married. And he's asked me to deliver his clarion call: he's urging others in the industry to join him in boycotting any form of participation in weddings.

There must be a few sympathetic priests, organists, hairdressers, makeup artists or florists who are just as fed up as he is. Surely others are pondering these thoughts, feeling the same discontent Adam has felt. Certainly, some of you are ready to stop supporting inequality.

Think about the power you have for just a moment. Straight people can't get married without you. Well, they can. But the events won't be nearly as fabulous.

Is there anyone out there today who would be willing to join Adam's fight? Is there one florist, reading this article, who's had enough? Who is ready to take a stand?

As you sit, surrounded by the beautiful wedding bouquets you've made for other people, I want you to pick one of them up. Hold it in your hands. Your hands that have been bloodied and scarred by countless rose thorns.

Now choose the grandest bouquet, the one you're most proud of. Admire your work. Think of all the skill, patience and love you put into creating it. Smell the flower's delicate fragrance. I'd like you now to carry those blooms to the front of your shop, open the door and go out onto the sidewalk. Hold the bouquet aloft. With all your might, hurl it into the street. And shout. Wail at the top of your lungs: "I'm mad as hell, and I'm not going to take it anymore!"

You've all seen the movie; I know you can do it.

I imagine that some of you reading this are thinking: Not a bad idea. But it doesn't affect me. I don't work in the wedding industry. I'm a plumber, or a banker or a cop. Love to help, but I'm off the hook.

Not so fast.

Adam and I have another request. We'd like you to stop attending weddings. (Unless the happy couple happens to live in Canada, Holland, Spain, South Africa or any country that offers marriage rights to all of its citizens.)

Since I can hear all seventeen of my loyal fans asking the question, I'll be very clear: Yes, I am serious. No, I'm not kidding.

This year alone I have attended five weddings. I have watched these couples, my friends, my family, as they've joyously entered into the sacred institution of marriage. I've seen them smile and weep. I've heard all the praise and toasts and cheers. And I have wholeheartedly given them my own. I have raised my glass, I have wished them happiness and health and long life. I have danced, celebrated, rejoiced. And now I am weary. I'm tired. I'm angry.

Yesterday, I received another invitation. I'm not going.

I can no longer laugh and make small talk. I will not kiss another bride; tell another groom what a lucky man he is. I refuse to be polite. I've no interest in feigning merriment.

I look at the invitation I'm holding in my hand. I feel the raised lettering beneath my fingers. Lucky me, another chance to dine at the matrimonial country club! Eat up, I'm told. I just better not think about joining the club myself. Everything will be fine, as long as I know my place.

My place, apparently, is cheerleader, not player. As of today, I reject this notion. I'm not jumping and clapping and shouting with joy. I'll no longer be sitting on the sidelines and watching. I've seen this game far too many times. If I can't play, I'm taking my balls and I'm going home.

For what does it say about a man if he refuses to acknowledge injustice? Who would rather be nice than righteous? Who chooses complacency over change?

The time has come for me, as a gay man, to stop attending weddings. My absence might have an impact, might make someone think. All my presence at the event can do is send the message that I approve of the current definition of marriage in America.

I do not.

Do you?

S.W.

Reprinted with permission: *The Gay New York Times*

CHAPTER TEN:
OH, THE *GAY* NEW YORK TIMES

Since Peter and Amanda live only four blocks from us, Adam and I left our apartment at 7:24 and arrived for dinner at their place as scheduled at exactly 7:30. Adam had wanted to bring champagne to celebrate the article, but I thought it was too much, so we settled on a great Pinot Noir we'd discovered recently.

As we approached their building we both noticed the news box stocked with copies of *The Gay New York Times*.

"Wow, I didn't realize it was right here," I said, suddenly excited at the prospect that Peter and Amanda had already read my column.

Adam smiled at me. "I guess I know what we'll be talking about tonight."

Amanda greeted us at their door wearing the most ridiculous oversized oven mitts—they were shaped like lobsters. She was also wearing a gauze bandage above her right eye.

"What happened?" I asked as I kissed her. Adam tried to hand her the wine, but the oven mitts made that impossible.

"I got hit in the head."

"An inch lower and you would have lost the eye." I looked to find my mother, but then realized the words had come out of my own mouth.

"How did it happen?"

"I can't explain it. I was walking down Amsterdam, coming home from Columbia, and a crazy man ran onto the sidewalk. He was screaming at the top of his lungs."

"Oh my God! You poor thing."

"Yeah, it was really scary. He was saying something about being mad as hell. And the next thing I knew, a bouquet of lily-of-the-valley came hurling at me. It was wrapped in French wired ribbon. That's what cut me."

I said nothing.

"I've got to get back to the stove," Amanda said, flashing her gigantic smile and her oven mitts.

"Not your fault," Adam whispered once his sister was back in the kitchen.

As if I didn't feel bad enough already, right then I saw Margaret standing by the window. I had been under the impression that it was just going to be the four of us for dinner. I'd been thinking a fun and relaxed evening. Seeing Margaret, I realized that the evening had the potential to be many things.

Fun and relaxed, however, were not among the possibilities.

When I first met Margaret, I was instantly wowed by her glamorous appearance. I remember she was wearing a cream-colored St. John suit. Her straight blond hair was tucked back behind her diamond-studded ears. She had sort of a Dina Merrill thing going for her. Immediately, I felt intimidated, anxious; I really wanted to make a good first impression.

As Adam introduced us, an oasis of sweat sprang forth on my palms. Before I could blot them on my pants, Margaret had extended her hand in greeting. I hesitated; I couldn't let her feel that hot clammy mess. So instead of shaking Margaret's hand, I leaned back, waved at her, like a germaphobe who just remembered he was out of Purell, and said: "It's nice to finally meet you, Mrs. More." Then I offered what I thought would be a compliment sure to make up for my egregious greeting: "You look smashed!" I shouted.

I swear to God, I meant to say, "You look smashing!"

Now, Margaret made her way over to Adam and me. "Darling." She hugged her son. "Steven," she said to me, without any of the brightness that had lightened her voice for "darling."

Margaret and I did the awkward dance of people who are supposed to be close but aren't. I moved in for a hug as she pulled away, she went for a peck on the cheek as I moved aside. Finally, we settled for warm-looking, put-on smiles.

Peter and Amanda have a spectacular loft-style apartment, which is uncommon on the Upper West Side. The wide-open space is wonderful for entertaining, but it's horrible when you're trying to find a private spot to gossip with your brother. I pulled Peter as far away from Margaret as I could, but we were still in her line of sight. "What's she doing here?" I asked.

"Meg? Come on, she's not so bad."

Meg? When did my brother start calling this woman Meg? It had taken me three years to get from Mrs. More to Margaret, and that shift had only taken place because I make such an awesome martini.

Across the room, in the open kitchen, I heard Margaret with her children: "Of course I read the paper today—terrible, horrible."

"What was so horrible about it?" Adam was irritated.

I was thinking a family fight within five minutes might be a record, but then I remembered last Thanksgiving.

"Oh, *The Gay New York Times.* Of course I didn't read it," Margaret said.

"Mother," Amanda snapped. Still clad in her lobster oven mitts. She stood, stirring a large pot on the stove.

"What did you think of the story?" Adam asked.

"I didn't read it," Amanda said. "But," she said turning to her mother, "I wouldn't say, *of course* I didn't read it!" Amanda looked over at me and smiled. All I really noticed, though, was the bandage. I was still huddled in the corner with Peter.

Peter who had given up extolling the virtues of his new buddy, Meg, said, "Oh right, your paper. I really need to find it and, you know…read it."

"It's available at the base of your building, and it's free." Why on earth had I thought this was going to be a fun and relaxed evening? "Who wants a martini?" I shouted.

I made a large pitcher for everyone but Adam. Adam is unfortunately allergic to juniper berries—a main ingredient in gin. When Adam was seventeen his parents decided that he was old enough to join their ritual of cocktail hour. Each evening at 6:00 (or 5:00 on the weekend) Margaret, her late husband Prescott, and Adam would sip martinis, and in low, civilized voices discuss their days and occasionally local and national politics. I never asked Adam to share the political views of his dad. My guess is Prescott and I would not have seen eye to eye.

As Prescott and Margaret were pouring martini number two, Adam would develop a migraine so severe that his father would have to carry him to bed. After several hours of excruciating pain and vomiting, Adam would pass out and slip into a coma-like sleep. In a day or two he'd be back to his old self and Margaret and Prescott would make him another drink.

When Adam's allergy was finally diagnosed, Margaret sent him a sympathy card. She could not imagine how he would be able to survive and get ahead in the world without the aid of the martini. When she handed him the somber card, she burst into tears. Years later, as he watched his mother at his father's funeral, he realized that she had cried more over his gin allergy than over the death of her husband.

Amanda was attempting to drink her martini without removing her lobster oven mitt. It occurred to me that maybe Peter and I were not the ones from the crazy family.

And then the doorbell rang.

"Expecting someone else?" I asked.

"Didn't I tell you? Mom is coming." Peter said this with an enthusiasm not usually shown with reference to our mother.

"No. I missed that fun fact."

The doorbell rang again. "Want to get it, hon?" Peter said, but Amanda ignored him and returned to stirring the giant cauldron on the stove.

Onda is a smothering hugger. Her hugs more closely resemble a linebacker's tackle than a tender show of affection. Believe it or not, I've never been tied into a straitjacket, but I imagine the sensation is similar to that of my mother's exceedingly long arms wrapped around me in greeting.

Peter was at the door, bracing against the hug. Onda was in her uniform: black dress, black hose, black shoes. Her hair, still mostly black, was pulled into a tight bun. She was four years younger than Margaret, she ate better and drank far less than Margaret did, but looked so much older. Maybe Margaret had had some work. But if so, it had been very good. Her face was expressive. There was none of that frightening Kabuki mask syndrome that so many of Margaret's peers suffered from—their faces stuck in perpetual, startled grins.

I made my way over to Onda. She let go of Peter and pulled me into her grip. Onda had tears in her eyes, which depending on her mood meant that she was happy, sad, anxious, overjoyed, confused, or melancholy. "My son," she said to me, squeezing out my last bit of oxygen. "My son...*The New York Times*!" She looked around the room as if she was waiting for someone to start a round of applause.

No matter how many times I correct my mother, she persists in her fantasy that I work for *The New York Times*.

"How's it going?" she asked, finally letting me go. "You know, Steven, I read the paper from cover to cover and I never find your articles."

"Trust me, Mom, they're in there."

Mercifully, Amanda did not adhere to the custom of a full hour for cocktails and she had us seated at the dining table moments after Onda arrived. At the time, I thought she was moving the evening along so quickly because she was having as bad a time as I was and wanted to get the night over with. Turns out, it was because she'd made risotto—and mistimed it. It was done, and when risotto is done there is no waiting—it's time to eat.

While the rest of us sat at the table, Amanda ladled the rice onto a large earthenware platter that Adam and I had given them for Christmas/their anniversary last year. We'd found it in Tuscany and Adam had carried it back home. I wondered if she actually liked it or if it had been pulled out for this sole occasion. She carried the exquisite platter to the table and I noticed that she was still wearing the hideous, lobster oven mitts that she'd been wearing from the moment we'd arrived.

Adam had been trying, unsuccessfully, to talk about "the movement" all through the brisk seventeen-minute cocktail hour and could wait no longer. Amanda had barely set down the platter when he said, "I'm sorry that no one read Steven's column today, because it was wonderful."

"It was fine," I said. I don't take compliments well. I was proud of the column and yet felt compelled to be dismissive.

"Where? Where was this column? I didn't find it." My mother was getting agitated.

"Adam, remember your old boyfriend, Tim?" Margaret said. She loved Tim. As far as Margaret was concerned, Tim was the great catch that Adam let get away. "Did you know Tim's writing for television now? He's been nominated for the prestigious Emmy award."

I had the urge to shout: *Daytime! Daytime Emmy award!* I did not, since I felt the comment would be more damning to me than Tim.

Here's the thing with family dinners: It's virtually impossible to tell a story from beginning to end. With the interjections, the asides, and the questions you end up with about thirty-five beginnings, eleven middles, and, if you're lucky, maybe two endings. Adam was determined to have his story be one of the two that got told through to the end. "So anyway," he carried on.

Amanda was still hovering alongside the table. She reminded me of my grandmother, my Maia, who throughout my entire childhood, never once sat down and ate with us. Maia was like an overly attentive waiter. Standing never more than a few feet away, checking to make sure every bite was satisfactory, refilling the breadbasket and keeping the glasses full. Actually sitting down and eating with us, I never saw her do once.

"*Ma!* Sit!" My mother would scream.

"For what? Let the children eat, I don't need anything. The children need the food!" Maia would shout back with her thick accent as she brought out another platter of pita. (This may explain why I was two hundred pounds in the eighth grade.)

Adam forged ahead, "The thing about Steven's column—"

"Before I sit down." Amanda interrupted with a theatrical flourish. "I must remove my oven mitts."

"Knock yourself out," Adam said, losing the momentum of his story one more time.

"Yes," Amanda said. "I will now take off my oven mitts." She started peeling them off in a sort of Gypsy Rose Lee style, which I found an odd choice, given the audience. I saw a somewhat embarrassed look pass across my brother's face. We were all silent, watching the bizarre striptease.

When the mitts were completely removed, Amanda started jumping up and down and screaming.

It was a minute before anyone knew the reason for this queer behavior. My mother added to the confusion by screaming right along with her and jumping onto her chair—she assumed there was a mouse in the room.

I was the first to realize what was going on. I saw the diamond sparkle as Amanda's hand waved by. Peter and Amanda were engaged. She was showing off The Rock.

This could not be happening.

I hadn't eaten a bite and already I was bloated. I looked at Adam; he was actually frowning. I forced myself to plaster a big wide smile on my face and Adam mirrored it.

By now, my mother was the only one still in the dark. From atop her chair she screamed, "Oh my God, what? What?"

"Mom," Peter said, pulling our mother back down to the ground. "I finally wore Amanda down. We're getting married."

Onda's screams instantly turned to tears. She gave Peter one of her signature hugs. "At last, a child of mine is settled."

"Meg"—again, with the Meg—"I hope you'll let me marry your daughter."

Margaret gave Peter a hug that almost rivaled Onda's. "Darling," she said.

Now I know I must be starting to sound like a whining brat, and I don't want to beat the proverbial dead horse—but did she have to say *darling*? I mean, *darling* was reserved for her children. I could justify the fact that I'd never gotten a darling, by telling myself that it was an endearment saved for offspring only. But here she was calling my brother darling. "Hey, lady," I wanted to scream, "where's *my* darling?"

"Darling," Margaret said *to my brother and not to me*, "I can't imagine a more perfect man." There was a long pause, at which point she stared over at me. I'm guessing she stared at me so that I'd know there was only one "perfect man" in the room and it wasn't me. She kissed Peter's cheek. "Of course you can marry Amanda."

Moments passed before I realized that everyone was looking at Adam and me. It was our turn to say something. "I thought you two were never going to get married. Antiquated institution…enslavement of women." I said in a joking, offhanded style that I hoped I'd delivered with a light touch.

Amanda's giddiness vanished. She was suddenly serious. "I've spent years lecturing about the history of marriage. Most of it focused on the plight of Victorian-era women. Those women suffered terribly. They were no more than property. Their husband's subjects. Shockingly, that still is what marriage is for some women. But that's not what it has to be." Her beautiful giant teeth flashed at my brother.

"When we were at the wedding last weekend," Amanda continued. "Sitting with that poor drunk woman whose husband left her for her sister, I thought to myself, thank God that will never be me. Because I have a soul mate. I have a real partner."

I noticed my brother, eyes downcast, tearing. A blush had spread across his cheeks.

"So Saturday night when we came home from the reception and Peter asked me to marry him for the thirty-ninth time, I couldn't think of a single reason to say no. And about a hundred reasons to say yes."

The mothers cooed and cried.

I didn't cry but was close. Whatever commitment I had to the marriage boycott evaporated. I was overjoyed for Peter. And Amanda, too, of course. "Congratulations," I said, my voice choking. I looked at my brother. In spite of his embarrassment, he glowed. I knew he'd asked Amanda to marry him in the past. I was unaware it had been so often.

As thrilled as I was for them, I felt sorry for Adam. He'd just made this major decision to stop planning and going to weddings and already there would have to be an exception. Obviously, Adam would be planning his sister's wedding. How could he not? It's his sister, after all—not some stranger. For my part, I knew I'd be Peter's best man. I am, after all, both the brother and the best friend.

Amanda looked toward Adam; he was the only one of us who was still silent.

He gave his sister a gentle smile but remained quiet.

"I'm going to need so much help," Amanda said. "Because now that I've, I mean we've, decided to do this, I don't want to wait. I want it to be the week before Christmas," Amanda shouted. "Because of when we met at your party. The date even falls on a Saturday, so it's meant to be. I know a December wedding is short notice. Sorry, Adam, you have your work cut out for you."

"Oh, you don't need me," Adam said, without quite looking at Amanda.

Fortunately Amanda's glee had blinded her to Adam's indifference. "What are you talking about? I want this to be the most over-the-top, out-of-control thing you've ever created." She'd certainly done a 360 from her "enslavement of women" days.

Adam took a long pause.

I looked at him and then at the risotto. It would be wallpaper paste before we ate it. I was hoping Adam would say, "I'll do whatever you want." I was starving. I almost picked up the platter and started serving the food, but since everyone else was staring at Adam and waiting for a response, I refrained.

"I'm really sorry that no one read Steven's column today." He was determined to tell the story. "If you had, you would have learned that I'm not a wedding planner anymore."

"What?" Margaret said. She directed her venom in my direction. I could see in her eyes what she thought: If it wasn't for me, maybe Adam would still be with Tim, then she could go to the Daytime Emmy Awards with them and meet Susan Lucci.

"Why aren't you planning weddings?" Amanda asked Adam. It wasn't really a question, though; it had more of an *en guarde* quality.

Margaret turned to her son. "Adam Prescott More." She had used the middle name, she meant business. "That is the silliest thing I have ever heard in my life."

I immediately started thinking of all the far sillier things I'd heard in my life. A few of them had to do with her beloved Tim, but I didn't share them.

"Last week you were a wedding planner," Margaret continued. "You will come out of this retirement of yours, for your sister."

"No, Mom." It was a whisper, but it was loud enough to be heard. Adam turned to Amanda, who seemed to be in a bit of shock. "Sorry."

Amanda started mumbling. It was rather disturbing. She clutched her bandaged forehead. "I was struck by a bridal bouquet. It's a sign. A bad omen. My face was slashed by the wire in a piece of peach-colored organza ribbon!"

My God, she had turned into Onda.

My mother quickly made the sign of the cross three times—Orthodox style. She spat on Amanda, who seemed to welcome it.

Peter grabbed his napkin and wiped his fiancée's face. "We don't care if you plan the wedding," Peter said trying to salvage the celebration. "All we want is the two of you to be there."

Of course we'd be there. I pinched Adam's thigh under the table. I looked at Adam, as I tried to tell the now less than "happy couple" that we couldn't wait for the wedding.

Adam cut me off. "We really want to be there, but the thing is—"

"Yes?" Margaret bellowed. I imagined she'd be calling her lawyer and cutting Adam out of the will. Maybe she'd leave Adam's share to the Daytime Emmy–nominated Tim.

I began flashing back to the years following the Second World War. Odd, you might be thinking, since I was born in 1974. But haven't you noticed that when you hear a story often enough, you begin to think you were there when it happened? And so I saw myself in Bridgeport, Connecticut, in my grandmother's six-family house: Christmas Eve, 1948.

Maia had just finished scrubbing the kitchen counters and was preparing to roll out the dough for *pita di spinak*, the sublime Romanian spinach pie that is the centerpiece of our cuisine. The smell of potatoes with roasted onion and rosemary filled the house. Through the kitchen window, Maia saw that the postman, Mr. Fitzpatrick, had delivered the mail and was heading back down the stoop from the boxes.

"Irish"—long pause and sigh—"but nice man," Maia would say

in the hundred retellings of the story. She had a little something for him for Christmas—a bottle. She ran down the stairs to give it to him, and caught him just as he was reaching the sidewalk. They exchanged holiday wishes as best they could—my grandmother with her broken English and Mr. Fitzpatrick with his brogue.

When she returned to the house, she removed the mail from the box and began going through it. And then she saw the postmark: Albania.

Just before the war, Maia's parents and her baby sister, Toya, fled to the mountains of Albania. There had been one letter just after they arrived there, but no news at all since 1941. Maia and her sister Reta (also now in Bridgeport) feared the worst.

My grandmother tore open the letter: Her family was safe. They were alive!

Clasping the letter, leaving the potatoes to burn in the oven, Maia ran through the streets of Bridgeport—crying and panting all the way—to deliver the news to her sister, Reta. (Years later I learned this part of the story was slightly embellished. Reta lived across the street.)

Maia pounded and pounded on the door, shouting Reta's name. "Reta, Reta, I have news!"

Eventually, Reta opened up a window on the third floor and shouted down to her sister, "What are you, crazy? Why you scream like that? You think I no hear you? I'm busy. Slide the letter under the door. I'll read it when I have a chance!" And with that, Reta slammed the window shut.

My grandmother was stunned and shocked by the callousness of her sister. How was it that Reta had not rushed from her house to hear the news of their parents? My grandmother had received joyous news that one sister was alive. But now, as far as Maia was concerned, her other sister was dead. Maia returned to her house and began cursing her sister, literally. Maia set out to give Reta the evil eye. I'm not exactly sure how that was accomplished, but I do know that most of the family photos from that period are riddled with pinholes.

Finally, Maia did *di ocui* on her sister and watched as the drops of olive oil sank like lead to the bottom of the glass of water. When the oil was completely dissipated she knew she had achieved her goal. "Now she's dead to me," Maia spat.

Throughout my childhood, I visited my grandmother often. On one particular visit, when I was about thirteen, I saw my Maia walking on the sidewalk in front of her house. I ran up to kiss her, but she put her hand up—as if trying to block an attack. She had no idea who I was. I was terrified; I thought she'd developed Alzheimer's disease. And then I realized my mistake, it wasn't Maia—it was Reta. Maia and Reta were twins. It seemed my Maia's attempt at killing her sister with incantations and pinpricked pictures had not exactly worked out as planned.

Forty years had passed since Maia put a curse on Reta. They still lived across the street from each other, still attended the same church— St. Dimitri's Romanian Orthodox—and still had not spoken a single word to each other.

The war between Maia and Reta was never talked about, at least not in front of my brother and me. In fact, the only story I ever heard about Reta was told to me by my mother. When my mother was pregnant with me, her uncle Dean died. Reta showed up at the wake. My mother, of course, knew who Reta was because of the clone-like resemblance to Maia.

Even then, at this time of sorrow, Reta did not acknowledge her sister. She marched up to my mother and demanded, "Who are you?"

"Onda," my mother said.

Reta eyed my mother from head to toe. "Onda? What happened to you? You look different."

"I went through puberty," my mother shot back, placing a hand on her swollen belly.

Was this what I had to look forward to with my brother? Would the day come when I'd attend his funeral (God forbid) and meet his children for the first time? Would we die, as our mother had warned us, no longer knowing each other?

As kids, when Peter and I fought, my mother would grab both of us, press us together, and forcibly wrap our arms around each other. Making us hug one another for what seemed like hours. During the time that Peter and I stood, squeezing each other as hard as we could, Onda lectured us:

"Don't you know someday Maia will be dead? Someday I will be dead. And then, you will only have each other. You *only* have each other. There is no one else. If you continue to fight with each other, you will end up alone. No one will care for you. If you have no family, you have nothing. Why do you fight? So you can stop talking? So you can lose the only brother you'll ever have? So you can die alone? Is that what you want? Kiss your brother right now!"

At the dining table, voices were elevated and tense. We were joining the ranks of warring families. I could see it happening but didn't know how to stop it. I was surprised that Adam was taking such a hard line, but I was just as surprised that no one seemed to care why Adam had stopped planning weddings and why we had decided to stop attending them.

We hadn't started saying things that couldn't be taken back, and I of course hadn't said anything—I don't do confrontation. But the tension was so thick and the risotto was so cold and congealed, it was only a matter of time before some ancient, never before mentioned, wrong was brought up.

"We're not attending your wedding," Adam said.

I thought about jumping in with, "Isn't he a kidder?" But there was nothing humorous in Adam's tone. I was angry with Adam for speaking for me. I was angry at everyone else for not caring at all about why we might not want to be at the wedding. But mostly I was angry with myself for saying nothing. I wanted to reassure Peter and Amanda, tell them that I would be at their wedding, because of course I would be there.

To me, nothing is more important than family—I'm no Reta.

CHAPTER ELEVEN:
TO WALK THE MIME'S PATH

A dam needed to take a walk after we—I like to believe that we—*chose* to leave the family dinner party. Others might argue that we were thrown out. Either way, I would have preferred going to eat since we'd been shown the door without a bite of risotto. Perhaps it was best we didn't get food. I know I would have ended up self-medicating with an entire Entenmann's Raspberry Danish Twist and a pint of Cherry Garcia.

That's how overwrought I was.

We walked for nearly two hours—mostly in silence. Then Adam spoke:

"Fucking cunt."

When you have lived with a man for six years, and aside from the rare lust-induced outburst, you have never heard an obscenity come out of his mouth, hearing him utter the above quoted line is shocking, and also a little terrifying. Once, absentmindedly, Adam walked out into the middle of traffic. When the taxicab screeched its brakes and stopped mere inches away from him, Adam jumped and screamed, "Holy cow!"

And now he was using the most vulgar words imaginable. He uttered them again—but I shall not.

Adam was seething as we walked home. "It's all about her!" He railed. "God fuckin' forbid I should get a little respect!"

I looked over at my boyfriend. In an instant he had morphed from my croquet-loving, Ralph Lauren–wearing Ivy Leaguer into a kiss-of-death-dispensing Michael Corleone. The only thing missing was the lush strains of "Speak Softly Love" playing in the background.

"You know, Adam," I said, "I'm sure Amanda just felt blindsided. I mean, you tell your brother, the wedding planner, that you're finally getting married, you expect a different response."

Adam said nothing.

I knew this was my opportunity. I had to tell Adam I was going to the wedding. "Maybe we should make an exception for them." Okay, I was not exactly forceful, but at least I brought up the subject.

"We agreed. This was your idea."

It was becoming clear that he was never going to let me forget that this had been my idea. But in truth, it wasn't, not really. It was just an offhanded sarcastic remark I'd made and he'd seized upon.

Adam continued. "Your problem is you never want to hurt anyone's feelings."

My only brother was marrying Adam's only sister. I was trying to point this fact out to Adam, stressing the uniqueness of the situation. But he had made up his mind and was not grasping how wrong he was and how obviously right I was.

I was hoping he'd see the necessity for compromise and realize that sometimes it's more important to do for others than for ourselves. Not only was Adam not seeing my point, he was goading me.

"You never want to hurt anyone's feelings." When he said it, it had a singsong quality, like a stuck-up girl in the schoolyard. He sang it several times. "You never want to hurt anyone's feelings." I half expected him to follow it up with *Nah, nah, nah, nah, nah, nah.*

"No, I don't want to hurt anyone's feelings. What's wrong with"— my voice cracked—"that?" I persevered, even though my anger had reduced my audibility to the level of whisper. "Maybe I love my brother more than you love your sister." *Good one*, I thought, although it was shockingly similar in tone and style to things I'd heard my mother say (she always spoke in full voice, though). I'd even snapped my head back at the end—her signature accent mark.

"What? I can't hear you," Adam sneered.

There was a long pause as we continued stomping toward our apartment. I was not speaking because I had lost the ability. Adam was not speaking because he was being unreasonable.

Finally, Adam broke his silence. "Have you ever noticed that when you're angry you turn into Marcel Marceau?"

I mean absolutely no disrespect to the memory of the incomparable Mr. Marceau, but I consider comparisons to mimes the lowest form of insult.

When I was in college, I began to come into my own as a person. I came out. I lost my baby fat (all seventy-three pounds of it). And I began to think of myself as a creative person—an artist. I dressed only in black. Not Onda black, I was working more of a '50s beat generation look. I even wore a beret (please cut me some slack, I was only twenty-one). I smoked Dunhills, or if I was really feeling festive Nat Shermans, and I talked about my angst with other young writers, actors, musicians, painters, and dancers. They discussed their angst, too. On warm days, we'd remove our berets. This gave us the opportunity to yank on our hair as we discussed, for example, existentialism.

Other, less evolved students called us "art fags." The girls were dubbed "Sartre's Sapphos"—which we actually thought was very cool and so we started saying it constantly. We even had T-shirts made. It's not that everyone in the group was gay, but in the minds of the other students we were all suspect. Guilt by association, I guess.

We welcomed all artists into our fold—even those that we felt had no talent. Interestingly, the only one of us to make it "big" was one of the actors in our clique who was fantastically atrocious (but my, was he beautiful). He's now a movie star. At the time he was openly gay, but that didn't really jibe with the box office success he coveted. He met a young woman and is now married with two lovely children. The last I heard, he'd converted to Scientology.

Toward the end of the fall semester of my junior year, one of the most angst-filled of our group, a gangly boy named Seth, announced that he was dropping out of school. He'd been studying to be a dramaturge. We were all shocked; he seemed so happy in his studies and in his faux beatnik lifestyle. He told us he was leaving to follow his dream—he was going to mime school.

I remember thinking at the time: If it was hard telling your parents that you wanted to go to school and study dramaturgy, what would it be like telling them you wanted to learn how to escape from an invisible box?

Suddenly our whole group of dreamers seemed downright practical, conservative, really. I mean, it might be hard, near impossible to achieve, but some actors, writers, and musicians do succeed and make a living at it. There is a chance—some hope. But to walk the mime's path, to step in his silent footsteps, is to subject yourself to a life of poverty, ridicule, and very bad outfits.

And now, Adam had called me a mime.

I opened my mouth and shouted, *"No!"* Unfortunately, no sound came out. I recognized that at the moment I looked exactly like a mime. All that was missing was the whiteface and the boatneck sweater.

Adam laughed at me. I pretended not to notice. We kept walking and my cell phone rang. I grabbed it. "Hello," no sound from me. I gave it another try: "Hello." Still nothing.

"Let me guess," I heard Brad shout from the other end of the line. There was so much background noise I could barely hear him. "You and Adam are having a fight, you've lost your voice, and so I'm forced to speak to dead air. Well, kiss and make up and give the phone to Adam so I can actually engage in a dialogue."

I handed Adam the phone. I was not thrilled that for the second time in a week Brad was calling after 10:00. What was it about the death phone concept that he did not understand? Was there even anything wrong? Maybe Charlie left him.

I glanced at Adam trying to discern the reason for Brad's call. It was definitely not a post-breakup call. Adam wasn't saying those "I'm so sorry" kind of things you say to the newly dumped. Actually he was mostly saying, "You have to speak up, I can't hear you." Fortunately, Adam only had to deal with noise coming from Brad's end of the line. Broadway was surprisingly quiet for a Friday night, so there was no street traffic noise—and I, of course, was temporarily mute.

"Where?" I heard Adam shout into the cell phone.

For several minutes, Adam struggled to communicate with Brad. Then he hung up, handed back my phone, grabbed my shoulder, and began dragging me to the curb. He was waving his hand in the air, trying to hail a cab.

Did I mention that it was 11:00? That's 11:00, as in P.M.

We don't go out at 11:00. It's rare that we come home at 11:00. Honestly, it's rare that we go out at all, but if we do, it's early.

There was a cab stopped alongside of us and I was climbing in behind Adam. I'm not in the habit of following Adam without asking where I'm going, but I was stressed, hungry, tired, and not thinking clearly.

"Where to?" the leather-faced cab driver, with a neck nearly twice as wide as his head and a voice like Brenda Vaccaro, asked us. He had an unlit cigarette tucked behind his right ear. And two packs sitting up on the dash. The car reeked of smoke. Not, I think, because he was breaking the law and smoking in the cab, but because he had smoked so much in his lifetime that the smell just oozed out of every pore. It was late, I was cranky, and I was sitting in the back of a giant ashtray.

Adam turned to me and asked, "Do you know where Man Land is?"

I didn't even know what Man Land was, but I knew whatever it was, I didn't want to be going there.

"How can two beautiful boys like you not know where Man Land is?" Brenda Vaccaro winked into the rearview mirror at us. "Don't worry, I know how to get there. I love that place. Impossible to get into, though. I've only been let in on a Monday, and even then it was tough. I waited for hours. But I'm sure they'll take one look at you boys and you'll get right in."

Brenda smiled lasciviously at us in the rearview mirror, revealing a row of tarred, decaying teeth. It was a terrifying image, best suited for the opening shot in a cautionary tale about the hazardous consequences of smoking. The smile was framed by dozens of fine lines around his lips. Just when I thought I could bear it no longer, he stopped looking at us in the mirror and sped away from the curb, heading downtown.

"Are you going to tell me why we're going to Man Land?" I asked Adam, my voice having returned.

"Brad asked us to."

"Why?"

"I don't know. I'm not sure?"

"Why didn't you tell him no. It's late."

"Because I didn't want—" Adam stopped abruptly before finishing the thought.

And then I understood: "Might it be because you didn't want to hurt his feelings?"

Adam was silent. Victory was mine. Funny how a little thing like vindication can alter your mood. Suddenly I didn't feel quite so bad about going out. I was even curious now where we were going—curious enough to engage our driver in conversation.

"Excuse me, Bren—" Just in the nick I stopped myself. "Excuse me, sir. Is Man Land a gay bar?"

Brenda let loose a big phlegmy laugh, which within moments transformed into a violent hacking cough. In spite of the fact that Brenda's huge neck and tiny head were reeling uncontrollably with each hack, he kept driving. Apparently the coughing was causing him to shake from head to toe because his foot kept slamming on and off the accelerator, sending the car into a lurching series of stops and starts. Horns honked and pedestrians scattered as we careened down Broadway. Five blocks, and one too-brief-too-self-absorbed-life-played-out-rapidly-in-front-of-my-brown-eyes moment later, Brenda's fit subsided. By the grace of God, his lungs were still inside his chest. I'm pretty certain mine were as well.

Brenda cleared his throat, popped in a Sucrets, and continued chatting about the nightclub, seemingly unaware that we'd all just narrowly escaped extinction.

"Man Land's been open about five months, I guess. It's in the meatpacking district. As you guessed from the name, Sherlock, it's a primarily gay crowd, but there's definitely a mix of people—lesbians, hipster straights. It has a very cool vibe. Great music. Beautiful people. You know how it is with the club scene…"

I had no idea, but I figured he was going to tell me.

"Places come and go. Man Land is the hip spot of the moment."

I was instantly drenched in flop sweat. I had never been to the hip spot of the moment before. I mean, I've been to hip spots, but only like five years after their glory period, when the place is empty and you sit there along with the two or three other patrons who've wandered into the joint, wondering what it must have been like back in the day.

My unfamiliarity with the trendy nightlife scene has something to do with the fact that deep down inside, I don't believe I will get past the roped-off door and be allowed into the inner sanctum. I have a little voice inside my head that says: "You're a fat boy, Steven Worth-less. You shop in the husky department. Your kind is not welcome here." It doesn't matter that I'm no longer fat or a boy anymore. Or that I have in fact a very good body, thanks in part to all the Hot Nude Yoga I do. The voice persists.

And it was coming in loud and clear as we approached the entrance to Man Land.

There was a bouncer on duty in charge of corralling the sixty or so people waiting on the sidewalk to get in. He stood about 6'7" and had a 50-inch chest and a 29-inch waist. I'm pretty certain that he'd managed this feat without the aid of a corset. This inverted pyramid of a body he had was both bizarre and fascinating to look at. I was obviously not alone in my opinion because everyone in line was staring and smiling at him—and not just because they were desperate to get into the club.

Just then, someone who I either recognized from his appearance on a reality show or from living in my neighborhood or, I suppose, possibly both walked up to the bouncer and offered a warm greeting. "Jackson," the reality/neighbor cooed as he kissed the bouncer's shoulder. I'm guessing he was aiming for Jackson's cheek, but considering the fact that reality/neighbor was about 5'6", that wasn't possible.

Jackson ushered reality/neighbor past the throngs and he vanished inside the club.

I did not want to face the humiliation of standing in this line for an hour only to discover that Jackson was not going to let me in. I looked at Adam; he seemed anxious, too. Adam also has a little voice in his head that pops up at moments like these. His, however, does not call him fat. His evil voice is more focused on his lack of true celebrity status. I'm sure that at this moment he was hearing something like: "Hey, you think you're going to get in here because you appeared on *The View* one time? Try again when you've been on *Oprah*."

"Let's go home," Adam said.

"Good idea." I was immediately feeling more at ease.

We got out of the line and started walking back to the curb.

"May I help you?" Jackson's voice came from miles above us.

I turned around and was staring directly into Jackson's chest. He wore a skin-tight T-shirt. I wondered how he got the thing over his gigantic head without stretching out the neck. I could see the outline of two large hoops dangling from his massive nipples. Some men refer to them as "eraser nips." I have always found both the term and the image revolting, but I must say that on Jackson it was kind of hot. I realized that with all the pectoral inspection I had not answered Jackson's question.

He asked it again. "May I help you?"

"Um…not really," I said, happy that I was short enough to talk to his nipples.

"We just wanted to meet a friend," Adam said.

"Are you on the list?" It was only then that I realized that Jackson was carrying a clipboard.

"I doubt it," I said as my inner voice screamed, "There's no way you're on that list, Steven Worth-Less."

"Would you like me to check?" Jackson offered.

"That would be so nice of you, thank you," Adam said as I nodded in agreement.

Adam and I just stood there. I noticed that Adam was as entranced by the nipples as I was.

"Do you think you could tell me your names?" I could tell by the slight edge in his voice that Jackson was beginning to tire of us.

I couldn't let that happen. I smiled widely. "Steven Worth and Adam More," I said.

And then the oddest thing happened:

Jackson didn't even look at the list. He just took our hands—first mine and then Adam's—and shook them. He told us what an honor it was to meet us. He was misty-eyed. I felt a little guilty that I'd devoted so much energy to objectifying his breasts.

"Please go right in, gentlemen, and enjoy your evening," Jackson said as he unhooked the rope that was blocking the front door.

In telling this story, I've been making a concerted effort to avoid gay stereotypes, but I have to confess, I felt just like Barbra Streisand in *Hello, Dolly!* (You know the moment. It's when Barbara, as Dolly, walks into the restaurant and, flanked by dozens of dancing waiters, does the show-stopping title number.) The crowds parted as we sailed into Man Land. I half expected Louis Armstrong to start serenading us. We had no idea why this was happening, but Adam and I were enjoying the moment. He grabbed for my hand, which I gave him happily, and the partying, dancing crowd enveloped us.

Wow, I thought as we danced across the floor, *this* is what other people are doing when we're home flossing our teeth. I vowed that we would do this more often.

It was 11:30, and I was out on the town. I live in the City That Never Sleeps, but that's never prevented me from having my jammies on by ten.

"We should look for Brad," Adam shouted into my ear.

I thought it would be an impossible task until I remembered his newly bleached hair. I looked for the straw-colored beacon and soon saw it shining at me from the bar.

I had forgotten to warn Adam about Brad's new look. He stared with his mouth agape at Brad so hard and so long and with such a horrified expression that I finally had to pinch him to make him stop. Brad re-introduced us to Charlie. I was relieved to discover that Charlie's presence in this liquor-serving establishment suggested that he was over twenty-one.

"You guys are awesome!" Charlie had leaped off the bar stool to simultaneously hug Adam and me.

We were both taken aback, but soon warmed to the young man's group hug. He was being so friendly and sincere that even though we were basically strangers, I experienced the gesture as completely genuine. I felt I'd been rash in my assessments of Charlie. His sweetness was refreshing and made me analyze my own often-cynical worldview. After the third or fourth "It's really great to see you guys again. I admire you so much," from Charlie, I was ready to bestow my blessings upon his May/December romance with Brad.

The shirtless bartender approached. He was built—he was no Jackson, but still very impressive. "I'm really sorry," he began. "Please forgive me for making you wait. I'm Ty, what can I get you to drink?"

He hadn't kept us waiting; we'd barely finished our three-way hug. That poor anxiety-riddled bartender. I studied him: those dark eyes, that nervous disposition. Romanian? Not possible. Not named Ty.

We ordered a couple of martinis—vodka for Adam and gin for me—and Ty hurried off to make them. The best part of a martini in my opinion is that it comes with its own built in-snack—olives.

As I sat on my bar stool between Adam and Charlie, I noticed there was a large rainbow flag hanging behind the bar. I will admit that years ago when I was still single, there were a few occasions when I was in foreign countries feeling homesick and blue and the sight of the flag displayed in a window brought me solace. I imagine it's very much the way a lost child might respond to one of those safe haven stickers that shopkeepers display. But in New York City where I feel safe and at home everywhere, I focus on the flag's many flaws. For starters—the colors are ghastly. I, for one, refuse to believe that any homosexual was consulted when the colors for the flag were chosen. They're garish, gaudy and, well, they're not even the colors one sees in a rainbow. I would have discarded the rainbow idea entirely and gone with something far more tasteful like a tone-on-tone beige (think Calvin Klein Home)—or maybe a subtle pin stripe.

I was pondering my design concept when Ty returned with our olive filled drinks. "Here you go," he said as he placed them down in front of us.

I reached for my wallet, but Adam beat me to it. Adam makes far more money than I do, so he rarely lets me pay when we go out. But I don't like to assume that he's going to cover the bill, and since it was only drinks, I was determined to get the check.

"Please," Ty interrupted us, each with wallet in hand. "You're our guests this evening." He walked away, refusing to take our money. Looking around the room at the swarms of gay men, I knew they couldn't be giving out the Club Member Discount. If they did, they'd go out of business in a weekend.

Okay, we really needed to be clued into what was going on here.

I was just about to ask Brad why he'd summoned Adam and me

to Man Land when the music on the dance floor stopped and the lights got brighter. Instead of the boos and hisses that usually coincide with an action like that, the crowd cheered.

As they subsided, the D.J. from up in his booth began speaking. "Tonight's a very special night, so we're going to have a few words from the owner of Man Land. Everyone, let's give it up for Ginger Beer."

My first thought was that I'd never seen a more beautiful drag queen in my life. Ginger was well over six feet tall; in her heels she rivaled Jackson's stature. When she walked, it was with grace and ease. There wasn't a hint of effort in her movements. Her frame was narrow with curves that seemed not at all exaggerated. She was womanly without any of the overdone femininity that I think gives men away when they attempt drag. The only false notes were her hair, an obvious wig, and of course her name. Which was pure drag but not nearly funny enough. If you're going to do it, really do it. I'd have gone with a name like Eva Destruction, Barb Dwyer, Anna Falactic or, better yet, Helen Backagain.

I leaned into Charlie. "She looks just like a woman."

"That's 'cause she is."

Funny how I'd rejected the obvious. It just hadn't occurred to me a woman would be the owner of gay club called Man Land.

"First of all," Ginger began, "forgive my hair. I ran out of the salon before they were finished with me. Hence this relic from the Eva Gabor collection I'm donning." I was pleased to learn the Carol Brady shag was not her usual style. "I literally ran out of the salon with my hair half-cut, because of what I read in the paper."

I wondered what it could have possibly been.

Ginger continued, "As most of you already know, today is a very important day. It's the day when, as a group we started to say no. *No. No, we're not going. We are not participating!*"

I realize that all of you reading this now know exactly what Ginger was referring to, but Adam and I were completely baffled. We looked at each other and shrugged.

"We came to this decision," Ginger said, "because one brave man decided that he'd had enough. And because his loving partner has spread the story. Ladies and gentlemen, I give you Adam More and Steven Worth!"

It was like Ginger was speaking a foreign language. I truly didn't understand what was going on. I felt Charlie's hands on my back. He was trying to get me to stand. I felt Adam take my hand. And then I realized what this was: *This* was the moment I'd played out a thousand times alone in my bedroom or while standing under the shower. The moment was always the same. Whitney Houston read the nominees' names: Aretha Franklin, Chaka Khan, Gladys Knight, Patti Labelle, and Steven Worth. And the winner is...all eyes on Whitney as she struggles to open the envelope...tension...butterflies...oh, we're all really winners. It's an honor just to be nominated...and Whitney speaks again...The winner is Steven Worth!

I don't want to mislead you. I have, in fact, never won the Grammy for Best Female Vocalist—R&B. This moment at Man Land was different. This was actually happening. Never before had my name been announced at the end of a long introduction. I've always been one of the people in the throngs cheering someone else. It was the most thrilling experience of my life.

Adam and I kissed each other and everyone went wild. Brad and Charlie got off their stools and pushed us toward the dance floor. People started chanting, "Speech! Speech!"

I was wondering what I should say, when Adam started speaking. It's funny, I can't really remember what he said. I remember that it was moving. I remember that people had tears in their eyes, and couples were hugging each other. But I don't remember what he said because I was too busy thinking about what I should say. I figured I'd deliver a modified version of my Grammy acceptance speech. I was going to keep the part about no man can do this alone and skip the section about my deep admiration for Aretha, Gladys, Chaka, and Patti. Ditto the line about being thrilled to be standing here next to Whitney.

I heard a lull, Adam had finally stopped talking—my turn. Yeah!

Just as I was about to open my mouth the D.J. started playing again. It was Diana Ross's "I'm Coming Out," and it was really loud.

It was just like a bad Academy Award moment. They were playing us off before I'd had a chance to make my acceptance speech. Maybe, if I was Julia Roberts, I could have gotten them to stop the music—the way she did when she won for *Erin Brockovich*. And then I could have carried on. But I'm not Julia Roberts. So I just smiled at the crowd—but not a Julia Roberts smile, a cursory little smile—and we walked back to the bar. Adam was on cloud nine. I, sadly, had my feet planted firmly on the ground.

By the time my bruised ego was settled back on the bar stool, I could feel depression blanketing me. I should have known that one can't lift spirits by consuming them. But when Adam asked me what I thought of his speech, I raised my empty glass and shouted, "Another round, Ty." Then I looked at Adam and said, "Your speech was beautiful." I almost added, "What did you think of mine," but fortunately—and unfortunately—my second martini arrived and I started drinking it.

As I drank, I started thinking about Peter and Amanda. Or more precisely, my future estrangement from them. These thoughts did not cheer me. I realized what I had to do. I was just about to tell Adam that we had to go to the wedding when Ty brought me a third martini. Had I drunk the second?

Adam leaned in and kissed my ear as I was eating one of my gin-soaked olives. The kiss was wet and I could smell the mixture of Stoli and vermouth. "Still want to go to the wedding?" he asked between nibbles on my ear.

Yes! I thought.

I said nothing. I kissed him on the mouth to keep him from talking.

"Stop!" He pulled away. "I can taste the gin."

I apologized. I mentioned nothing about Peter and Amanda's wedding.

Let Adam have this magical night, I thought. I'd tell him my true feelings in the morning. I reached into my glass, plucked out the last of my gin-soaked olives, and devoured it. I was still hungry and there wasn't a pretzel or peanut in sight.

Maybe another drink.

CHAPTER TWELVE:
TO OUR LIFE TOGETHER!

O lives are no substitute for a healthy dinner.
I thought I'd be fine. I didn't think that the alcohol would have any effect on me—I'd eaten twelve olives, after all. I had not focused on the fact that twelve olives equals four martinis.

Four martinis equals waking up naked on the bathroom floor at three A.M.—your parched lips pressed against the cool tile. At three A.M., the tile is the only thing keeping you from sliding straight down into the fiery pits of hell. You pray to the tile, respect the tile, you bargain with the tile. "Oh dear tile, if you prevent the top of my head from flying off, I'll never again clean you with anything but Softscrub."

Rational thought, when it finally re-appears, between one of nausea's many waves, is always focused on some variation of the "how did I get?" question.

How did I get out of Man Land? How did I get into a cab? How did I get to my address? How did I get up the stairs? How did I get through the door? And, how did I get out of my clothes?

The answer to all these questions—*Adam!*

This was only the second time I'd ever been drunk. The first time was my last semester of college, years before I'd met Adam.

I'd decided to move off campus. I was never really a dorm guy, and I took a lot of abuse when I lived in student housing. Not for being gay. I was spared most of that—I think because of my bass voice and five o'clock shadow that even back then always appeared by noon. It made me seem manly and so the guys didn't quite know what to make of me. My machismo did not extend to my wardrobe. The pretentious black turtlenecks and berets got me into a lot of trouble. It was worse than looking like a fag; I looked French. So I filled my black bag with all my black clothes and I found a cheap apartment.

In retrospect it was not really so inexpensive, since the building seemed to be made entirely of cardboard. Every sound and word from the apartments above and below me was broadcast in stereo into my tiny studio. I wondered what conversations of mine my neighbors were enjoying. To be on the safe side, I began studying American Sign Language.

After I'd been in the building a month, a young Russian named Gregor moved into the studio next to mine. I never heard a word out of him—except the day he answered his phone and said: "Yes, this Gregor." He was hesitant, almost cagey when he spoke.

I imagined that he'd defected. "That's why he's so quiet! He's afraid of getting caught and being deported." I said this to a whole group of Sartre's Sapphos. It made perfect sense to me.

That was just the beginning of my elaborate fantasy. Gregor (or Greg, as I liked to call him) had been a principal with the Bolshoi Ballet. One evening after a performance of *Swan Lake*—it had to be *Swan Lake* because it's the only ballet I know other than *The Nutcracker*, and it was the wrong season for *The Nutcracker*—Greg failed to get back on the bus taking him to his next performance. Instead, he hitched a ride to Storrs, Connecticut—an obvious choice for defection. He was now my next-door neighbor. I allowed the fantasy to expand until Greg and I had taken the cardboard wall down between our two studios and we were living happily together making silent love each night.

And then one night the wall really did come down.

He had been sobbing and beating his fist against his wall. As I approached on my side, his fist came slamming through. He pulled his arm back through the hole and replaced it with his face. "I am Gregor," he said. "I am sorry."

"It's absolutely fine," I said, wondering if the hole would provide an unobstructed view of his bed.

"Is not fine. Please to let me make it up." The accent was adorable. "I have vodka, come have drink."

Who could refuse? I offered to bring the cranberry but he didn't seem to understand what I meant, so I let it drop.

Gregor's studio contained two folding chairs, a milk crate that served as a coffee table, and a futon without a frame. He directed me to one of the chairs and I sat, filled with regret that he hadn't pointed at the futon. He pulled a bottle of vodka from his freezer. He took one very nice crystal old-fashioned glass from the cabinet over the stove and one plain white coffee mug. He poured shots into each. He handed the nice glass to me.

"To my American friend. Na zdorovye!"

I realized he didn't know my name. "Steven," I said.

"Drink with me, Steven."

And then Gregor wept.

I thought about hugging him. I wanted to hug him. Decided to wait for a few more drinks.

"Today's my anniversary," he said.

"Wedding?" I felt the hairs on the back of my neck stand up.

"Da," Gregor said through his tears.

"Where's your wife?" I tossed it off like I couldn't wait to meet her.

"Dead."

My initial plans for conversation had been along the lines of "Your ass is really hot, are you a dancer?" But now, that seemed a tad inappropriate. Instead, I opted for, "I'm sorry."

"To my wife." We drank our second shot.

Gregor slammed his mug down on the milk crate and refilled our glasses. "To our life together!"

I was ecstatic; I knocked back my third shot. I had gotten confused; I thought he meant *our* life together—not his with the dead wife.

By shot five, I was drunk and hysterical. Gregor was a young man—older than me, but under thirty. How old was his wife when she died? She must have been very young, like Ali MacGraw in *Love Story*, and he was Ryan O'Neal except that he could barely speak English. Of course, that was it. Unless he was Raymond Burr in *Rear Window*. It was all clear now.

He'd murdered her! I had been dreaming of a life, or at the very least some really sweaty sex with a man who'd killed his wife. It occurred to me that I had the potential to turn into one of those desperate women (except that I'd still be a man, of course) who spend their whole lives writing letters to their misunderstood lovers on death row. Gregor was on the lam because he'd killed his wife. He wasn't Ryan O'Neal, he was Raymond Burr—except that Raymond was fat and Gregor was a total hottie.

I cannot tell you which shot we were on when he told me about the tumor because by then, I'd started blacking out—but many more drinks had been consumed. "Liar!" I'd said in response to the news of her malignancy. "I know the truth. Murderer!"

I waited for Gregor to respond, to make some attempt to deny my allegation—he did not. I took this as an admission of his guilt, until I realized that he was out cold. I must have been very, very drunk because it didn't occur to me that he might just have passed out—I was certain that he was dead. My words had killed him.

I had to flee the scene. I hightailed it back to my apartment. I'd be safe there. No one would find me right next door in my apartment with the big hole in the wall. At 3:00 A.M. I awoke. I was naked and I was vomiting. I never learned how I got out of my clothing, but Gregor was very awkward around me after that night.

Two days later he repaired the wall.

Two months later he had a girlfriend.

❖

"Who's Gregor?" Adam said as he applied a cool compress to my forehead. I was still on the floor in the bathroom. I had vomited and Adam had cleaned up the mess. I was still way too sick to be embarrassed, but I was aware that I would be. The shame would be arriving any time.

It's terrible being a caregiver. Of course most of us will nurse our loved ones, if we have to. But no one should have to assume that role because of a night of excessive drinking. I had been so irresponsible.

"I'm so sorry," I cried. "I loved him."

"Who?"

"Gregor."

"Okay. When?"

"College. I'm so, so sorry." I spat out the words, still in a sloppy, drunken stupor.

"Sweetheart, you didn't even know me then," Adam said softly.

I cried some more, remembering that once there was a time when I didn't know Adam, and recalling how much emptier my life had been.

He removed the underwear he had on and scooped me up. He turned on the shower and together we stood under the warm spray. He washed me. I realize that my parents washed me as a baby, but I have no memory of that. This was a new experience—and the tenderness of it made me weep again.

After a few saltines, a can of ginger ale, and four aspirin I got into bed. Vincent and Theo curled around my head, their soft purring a balm to the pounding going on deep inside my skull. Adam pressed up against me and put his hand on my heart. Theo stretched a paw out and put it on Adam's head so he wouldn't feel left out. We stayed like this until we woke.

❖

I didn't get out of bed until 2:00 on Saturday afternoon. It was only then that I realized Adam was as sick as I was—minus the vomiting. He had managed to take care of me while he was barely coping himself.

"The kids are starving and I don't think I can face a can of their food," Adam said.

"I'll do it." *How do they eat this dreck*, I wondered, holding the can with its liver and sardine contents at arm's length. While Vincent and Theo enjoyed a late lunch, Adam and I did our best to drink some coffee.

"You scared me last night," Adam said. "I don't want anything to ever happen to you."

"I didn't think I drank so much. I was starving. I wanted more olives."

Adam laughed and then grabbed his head in agony. "No jokes. They hurt too much."

We had a brief discussion about soothing our hungover state with a little hair of the dog, but decided against it. The thought of drinking alcohol was disgusting. We had lemons and cayenne pepper in the house, so instead we began a two-week liver cleanse. We stuck to it for three hours, and then ordered in cheeseburgers, rare. The burgers had a profoundly healing effect and we briefly considered going out to a movie. That would have required shaving and dressing and leaving the house, which seemed like an awful lot of work, so instead we had a Katharine Hepburn and Cary Grant double feature at home. Between *Philadelphia Story* and *Bringing Up Baby*, Adam once again brought up how my sickness had scared him.

"I wouldn't survive without you," he said.

"You would. You don't think so, but you would."

"I don't think—"

I cut him off. "Adam, I'm not going anywhere." I pulled his head to my chest and let him curl up on the couch as I sat up straight at one end, running my fingers through his hair. "I'm right here," I said. We watched Katharine and Cary's zany antics, with no more talk of illness or survival.

We hid from the world, locked in the apartment—screening calls and ordering in, until we were forced to go to work on Monday morning.

There was no talk of weddings.

CHAPTER THIRTEEN: A CARD-CARRYING MEMBER OF THE SOCIETATEA FARSAROTUL

It seemed Adam and I missed a lot of activity, spending the weekend sequestered.

I phoned the paper seven times on Monday morning to see if Gail wanted me to bring her a nosh. And each time I rang, I got a busy signal. I assumed that something had happened to the lines and that the phones were out of service.

As I marched up the stairs from the fourth to fifth floor, carrying the bag of muffins I'd bought for both Gail and myself, I heard something I'd never heard before: The phones were ringing.

It's not that the phone never rings at *The Gay New York Times*—but never three phones all at the same time. As is my way, I imagined the worst. Something must have happened to Brad. My heart was pounding as I walked through the door and into our office.

"*Gay New York Times*, please hold. *Gay New York Times*, please hold. *Gay New York Times*, please hold," Gail was saying.

When she saw me, she tossed the phone receiver to me. Actually it was sort of *at* me but I think that's because she has really bad aim. "You talk for a while."

"*Gay New York Times,*" I said, eyeing the coffee and muffin I'd let drop to my desk when the phone had come hurling at me. "Can you please hold?" I held the receiver to my chest. "Gail, I brought you a muffin," I said and returned to the person on the phone. "How can I help you?"

It was someone from a local news channel doing a report on the wedding boycott. I told Gail about it when I got off the phone.

"Big deal," she said. "I was on the phone with *The Today Show*. They want to cover the story."

"You're kidding! *Really?* Matt Lauer wants to cover this story?"

"No. I think Ann Curry."

"Oh," I said, a bit crestfallen. "Well, still good, right?"

And then another round of ringing began.

I was about to answer the phone when Gail reminded me how little money we made and said, "If we were smart we would just turn the ringers off and the answering machine on and ignore everything until we'd had our breakfast." It seemed logical to me.

I was halfway through my carrot muffin when Gail informed me that she hated me.

"Okay, I don't really hate you. But you are getting me into a lot of trouble with my family."

"Why?"

"My cousin Claude is getting married."

"Not going?" I asked.

"Nope. Only problem is I've been trying to find a way to wiggle out of it since they announced their engagement. I almost scheduled some elective surgery to coincide with the occasion."

I laughed, thinking of the lengths I'd gone to get out of a few weddings.

"The point is now my family is really not buying this discrimination angle I'm trying to work."

I was still thinking about the elective surgery. "What were you going to have done?" I asked, making a vague gesture toward her chest. Gail's large breasts are a constant source of back pain.

"Never mind," she said as she finished her last bite of breakfast.

"Steven!" a voice shouted.

The voice was coming from the fifth-floor landing. It sounded just like my mother, but it couldn't be—

"It's your mother," my mother said.

I looked at Gail, panicked. "My mother's here."

"So?"

"How did she find me? My mother thinks I work for *The New York Times*."

"You told your mother you work for *The New York Times*?"

"Never mind."

My mother was pounding at the door.

"Want to get it?" I asked Gail in a tone that suggested it would be fun for her to do so.

Mistress Gail was not buying it. "Be a good boy and open the door for your mother."

"Hi," I said as I obeyed Gail's order. I thought about Gail at home with Liz as she figuratively (literally?) cracked the whip.

"Stavri." Stavri is Romanian for Steven. My mother calls me Stavri on very rare occasions as an endearment or when she's really annoyed with me. At the moment, she was finding nothing endearing about me.

My mother came toward me and I braced for her embrace. Instead she just passed by me and walked into the office. "No hug?"

"I'm being withholding, Stavri. I'm so disappointed in you. I bumped into Teddy Balamaci at church yesterday."

"Who?"

"*Who?* He was almost your father-in-law. Tina's father."

"I dated Tina for six weeks during high school."

"Anyway, Teddy's the new treasurer of the Societatea Farsarotul and he told me your membership has lapsed."

"My membership lapsed about a decade ago."

"Well, that's why I'm here."

"*That's* why you're here?"

"Yes. I told him I'd get a check from you. It's eighteen dollars for a year! Which, let's face it, is a bargain. And that's why I'm here. Why else would I be here? To tell you that this stunt of yours is killing me?" My mother was screaming. Tears rimmed her eyes.

And then my mother noticed Gail and realized we were not alone. Miraculously, her eyes were dry. She smiled, reached for Gail's hand. "Who's your friend, *Stavri?*"

"Onda; Gail. Gail; Onda." I said as introduction.

"Gail, please accept our apologies. Mothers and sons, what can I say?" My mother shrugged and chuckled lightly.

Then my mother did that thing she always does. She started chatting with Gail, like she'd known her all her life. They were having girl talk, laughing. They were instant chums. After my mother had recommended a brand of bra that Gail just had to try and Gail had thanked her instead of saying, "Hey, lady, mind your own business, you don't even know me!"

I asked my mother what had really brought her into the city. I knew what had brought her into the city. But I figured we might as well cut right to the chase. And besides, with Gail here, it was unlikely my mother would actually murder me.

My mother got quiet for a moment. Placed her hand tenderly atop

Gail's, "Gail, dear, would you mind terribly giving me and my son a few minutes?"

"Mom, she's working." I tossed this off in an attempt at nonchalance, as my eyes darted over to Gail and scrunched into a position that I hoped communicated: *Stay with me, please. You're my only chance for survival.*

Gail missed or ignored the scrunched eyes. "Of course not, Onda. You two take all the time you need. I'm going to run out and get that bra. *Stavri* will give you my number. Call me sometime!"

Was she kidding? Gail headed for the door, but first turned back to me and mouthed, "I love your mother!" And then she was gone, leaving me alone facing my executioner.

Onda was silent. She stood before me, staring and shaking her head. She looked like a bobble-head doll.

"How did you find me, Mom?"

"You work for *The New York Times*. You don't think I can find *The New York Times*?"

"But I don't work for *The New York*..." I let it drop. I couldn't have that particular conversation one more time.

"I have one thing to say to you." My mother's voice was shrill and strident. "If your father was alive, this would kill him!" Her hands were clasped in prayer, and her eyes fixed toward heaven. She started screaming, "Thank God your father can't see this."

Statements like these might lead you to believe that my father is deceased—he's not.

When my father left my mother, she chose to believe that she'd been widowed—it had a nicer ring than *abandoned*. She didn't actually have a wake or funeral (the priest would have no part of it), but she did observe the traditional Romanian Orthodox forty days of mourning. That's correct—*forty*. She stayed in the house, mirrors were covered in black cloth, and my brother and I were forbidden to watch TV or listen to music. Her friends indulged this fantasy by paying their respects and bringing meals. Her traditional friends brought lamb *gella* (a hearty lamb stew) or *koulash*. In Romanian, *koulash* has two meanings: It's a tomato soup with meatballs that's delicious but quite simple to make, and it's also one of our many words for tired. So, for example, one might say: "I am so *koulash*, I think I'll just make some *koulash*."

My mother's more modern friends fell into two camps: the crock-pot girls, who thought waiting fourteen hours for a meal to be ready was a fair trade-off for never having to stir the pot. I strongly disagreed with them. And worked very hard to mask my disappointment when one of them arrived carrying a scorched and lifeless stew.

The other group consisted of the casserole ladies. I loved these women. They delivered comfort in a greased 13x9. The dishes they created were so creamy and soft that you barely needed to chew. Which is really a plus when you're spending your days watching your mother try in vain to make funeral arrangements for your still-living father. The long hours of responding to sympathy cards and listening to my mother's friends call me "a brave little soldier" was truly exhausting. It was nice to know that when dinnertime rolled around all I had to do was inhale.

At the end of the forty days my mother made *gud*—a sweet, wheat and raisin salad. It's one of the tastiest things you'll ever eat. Unfortunately, if you're in the mood for *gud* you have to start praying that some old Romanian will hurry up and keel over, as it's only served at forty days. After the *gud*'s been eaten by the now no longer mourning friends and family, the leftovers are tossed out for the birds to take and eat. Which somehow is supposed to have a connection to life continuing, but I never quite grasped it. No matter, because we didn't have any leftovers—not with me around—and my mother's grieving hadn't ended, it had just begun.

"Daddy is alive." We were like Albee's George and Martha, and I'd dared to bring up the baby.

"He's dead to me!"

"Be that as it may," I said, not about to let it drop now. "He lives in Palm Springs."

"I'm sorry, dear. Did you say something?" My mother has hysterical deafness. I know I shouldn't throw stones since I have hysterical muteness, but *I* really can't speak. I find my mother's auditory woes highly suspicious. "Listen to your mother. You want to die alone? Go to Piriclui."

Piriclui is Romanian for Peter. Based on the lilt that came into her voice when she uttered his name, she was finding him particularly endearing at the moment.

"Go to your brother," continued my mother. "Beg his forgiveness. If you don't do this, your guilt will destroy you."

"Right. Or you will."

"I'm sorry, I can't hear you. Did you say something?"

"No." I signed the word. It was one of the few ASL symbols I still recalled from my days in the cardboard apartment complex. My mother was not budging; she wanted some sort of guarantee that I'd be attending my brother's wedding. I finally muttered, "I'll be there."

That my mother heard.

She bruised my ribs as she hugged me. When she finally let me go, she began surveying my dismally dim work place. "You'd think *The New York Times* could spring for a nicer office."

❖

Later that afternoon, I decided to heed my mother's advice and make things right with my brother.

I was about to leave the office when Gail walked in, grinning and pointing at her breasts. They were perkier than usual. There was increased definition. A superior lift. More separation.

"When I think that I contemplated surgery." Gail launched into a litany of praise for my mother.

This has happened to me before. When people meet my mother, they look past the black nylons paired with sensible black flats and are instantly charmed by her.

I had now added Gail to the long list of friends who thought my mother was amazing, funny, delightful, and intuitive and thought I was critical, hypersensitive, and completely blind to my mother's obvious charms.

"Do you realize that I am without pain in my upper back for the first time in months. Oh my God," Gail exclaimed. "If she was my mother, she'd be my best friend!"

"If she was your mother, you'd shoot yourself." I saw the look of disapproval cross Gail's face. Of course she'd given me disapproving looks before, but never like this one. It was like she'd encountered a heretic—a blasphemer. I had sullied the name of Saint Onda.

I couldn't tolerate another word of devotion to my mother. I needed to go apologize to my brother for the dinner party debacle. I left Gail as she was calling my mother.

"Girlfriend? It's Gail," is how their conversation began.

❖

"Work the counter," my brother barked at me the instant I walked into the bakery. He then proceeded to do the crossed-leg hop to the bathroom that I thought only women did. I wondered where Barney was. Sick, I imagined.

When Peter was finished relieving himself and he returned, now walking like a normal person, I said, "Hi," sheepishly while staring at my shoes.

"I have a very unhappy fiancée," was the only greeting returned.

"Sorry, I..."

A customer walked in. Peter's glower vanished. He was his usual warm and charming self as he waited on the woman. Thankfully, he sold her the carrot cake I'd been eyeing every time I allowed my glance to rise above the level of my footwear. It's the stress; it always makes me jones for sugar.

When the woman left, so did my brother's warmth. "So...you were saying?"

Was I saying something?

"I..." I stammered, stopped.

"I..." I started again, failed. "Where's Barney?" I asked as a way to avoid our confrontation a minute longer.

With the possible exception of *How do you really feel about me skipping your wedding?* It was absolutely the worst question I could have asked him.

"Barney? You want to know where Barney is? I fired him."

"Why?" I thought perhaps that listening to "Quando Quando Quando" had finally become more than my brother could bear.

"You're asking *me* why? Why do you think?"

"I really don't have any idea." I really didn't have any idea.

"Because he refuses to make wedding cakes."

"So you fired him?" I was upset, both by my brother's actions and by my unwitting involvement. It took all my strength not to grab one of the flourless chocolate cakes right off the shelf and bite into it. I didn't need a knife. I'd just eat the thing whole.

Peter was shouting at me about my article and all the trouble I'd caused him. Peter never shouts. It's not that he's like me and is unable to. He's just calmer, mellower. He's an anomaly that way. We're not a mellow people. I often wondered if he was only a half-breed Romanian. Maybe our mother had an affair with a man who came from someplace where its citizens tend toward sunnier dispositions. Monaco, maybe. Or

Switzerland. Looking at Peter now, with his pupils dilated and the veins in his neck bulging, I was certain of his paternity. He was, without a doubt, a card-carrying member of the Societatea Farsarotul.

"It's because of you, I had to fire Barney!"

That was not fair. For one thing, he did not have to fire Barney. Making wedding cakes was not the only job to be done. Had my brother never heard of a birthday cake? Let Barney make those. And for another thing, as long as I was focused on, if not actually voicing, my rage, how about showing a little appreciation for all the support I'd given him over the years?

As far as I'm concerned, if it wasn't for me my brother wouldn't even have a business. Well, technically, he'd have no business without Adam—which, indirectly, means he'd have no business without me. Adam used Peter for every wedding he planned. I don't mean to suggest that Peter is not a very talented pastry chef—he is. But there are many gifted pastry chefs in this city. Adam helped put him on the map. If it wasn't for my partner, my brother might be stuck in some industrial kitchen making sheet cakes for Costco instead of being hailed as *New York* magazine's Tastiest Looking Chef!

"What am I going to do now?" Peter's anger was beginning to mix with panic.

The impulse to say "Figure it out for yourself! That's not my problem" was overshadowed by images of my mother. I saw her taking our arms, wrapping them around each other, pushing us into each other, and making us stay that way until we were friends again.

I wasn't ready to go that far. I wasn't prepared to grab him and squeeze tightly till everything was better. But I did decide to defuse the situation. It needed to be done.

I was just about to ask for Peter's forgiveness and tell him I was coming to the wedding when Barney's theme shoved its way into my brain.

I wasn't actually humming the melody. But the words, which I don't understand because I can't speak Italian, and the music, were filling me up, pulsing away inside of me. The song took on an anthem-like quality—a revolutionary call. I wondered if I, like Barney, might have "Quando Quando Quando" looping forever in my head. Suddenly it didn't seem like such a bad fate.

The instant I resigned myself to a "Quando"-filled life, the song was silenced in me. In its place came thoughts of Barney. Barney, who aside from his singing and his uncanny ability to make roses, lilacs, and delphinium out of butter cream, was not someone I ever thought particularly exceptional. Barney, it turned out, was a very brave man. I never would have guessed he was the caliber of person who would risk his job—his security—for his beliefs. He'd never seemed the type.

Who was the type, I wondered? There was…No, maybe not. I paused…I thought…I…

"Say something, Steven!" my brother shouted. He stared at me, exasperated.

Have you ever had the experience of going to the diner and, when you get there, you don't even bother looking at the menu because you know exactly what you're going to order? You knew what you were going to have before you even left the house. The sole reason you went to the diner was because you were in the mood for a cheeseburger deluxe. You always get the cheeseburger deluxe when you go to the diner. But then the waiter walks up to the table and you hear yourself saying, "I'll have a tuna melt on rye, please." Disbelief is instantly registered on the face of your fellow dinner companions who are both surprised and baffled by your atypical behavior. Because *you* never get the tuna melt on rye.

This was one of those moments. Though I realize the situation was far more portentous than sandwich selection ever could be.

I smiled at my brother, fully prepared to tell him I'd be there, and instead I said, "Peter, I'm really sorry. I won't be at the wedding."

CHAPTER FOURTEEN:
THIS IS ABOUT STUFF, ISN'T IT?

Wanting to avoid facing the ensuing familial fallout, which was sure to follow my fight with Peter at Great Cakes, I decided to fully immerse myself in the movement by reporting directly from the front lines. Like so many before me, I was embedding myself for the good of the story. Placing myself right in the thick of it all—harm's way, if you will—determined, as I was, to uncover the facts firsthand.

In other words, I decided to hang out with my boyfriend at his plush offices, in the heart of Greenwich Village, feet from Washington Square Park instead of sitting forlornly in my grim tenement digs, situated in the middle of nowhere.

Strolling down lower Fifth to Adam's building, I immediately noticed the spray paint had been scrubbed off the wall and a lovely new stainless steel plaque had been installed. It read: *More Parties!*

I walked into the reception area and was greeted by Vanessa. "Welcome to More Wed—Parties. Damn. I've been saying 'weddings' all day long. Old habits, I guess."

After we smooched and I admired her shoes, it was time to get down to business.

"Okay. I don't want to get in the way," I said. "I'm just here to observe, report. I'm going for a whole day-in-the-life kind of thing. Just ignore me." I pulled out the new pad I'd purchased for the occasion and got ready to work. I felt like I was missing something. Then I realized I'd forgotten to bring a pen, so I took one from the cup on Vanessa's desk.

Now I was ready.

"Where's Max?" I asked.

Vanessa stared at her computer. She didn't look up. She didn't answer.

"Vanessa?"

"I'm doing what you said. I'm ignoring you."

"Could we maybe go a little more with the spirit and a little less with the letter?"

Vanessa looked up from her computer screen. "He called in sick. Hey, Steven, could you do me a favor?"

"Sure."

"Will you go into Adam's office and bother him instead?"

❖

Adam applauded my initiative. He thought that my idea to chronicle the transition from More Weddings to More Parties! was a great one.

I returned the praise, telling him that I thought his addition of an "!" to the new moniker added a great jolt of enthusiasm.

Then we sat. I waited for things to start happening. I really wanted to run out for a cup of coffee, but I didn't want to miss the action. To avoid being idle, while I was waiting for it all to begin happening, I made a grocery list on my new reporter's pad.

The phone rang several times, which got both of us jazzed. With each call I grabbed my pad and Vanessa's pen. Alas, disappointment followed each telephone conversation. For all the callers were women trying to hire Adam to plan their weddings. Actually, there was one call from someone wanting help with a silver anniversary party. This gave Adam pause. Should he grandfather in the already married or banish them as well? He couldn't decide, but promised he'd get back to the woman later in the week with a ruling.

The atmosphere in the room became increasingly Beckett-like as Adam and I looked at the phone. Certain the next call would be the one to propel us into wedding-boycott action! Any second now that call would come. Neither of us moved. After a particularly long stretch with no calls whatsoever, I lifted the receiver to confirm that the phone hadn't gone dead.

It hadn't.

We began feeling hopeless, sitting silently, waiting for something to happen. We waited. And we waited.

Then Adam snapped from his malaise and decided to strategize.

"Why wait for something to happen?" he said. "When we can make something happen."

That's the spirit. I tore out a sheet of paper from my pad and gave it to him. Luckily, he had his own pen. Two or three times, I noticed him put pen to paper and then immediately pull it away and tuck it behind his ear. But at last, I saw that he was indeed writing away on the page. Progress was being made.

I moved closer to him. Not so close as to disturb. But close enough to see what he was writing so I could "report." After peering at the page, I decided to allow this moment to remain off the record. Adam was just making doodles. Apparently, he wasn't sure what the next step in the movement should be.

I didn't know either, so I told him to give it time. It would happen. There would be more press. More people would join. I pointed out that already it was a sizeable group. All the people at Man Land were committed. Barney had been fired for his beliefs. And, of course, there was the crazy florist on the Upper West Side who maimed Amanda. Things were happening!

Time was passing even though we weren't accomplishing much. In another hour we'd be able to go out for lunch. My eyes started getting tired. I was thinking maybe a nap would be good. And since I'd already decided that Adam's scribbling was not the breathtaking story lead I was looking for, I had nothing to write about. I felt my chin knock against my clavicle. My head bobbed back up. Almost immediately my head started falling again. My eyes were getting heavy. By the count of ten I was either going to be asleep or hypnotized.

"How do people stand this?"

Adam's voice pulled me from my trance.

"Stand what, honey?" I asked.

"I'm just sitting here. I don't sit. I go, go, go. I'm a doer. How do people sit around all day doing nothing?"

Having never had a problem with that concept, I was at a loss. I decided to act like it was a rhetorical question. I nodded vaguely.

Then I heard Vanessa shouting in the outer office. "Excuse me, ma'am. Sorry, you can't just go in—"

Adam's door burst open.

Margaret barreled in. The wool crepe cape she was wearing billowed behind her, creating a Batman meets Blaine Trump sort of effect.

"Darling!" she said through her newly whitened teeth. "How are you?" The tone was bright, loving—a bit of a surprise in light of recent events. Then she noticed me. "Steven!" Just as bright. Just as loving.

So clearly, her behavior was all part of some elaborate ruse.

"Mom. What are you—?"

"My goodness, what an efficient secretary you have. I think she thought I was one of the terrorists." Margaret let loose with a big throaty laugh.

"She's not my secretary, mom. She's my assistant."

"I see. Does she answer the phone for you?"

"Yes."

"Schedule your appointments?"

"Yes."

"She's your secretary, darling."

Point to Margaret.

Again, she grinned. First at me, then she gave a wide smile to Adam. He refused to acknowledge her newly dazzling smile. He seemed on guard.

"My, your secretary is awfully pretty." Margaret did this kind of thing constantly—make the suggestion that there might be a great woman out there for her son, if he'd just open his eyes. Of course, she also brought up other men, too—like the beloved Daytime Emmy–nominated Tim.

Basically, anyone would be an improvement over me.

"Yes, she is awfully pretty. Her girlfriend thinks so, too."

This Margaret could not believe. "No! She's so feminine," Margaret whispered. She made a point of motioning toward the door with her head. Which I guess was her way of suggesting that Vanessa might be listening in at the door.

"Mom, much as I don't want to, I'm going to have to cut this visit short."

"I'm sorry, darling. Do you think this is a social call? It's not. I'm here on business. I need your help with a party I'm organizing. Now that you're a party planner, exclamation point," Margaret drew the punctuation mark in the air with her finger and tittered like one of the three little maids from school. "I thought to myself: I must hire my son for the launch of his new business!"

I wasn't sure where she was going with this. But it seemed pretty clear to me this was a charade. She'd used the same WASPy, cucumber sandwich caterer for every party she ever threw.

Adam was generously giving her the benefit of the doubt. "Thank you. What party are you talking about, Mom?"

"It's not the wedding."

"Okay. I didn't say it was."

"It's an evening formal for two hundred or so. I want nothing but the best."

"What kind of party is it?" Adam asked.

"Kind?" Margaret had apparently been thinking that Adam was going to be blinded by her new smile and offer no resistance.

"Yes, *kind*. You know, what sort of a party is it?"

"It's for charity." Margaret said it with finality. Hoping, I guess, that this would end the conversation.

It did not.

"That's so philanthropic of you. Which charity?"

Adam had Margaret on the ropes. She stammered, faltered and finally blurted out, "Orphans."

"Great. What orphans?"

"The ones without parents!" Margaret was perspiring. She never perspired—she removed her cape and let it drag from her hand, like a child with her security blanket. Her mouth opened, the beacon of white teeth shone a moment. Words were forming, but then she closed her mouth again. Whatever tack she'd been thinking of trying, she abandoned. She stood quietly, clutching the cape. She looked defeated.

Point to Adam.

I found their exchange fascinating. My mother never would have employed a strategy this nuanced. True, just as my mother had been, Margaret was being deceitful. She was trying to trick her son into planning his sister's wedding. But I found it refreshing to witness a scenario that didn't rely solely on tears and guilt for its success. Margaret was being creative. If she'd been a little better rehearsed, she might have actually gotten away with her plot.

"I'm not planning the wedding. I don't plan weddings."

Now that all pretenses had been tossed aside, things were really heating up. I grabbed my reporter's pad and started transcribing their row, so as not to miss a word.

Margaret's voice dropped. "We don't have to tell anyone. It can be our little secret. Who's going to know you planned the wedding?"

"I will," he said solemnly.

"Adam," Margaret pleaded. "How do you expect me to face my sisters and tell them that although you were absolutely delighted to plan their weddings, you refuse to plan mine?"

"You do realize that it's not actually *your* wedding I'm refusing to plan."

I noticed Margaret's eyes now. They were wide, angry. Her shining new teeth were hidden behind a snarl.

"How sharper than a serpent's tooth it is to have a thankless child!" Margaret managed, remarkably straight-faced.

"Okay, Mother. You better go," Adam said sternly.

"Wait. Wait. I'm not finished yet. Listen to me." Margaret caught sight of my furious dictation and glared at me until I dropped my pad and Vanessa's pen.

"This is about stuff, isn't it?" she said disgustedly, returning her attentions to Adam.

"What are you talking about?" Adam asked.

"Don't play coy with me—stuff. You're jealous that your sister gets to register for wedding gifts and you don't! You want the china. You want the crystal."

"This is not about stuff, mother. I have china and I have crystal. I bought it for myself." He danced on the balls of his feet, ready to respond to what ever she lobbed at him.

Margaret slammed back with: "Not Lalique. You want Lalique? I'll buy you Lalique."

I noticed Adam sway as his knees buckled. Or maybe that was me. I'm ashamed to admit it, but I felt this was an offer worthy of serious consideration. Attend the wedding of your own flesh and blood and in exchange receive fine French crystal. That was a good deal. It's true, we do already have stemware. But we own Waterford—it's lovely but it's *not* Lalique.

I looked at Adam, trying to figure out if he'd take the bribe. Would he consider abandoning his principles for fine imported housewares? I felt like I was in the studio audience of a game show. It took every ounce of my self-control not to screech: *Take the glasses! Go for the prize!*

I didn't, of course. I remained silent, watching.

Adam would not be bought. "Mom, you have to leave right now!" he shouted.

I shoved dazzling images of sparkling champagne flutes from my brain.

Margaret stood there a moment, defeated. She turned and marched out of the office, leaving the door open behind her. I watched as she made it as far as Vanessa's desk, pausing to look at her. Margaret shook her head morosely at Vanessa. "You're so pretty," Margaret sighed.

Then Margaret turned on her heels and marched straight back into the office.

"All right," she shouted. "This is my final offer. If you come to the wedding, I'll buy you Baccarat!"

CHAPTER FIFTEEN:
TALKIN' 'BOUT A REVOLUTION

My tenure at More Parties! was turning out to be quite a bit less live-from-the-trenches than I'd originally anticipated. Most days Adam and I showed up at his office, had coffee, and talked about how today would certainly be busier and more challenging than the day prior. Each day, when the challenges failed to materialize, we'd sneak out and go to the gym, or for a long walk. One day, I even dragged Adam to a Hot Nude Yoga class. In the afternoon, we'd try a new restaurant for lunch, or I'd pack up leftovers from the night before and we'd picnic in Washington Square Park.

It had been years since we'd spent this much time alone with each other, and I was loving every minute of it. We'd had a period of this kind of intense together time when we first met and were imprinting on each other. I think it lasted about four months. Ignoring friends and work (well, I ignored work), we spent every moment together. Talking, learning about each other, laughing, making love. And then, sometime around week seventeen, the inevitable happened. We realized we had other friends and family members and obligations before we met each other. They could no longer be ignored. And so we emerged from our love cocoon and once again began attending to all the other people and responsibilities in our lives.

Now, six years later, the time spent "working" with Adam during the day, followed immediately by evenings spent alone with one another at home, brought up all kinds of great memories of our earliest days together.

Adam and I first met on the sidewalk in front of St. Patrick's Cathedral. It's funny how memory works; some moments of that day are etched into my brain, others are gone completely. It was January fourteenth, and a light snow was falling—that I know with certainty.

I was standing in front of the cathedral as part of a protest group. We were angry about something the Cardinal had said the week before, but I can't for the life of me recall now what it was. It must have been offensive, though, because it was a very sizable group. We filled the sidewalk on Fifth Avenue, making passage for the pedestrians who were not part of our rally virtually impossible.

I believe I saw Adam before he saw me, but this point is always debated when we retell the story—since I'm telling it now, I saw Adam first. He had a chocolate brown shearling coat on, and the gloves that he wore matched the shearling exactly. I remember wondering if he had gloves to match every coat he owned, and hoping that he didn't. I would have found that excessive.

He was (and continues to be) spectacularly handsome. I remember thinking, "Wow, he looks smart," but what does smart-looking mean? He didn't have horn-rimmed glasses on, he wasn't carrying a calculus textbook. Still, smart was the overwhelming feeling I had about him. I really like smart, so I decided to make my way through the crowds of people carrying signs about the important matter I no longer recall so I could stand next to him.

Adam saw me pushing my way toward him and he smiled at me.

He was the first to speak. "Impressive work there, getting through the crowd."

I had not thought of an opening line in advance—a mistake. I thought I would appear next to him without being noticed and convince him later that it was only fate that had brought us together. I looked at him and said, "I'm not usually that aggressive." I said this rather meekly.

If I knew at the time that I'd be spending the rest of my life with this man, I'd like to believe that I would have said something funnier or wittier or more profound. I wish that I had not opened with that tragically true comment about my personality. But, alas, one does not know the important moments of life until months or years after they've taken place. On reflection, I realize I have frivolously used all my best opening lines on one-night stands and shopkeepers in foreign countries to which I will probably never return.

"Can you help me?" Adam asked.

"Sure," I said, grateful that my opening line hadn't ended our conversation.

"I need to get through to the other side. It's extremely important."

"Okay," I said. Not exactly scintillating dialogue, but I was flustered.

I looked toward Fiftieth Street and wondered how I was going to get him there. I was wearing a waist-length down jacket and a pair of easy-fit jeans. (Romanian men tend to be a little pear-shaped. Levi's are a bad idea for us.) I had, regrettably, dressed for a rally, not to meet my life partner.

"Hang on to the back of my pants," I said, and I began pushing through the crowd with Adam's fingers clutching my waistband. "Excuse me, pardon me," I shouted. And people did excuse me. It was very *parting of the red sea*. We passed through the crowds effortlessly.

"Thank you so much," Adam said when I'd delivered him safely to the other side of the street.

"Happy to do it. So you're not here for the rally?"

"No. I don't do protests. Although the first CD I ever bought was Tracy Chapman, you know, remember that song, 'Talkin' 'bout a Revolution.'" Adam sang this and smiled. "Does that count?"

"That was my first CD, too," I said, and it was. "I bought it for 'Fast Car,' which is kind of funny because I hate driving."

I had crossed the street with him and found myself standing in front of Saks Fifth Avenue. "I'm here for a sale," Adam said, pointing at the department store.

Adam had to get through the crowd because he wanted to go shopping. That was his extremely important reason?

It is with Adam's help and guidance that I've wisely accepted couture as my personal savior. However, when we met, I thought fashion was rather frivolous. To my mind, I was out on the street trying to change the world. And Adam was on the street trying to change his wardrobe. "Oh. You're here for a sale?" There was a hint of disapproval in my voice.

I guess he picked up on my tone. "It's not just any sale," he said. "Etro." He paused to allow me to fully grasp the importance of what he'd just said. "I have my eye on a shirt—you know how gorgeous those Etro shirts are. I've been waiting for one in particular to go to fifty percent off."

Since Etro was not available at the Gap, I had no idea what he was talking about.

"I'm Adam More," he said, removing his right shearling glove.

"I'm Steven Worth," I said, removing my right wool-acrylic blend mitten.

We shook hands; Adam's was warmer than mine. "Thank you, Steven Worth, you've been most kind."

"Most kind." I found that phrase both formal and flirtatious. A chill, not caused by the falling snow, ran up my spine.

He gave my hand a little squeeze, which I returned. We hesitated, not sure what to do next. I fantasized about walking together into the sunset—but it was only noon. Even if it had been later in the day with the precipitation and the midtown high-rises, no sunset would have been visible.

He walked to the store and waved at me through the revolving door.

"What just happened?" I asked aloud. Of course, no one answered me. It's New York, we're used to folks talking aloud to themselves on the street. At least I wasn't muttering obscenities.

I stood at the edge of the rally, no longer interested in it. After all, the Cardinal was always saying something that offended somebody. "Who cares?" Again, I spoke out loud—this time I got a response. I received a chorus of hisses from the militants on the sidewalk.

I had made a terrible choice; I had opted to stand in the freezing cold, in the snow—accomplishing nothing—when I could be shopping in Saks with Adam. And then I realized I didn't know his phone number. If I didn't go to Saks, I might never find him again. I turned to walk back toward the store and saw him walking toward me. He was carrying a shopping bag.

"Did you get the shirt?" I asked, my voice suddenly high and giggly. It was not at all the masculine tone I'd been hoping for.

"I did." He handed me the bag.

I thought he wanted me to take a peek inside at his new purchase.

"It's for you," he said.

"What? No," I said, my voice now a bit more restrained.

"You have to take it. The color is completely wrong for me. I don't know what I was thinking. It'll be perfect with your brown eyes. Hold it up. Let me see."

I was embarrassed but very flattered. He'd noticed my eyes. I pulled the shirt from the bag and gazed longingly at it, thus beginning my sartorial conversion. I held the shirt at my neck. It was a series of blue and green stripes woven on the softest cotton I'd ever felt. It was gorgeous!

"That looks great on you. Look." Adam turned me around to

face the store. I saw the shirt reflected back at me from Saks' main window.

"Thank you, but I'm sure it will look great on you, too." As much as I wanted to, I was afraid to take the shirt—what would he want in return? I thought of the possibilities, which excited me, but I was not raised that way.

Adam took the shirt and held it under his neck. It didn't look that good. I mean it was fine. He's very handsome and it was a magnificent shirt, but I had to agree it was better looking on me. Somehow the blue in the shirt looked washed out against his fairer coloring and the magnificent violet of his eyes.

"See? Bad. Right?" He handed it back to me.

"This is too generous. I can't accept it. You should return it." I rattled the three sentences off without taking a breath, as I pushed the shirt back into his arms.

"Fifty percent off. Final sale. You have to keep it," he said just as fast, shoving it back to me.

Adam pulled his hands away leaving me, literally, holding the bag. "I gave you the shirt, you give me something?"

"Okay, what?" I asked through another round of nervous giggles, my cheeks suddenly hot.

"How about your phone number," Adam said.

I happily obliged.

"I don't feel like that's quite enough," I said. "I should give you something else."

"Like what?"

"Since you've been"—(long pause)—"most kind," I said, now in love with the phrase, "may I give you a kiss?" I cannot begin to express how uncharacteristic and extremely bold this was for me. I am much more of a "pine for and remain frustrated" kind of a guy.

"You may kiss me." Adam blushed.

I moved toward his lips with the intention of giving him a mere peck. However, the softness and fullness I felt when our lips touched inspired me to give him a far more significant kiss.

Adam responded to it.

We stood there unaware of the crowd around us. If the moment had been shot for a film, the camera would have done one of those 360-degree rotations around us, immortalizing our blossoming love from every angle.

I'm not sure how long we'd been kissing but at some point we both became aware of the loud cheers and applause we were hearing. It was only then that Adam and I became aware of the social and political significance of our first kiss: We had been making out in front of the entrance to St. Patrick's Cathedral.

As our lips parted, and the cheers began to subside, I noticed other couples—gay, lesbian, and straight—all kissing. It seemed that we had started something.

I moved my mouth to Adam's ear and began singing "Talkin' 'bout a Revolution." It became our song.

❖

I found myself gazing at Adam, and humming our song softly, that last day that I was stationed at More Parties!

It had been, without a doubt, time well spent with regard to my relationship. I can't really say the same for my reportage. Aside from completing one piece about Adam's run-in with his mother, I didn't have much material for future columns. I had abandoned the notion of writing about Barney getting fired—partly because I didn't want to create more bad blood between Peter and me. But mostly because I didn't think informing my readers that they risked unemployment by joining the movement was a smart way to rally the troops.

Facing another day of inaction, I had a brain wave. I called Gail at the paper to find out if there was any news from *The Today Show*. Surely there must have been some word.

"You must be psychic. I just got off the phone with them," Gail said when I finished asking for a progress report.

I quickly flipped on speakerphone so Adam could hear the news, too.

"Great. What's going on? Do they want to interview Adam and me?" I asked flashing a big grin at Adam.

"Here's the thing…"

I immediately knew from Gail's grave tone that the word wasn't going to be good. I reached over to switch off the speaker option, but Adam blocked my hand.

"I talked with the producer. They're still interested. But the story has been pushed to the back burner. Anne Curry's camped out in the Hollywood Hills indefinitely. It seems not one, not two, but three celebutantes, all under the age of twenty-three, have escaped from rehab and are somewhere on the lam in Southern California."

I was dying to know which three exactly, but it seemed off point. Besides, I'd find out on *E!* later.

Adam slumped down in his chair and cradled his face in his hands. "I better go, Gail."

"Wait. I miss you. When are you coming home?"

"I'll be in Monday. I promise."

"Good. Brad's been wearing a new Kangol cap. Trust me. You don't want to miss it." Gail was still cackling when I hung up the phone.

Adam's posture was unchanged. He continued shielding his face with his hands. "Honey," I said. "Everything's going to work out."

"How?"

I had no idea. Adam's spirits were sinking. There was only one hope. Endorphins needed releasing.

Once I convinced Adam that going to the gym was a good plan, we sat in his office debating whether we should work out back and biceps or chest and triceps. We couldn't agree. So Adam, with stunning diplomacy, suggested shoulders and legs, which we both have an aversion to. Torturous as the notion was, I concurred. I knew I'd be happy with the decision the next time I put on a pair of shorts and a tank top.

We'd gathered our gym bags and were heading for the door when we heard a knock.

"Come in," Adam said. He walked back to his desk and slid his gym bag beneath it.

I also dropped my bag and took a position on the love seat opposite the desk. I picked up my pad and Vanessa's pen, just in case.

Max walked in. His first day back to work after being out sick for days.

"How ya feeling?" I asked, having abandoned my earlier I'm-not-here-just-ignore-me stance.

"Much better," Max said, his eyes darting guiltily to the floor. Then, as if on cue, he offered one brief, Camille-like cough. "But I'm not a hundred percent yet," he added, his glance still averted.

I found it rather sweet that Max was such a terrible liar. I wondered what had kept him from work for a week. Based on the performance he'd just given, it wasn't related to illness.

"Adam, I wonder if I could talk to you for a minute?" muttered Max.

"Sure, of course."

Max, at last, looked up from the floor and glanced at me. He gave me an awkward smile that accentuated the Karen Black–cross of his eyes. "It's kind of personal," he said.

"Oh, don't mind me," I said brandishing pad and pen. "I'm not here," I said. Opting to return to my I'm-not-here-just-ignore-me stance.

"What's up, Max?" Adam asked.

"I want you to know, I think what you're trying to do is great."

"Thanks. That means a lot. I know it's been quiet, but once people get used to us as more general party planners, we'll be busy again."

"Yeah," Max said. "About that…"

I wasn't sure what Max was leading up to, but I was pretty sure it wasn't going to be good.

"I've been very happy here. But I've decided to go out on my own. Start my own business."

"Oh?" Adam paused. "Well, I'm sorry for myself. But I'm happy for you. Congratulations. You've done amazing work for me. I'm going to miss you. I'll look forward to the opening of…What are you calling yourself? Parties by Max?"

"Something like that."

"What exactly," I chimed in. "I'll give you a plug in the paper."

Perhaps Max really had been sick. His skin went completely ashen. "Max's Weddings," he stammered.

By the time Max had cleared out his desk and fled the scene, Adam was beyond being helped by mere exercising. I suggested a far more healing endeavor.

"How about shopping?"

"What would be the point of that? I don't need anything," he sighed.

Oh my God. Since when did shopping have anything to do with need? I was terrified.

I considered an intervention of sorts. Maybe I should go to Etro and buy a few shirts, maybe a cute sweater, and bring them to him. Of course, with Adam generating no income at the moment, perhaps it would be better to be a little more budget minded. Instead of buying him something snazzy, I could… *What? I could what?* I was at a loss.

I was wondering whether curing Adam's mental health while

simultaneously incurring credit card debt was a good idea or not when suddenly Adam leapt from his desk and slapped his forehead like they used to do in those old V8 commercials. He ran to me and gave me a sweet kiss. He seemed completely fine. "Were you saying something about going to Etro?" he inquired gleefully.

"Not so fast. Why are you happy?" My tone suggested that this alteration in mood was not to my liking. That was not the case. It was just the swiftness of the swing that I found so troubling. It was far too reminiscent of experiences I'd had growing up with my mother.

"I'm happy because I just had a brilliant idea!" He pulled a sheet of paper from the top of a stack on his desk. He gazed upon the form like it was a winning lottery ticket. With a flourish he extended his arms. Bowing regally, he presented me with the paper. "Take a look at this." It was a flyer for an event called the International Wedding Expo. I knew from past years that the expo was the annual New York trade show for the wedding industry.

How could this piece of paper be the source of Adam's instant joy? "What?" I asked, studying the form for clues.

"It's the wedding expo at the Javits Center. Don't you see?"

I did not see. I shrugged and raised my eyebrows—the universal sign for what are you talking about?

"You do realize what this means? I have a confirmed booth at this event. I've already received my entrance badge. I'll be there along with another four hundred or so involved in the business!" He was elated.

"Why are you going? Are you going to start doing weddings again?"

Adam's eyes were scornful. He didn't even dignify the question with a response. "Don't you see?" (Again, with the don't you see.) "I have figured out our next step! We are going to gather an angry mob and storm the expo!"

"I don't think so." I said it calmly, but I wanted to make it crystal clear that there was no way we'd ever be doing that.

Adam was instantly pouty. He, like most of us, prefers it when people think his ideas are terrific. "I think it's a great idea," he said as he kicked his Cole Haan boot against the leg of his desk. "Why shouldn't we storm the expo?"

"Because the reality of getting gang-banged in prison is probably not nearly as hot as the fantasy is."

I could see that he thought what I said was funny, but he would not laugh or even smile—he continued to kick and sulk.

"You're going to scuff your shoes, sweetie."

"So," he said, holding the "o" of "so" for about twelve seconds.

Adam flung himself onto the love seat. His head landed on my shoulder. Then he burrowed into my neck and sighed heavily and with exaggeration. This he did in case I had missed the earlier displays of petulance.

"Honey, you're regressing," I said. "It's not really attractive and it's not necessary. I think I have an idea."

"What?"

"We can try to get a permit to hold a peaceful rally."

"How do we do that? You know how to do that?"

Had I really changed that much in the years since we'd been together? Adam seemed to have forgotten that long before I knew anything about Etro or Prada or Gucci, I knew a whole lot about civil disobedience.

"These permits," Adam said. "Will you get them? I'm really more of the…" Adam faltered, unsure how best to finish the sentence.

I helped him out. "Big picture, center of attention, let others do the menial work, type?"

Adam recognized this about himself and smiled. "Exactly!"

CHAPTER SIXTEEN:
ONCE UPON A TIME I HAD AN EDGE

On Sunday there was a downpour so heavy that streets flooded and even subways were thrown out of service. To the delight of the kids, Adam and I decided to alter our plans and stay in. With a whole day at home, I set out to accomplish a big project: I cleaned out my closet. It was a task I'd been dreading and putting off for about six months. I wasn't dreading the cleaning part. I could do that in my sleep if I ever slept. It's the parting with things that I find challenging. But today, I was making real progress.

I already had three bags full of clothing to take to Goodwill when I came across a stack of ancient T-shirts buried in the back on a ridiculously high shelf. I struggled to reach them and they tumbled to the floor, sending Vincent and Theo, who had been serving as my assistants, darting for safety.

The first one I picked up was my old Sartre's Sapphos T-shirt. A wave of nostalgia rolled over me. Ah, my carefree youth! I pulled off the shirt I was wearing, dropped it to the floor, and pulled on my college-era shirt. The cotton had become so faded and thin that I could see my skin beneath it. My impulse was to take it off, fold it back up, and return it to the shelf. The shirt would become important, I reasoned, if I ever became the president of the United States. It would be an integral part of the Worth Library—part of the president-as-an-angst-filled-young-man collection. I took the shirt off and held it, clutching it to me like a lover about to head off to war. Just as I was about to preserve it for the good of the nation, I came to my senses. It was time to move on.

It didn't even make it to the Goodwill bag. It went straight to the trash pile, which Theo was now napping on. I was sure even a homeless person would prefer to go topless than to wear that ancient, tattered garment. I glanced at the other shirts littering the floor. They were all embossed with political maxims.

There was a chartreuse Farm Aid tee stacked atop an oatmeal-colored, oil-stained shirt proclaiming, *I'm pro-choice and I vote*. The last one I looked at was black with pink lettering; *Silence=Death*, it read. A pink triangle was centered beneath the words.

The T-shirt looked brand new. I'm not sure that it had ever been worn. I would certainly never wear it now—too aggressive for me. I tossed it into the giveaway pile. I glanced over at the dozens of new shirts hanging on my clothes rack, all of them gorgeous. But one sleeve of fabric looked out of place. I grabbed the shirt—it was from the Gap. Wow, the shirt had to be old. It must have been purchased pre-Adam. It was instantly jettisoned to the Goodwill bag.

❖

The next day, I made my triumphant return to the offices of *The Gay New York Times*. After Gail and I kissed and caught up on gossip, I asked her if she thought I'd lost my edge.

"By lost, are you implying that once upon a time you had an edge?"

"Once upon a time I had an edge. I was very edgy!"

"If you say so."

"It's just that I was cleaning out my closet and I came across all these old political T-shirts."

"You mean shirts with slogans?"

"Yes," I said.

"Wow. You are edgy." Gail laughed hysterically.

She was right. I never had an edge. Even all my youthful protesting was the result of my following the lead of more socially aware friends. *They* were political; I just succumbed to peer pressure. I'm not radical. I'm a conformist. My idea of bucking the system is insisting on saying "large" instead of "venti" when I order my Starbucks coffee.

I guess Gail could see my ensuing despair. "We fought some good fights together. You've done a lot more than most," she said. "What's going on with you?"

The truth was that I couldn't figure out why I wasn't as passionate about this wedding boycott as Adam was. Adam was so committed. He was of such single focus. As for me, in spite of what I wrote in the paper, I really didn't see how our actions were going to make any difference.

I certainly believed that I should have the right to get married. I guess I didn't want the right bad enough to really fight for it. Besides, there were other, more important things to fight for. (Not that I was fighting for those things either.) How apathetic. What happened to me?

In that instant, I realized that Adam and I had swapped roles. He was now the committed activist; I was the conspicuous consumer. He wanted to storm the wedding expo—misguided, yes, but energetic. And then I remembered:

"Shit!" I shouted, glad Adam wasn't here to hear me swear. "I need to apply for a permit to protest the International Wedding Expo!"

"When is it?" Gail asked.

"It's right after Thanksgiving."

"Of this year?"

"Yes. Why? Is that too soon?"

"Yes. It's not possible. Not to mention the fact that the city would never grant a permit to boycott a harmless event that also happens to be a major source of revenue for the city."

Of course she was right. It had been foolish for me to think otherwise. I would have to tell Adam. Perhaps he was right; we should just gather an angry mob and storm the thing. It was nine weeks away; I planned to start eating a lot of very fattening food and stop doing any form of exercise. If we ended up in jail, best not to be so cute.

As I was pushing the image of Ned Beatty in *Deliverance* from my brain, Gail dropped a slip of paper onto my desk. "If only you had an in at City Hall," she said.

I looked at the paper. She had written the name *Liz* and a telephone number. "Your girlfriend?" I asked.

Gail nodded her head. "She has a job, you know. She doesn't spend every hour of the day doing my bidding."

❖

"Liz," I said when she picked up the line. "This is—"

"No names."

"Excuse me?"

"We're not talking to each other."

"Oh, okay. Do you want me to hang up the phone?" I hadn't the foggiest idea what she was talking about.

"We're talking to each other, but we're *not* talking to each other."
For a submissive, she had a very bossy tone in her voice. "I've had
contact from our mutual friend."

"Who?" I asked.

"Gail," she sighed. "No names!"

"Oh, right. Sorry." I sounded contrite but I felt she was being
excessive. It wasn't like I was hiring her to carry out a hit.

"Our mutual friend and I spoke on a more secure line. This thing
you need done, I believe it's possible."

"Great! How—?"

"No details!" she barked.

I had to have a conversation with Gail about this woman. No
matter how clean she was getting her bathroom—she had to go.

"This thing you want…"

"The permit?" I asked.

"Are you doing this on purpose?" Liz screamed full force. I
wondered if it was possible that her line was really tapped, or if it was
just the paranoia screaming. "Don't say anything, please!"

"Sorry," I said, deliberately disobeying her orders.

"If you see me, pretend we don't know each other."

"We don't know each other."

"Great, let's keep it that way."

The line went dead.

❖

I called Adam at his office to tell him the good news. Instead, he
told me about the bad news at More Parties! It seemed that not only
did Max quit, but when he left, he took all of Adam's wedding clients
along with him.

I tried my best to accentuate the positive. "Now no one is going
to sue you. All of the weddings you had booked will be carried out by
Max."

"But now all those couples aren't even experiencing any mild
inconvenience. There's just a different gay guy running the show. I
thought Max was committed to the cause," said Adam.

"The cause doesn't have a 401(k) plan," I pointed out.

I knew Adam could see my point. The reality was that eventually
he would have been forced to let Max go. He couldn't go on paying
salaries forever without any new income.

Adam sighed. "I thought every gay person in America was going to come on board when they heard my plan."

"Honey, you'll never get every person, gay or straight, to agree on any issue, especially if it affects them financially."

"People should—"

I cut him off. "Adam, if this had been one of your competitor's ideas, instead of your own, you'd be thinking of ways to contact their clients and plan those weddings." It was perhaps too harsh a thing to say, but I knew it was true.

"You don't have to be *mean* about it."

"You're right. I'm sorry," I said. "Sweetie, you just need to stay focused. Remember why you're doing this. And don't worry about what other people are doing."

"I'm trying," Adam said. "But it's so much easier being a leader when you feel like there's someone following."

That's for sure.

Chapter Seventeen: And That's How Things Went, Right up until Halloween

First, some good news.

With six weeks until the rally at the International Wedding Expo, I mentioned the event in every one of my weekly columns. Even though I was not feeling particularly militant, I always managed to sneak in a reference. One week, I wrote a piece about the importance of finding a quality sunscreen that's protective, long lasting, and doesn't leave any unsightly white streaks. Then I cleverly mentioned that while one should wear sunscreen daily, it's especially important on those days when you plan on being outside for long periods of time. For example, when you've jetted down to South Beach for the weekend or you're standing in front of the Javits Center chanting and shouting, "Hey, Hey! Ho, Ho! Marriage rights are the way to go!"

The day I wrote the column about tasty sandwiches that are easy to carry and pack and aren't too messy to eat with one hand while you're carrying a picket sign in the other, Brad approached my desk. He was ecstatic.

"Tell me what day it is?" he asked.

"Tuesday," I said, wondering why he'd interrupted me with such a mundane question when I was busy writing out my recipe for spicy black bean burgers.

"That's right, Tuesday!" he said, raising his arms in a show of victory. The velocity of his arm movement caused his bling to start clanging. When finally the gold chains were silenced, Brad continued speaking. "It *is* only Tuesday. I have spent the last day and a half searching the city for Friday's edition of the paper, and have come up empty-handed. We're completely sold out!"

Being that we give the paper away for free, *sold out* was a bit of a misnomer. Still, I was delighted with the news.

"We're printing more copies. I'm adding extra boxes in additional neighborhoods. I have a meeting with some potential new advertisers this afternoon."

"On the phone or in person?" I asked.

"In person. Why?"

"No reason," I said, staring at the four inches of boxer shorts I could see rising above his pants. He'd also purchased a new hat. The Kangol cap had been replaced by a Yankee one. If Brad's nose was pointing north, the cap's brim was somewhere in the great Southwest.

"Steven," Brad said, hoisting his pants. "Thanks for everything. None of this would be happening without you. I really appreciate how hard you've been working lately."

That was a very good day.

Now, for some bad news.

One of the main reasons I'd been so diligent at work was because I was trying to ignore the fact that I still hadn't spoken to Peter. A month had passed. We never went that long without seeing each other. Since Peter and I no longer lived under my mother's roof, she could not orchestrate one of her forced embraces. Therefore, she'd come up with a new method of intimidation designed to coerce a reconciliation. She'd taken to leaving threatening messages on my answering machine: "Steven, have you spoken with Peter yet? I'm curious because you're the two strongest men I know. So I'll need both of you to serve as pallbearers at my funeral, which I'm assuming will be in the next week or two."

By screening my calls and dedicating myself to work, I tried telling myself it was only because Peter and I were both so busy that we were out of touch. As long as I wrapped myself in this warm blanket of denial, and erased my mother's messages the instant they were played, I could almost convince myself that this was true.

As long as I kept busy with the movement, I could justify that what I was doing was more important than standing up for my brother on his wedding day. Some moments it was actually easy to believe I was doing the right thing. For instance, there was the day an official-looking envelope arrived from the city. Adam and I were both home. He grabbed the letter and opened it. Adam cheered as he waved the rally permit over his head. It had actually arrived. Liz had come through for me and the event was officially on. I was so proud of the accomplishment that I jumped right along with Adam.

Regrettably, this moment of joy was short-lived. When I continued sorting through the rest of the mail, I came across something addressed to Adam More & Steven Worth. I knew immediately it was the invitation to Peter and Amanda's wedding.

Being my mother's son, I didn't think this was mere coincidence. Why should I, when I could find a darker, far more ominous explanation for events? It was clear to me that the permit and the invitation arrived together as a way of sending me a message. It was Adam who opened the permit. *I* opened the invitation. What more proof did I need to realize I'd been making a tragic mistake? My old friend panic raced through my core. My upper lip began quivering so intensely that I could feel the nerves in my face twitching all the way up into my temples.

Then Adam, blind to my torment, handed me the permit. "Steven, thank you for this. This wouldn't have happened without you. We're going to make history. This is the best day of my life!"

And that's how things went, right up until Halloween.

❖

If I were making a movie out of this life of mine, perhaps I'd "smash cut" from my quivering lip to my face bobbing for an apple. Don't you love the imagery? I'm drowning. I'm at sea. Get it?

In reality, though, I have not bobbed for apples since I was ten, and there was certainly no apple bobbing going on at Brad's Halloween party—he would never tolerate water spilling onto his newly stripped and waxed oak floors.

Adam has always gone all out for Halloween. He's so creative in that way—he is, after all, king of the glue gun. He can make anything.

One year he made a giant mountain with a papier-mâché Julie Andrews on top. The two of us were inside the mountain, manipulating the miniature Julie so she could twirl around. It was impossible to eat or socialize from inside the mountain, so we spent the evening necking and pulling Julie's strings. It was by far the best Halloween of my life—lots of romance and no sugar hangover.

If that was the best, this Halloween at Brad's was without doubt the worst.

Because Adam gets such enjoyment out of creating our costumes, I give him free rein and always look forward to the surprise that awaits me on October 31. I have only one rule: No drag. (I guess I'm not secure enough in my masculinity.) Anything else, though, is fine with me.

When I came home, I found Adam dressed in a tuxedo. He was standing, looking out the living room window, and he slowly turned to face me. There was something about the sly smirk he gave me, paired with an effortless Bond-James-Bond kind of elegance, that made me instantly want to jump him. It was a nice feeling because with all the stress about our siblings and the movement in general, there had not been any "jumping" going on in quite a long while.

"You look great," I said as I pawed him.

"Thanks. Sweetie, get dressed. We don't have time," he said, holding my hands away from his body.

"I only need about two and a half minutes." I was *not* referring to the amount of time it would take me to dress.

"Later. When we get home. Start getting dressed. I'll be in to help you."

I gave up and went into the bedroom to get into my costume. Hanging from the closet door was my tuxedo.

Adam came into the room behind me. "What do you think?"

"I don't get it."

"That's because you haven't seen it all."

Adam went into the closet; he emerged with two masks that resembled the drama tragedy masks. These masks had the additional touch of giant tears coming down from the eyes. Adam pressed the masks toward me. In stark contrast to his creations, he had a huge grin on his face. "Great. Right?" he said.

I gave him a vague smile. The masks did not provide me with any clue to this costume riddle.

He put on one of the masks and stood in front of me. He was frowning, crying, and wearing black tie.

"I give up. I don't get it," I finally admitted.

"How can you not get it?" His voice came at me muffled from behind the grim mask. No mouth opening, terrific—this was shaping up to be another party where I wouldn't be able to eat. "Steven, we are two gay guys, sad because we can't get married. It's a statement."

"That's the costume?" I asked it like an innocent question, but of course he'd just told me it was the costume, so I was really just being passive-aggressive. I was hoping to have fun tonight, not spend it lecturing the other guests on the evils of attending weddings.

"Don't wear it if you don't want. I don't care." He said this in a voice that told me it would crush him if I didn't wear it.

"I want to wear it. It's just not your usual style. I think it's great."

"There will probably be forty people at the party—that's forty people we can get to the protest rally!"

I slipped into my tux shirt, extended my arms, and waited for Adam to insert the studs.

❖

We were the first to arrive at Brad's. We're always the first to arrive places, except when the hosts have also invited their parents or grandparents—in those instances we show up about three minutes after they do. We've tried everything we can think of to be fashionably late; still, everyone else manages to be more fashionably late.

Brad throws the kind of Halloween parties where about half the guests commit to wearing costumes and the other half absolutely refuses.

When Brad opened the door, he was dressed as Brad—as in, *I may live off Sutton Place but I shop for clothes in a different 'hood.* I couldn't believe he was persisting with the hip-hop wear. At least on Halloween he should have given us a twenty-four-hour reprieve. But no. The hoodie, the cap, the pants so baggy and long I couldn't see his feet; he was wearing the whole uniform.

"No costume?" I asked after we'd exchanged greetings.

"Charlie asked me to dress like this. He didn't want me in a costume."

Just then Charlie walked in wearing almost nothing, which is exactly the kind of thing young and hot guys do as an excuse to show off just how young and hot they are. He paraded around in a jock strap with some sequins sewn on it.

"He's a stripper." Brad beamed.

"How original," I said.

I think Brad sensed that I was being less than my usual charming self. "What's up with you? What are you decked out as?"

"I'm a sad gay guy who can't get married."

"The 'hills are alive' costume was funnier," he said as he left me to greet an arriving guest.

I picked up one of Brad's famous crab cakes and smashed it against my mask. I'd forgotten I didn't have mouth access.

"I'm hungry, too," said the other sad gay guy who can't get married. "Let's take off our masks and eat something."

Adam and I surveyed the buffet. With the exception of the crab cakes, everything looked really healthy. Non-fat yogurt had been used as a substitute in a variety of recipes that would normally call for sour cream.

"Brad" I asked, "Did you use yogurt instead of sour cream in the onion dip?"

"Yes!" he said proudly. "It's impossible to taste the difference, isn't it?"

I wanted to say that if it were impossible to taste the difference, I wouldn't have asked the question. I decided instead to inquire about some of the other treats he was serving. There was a platter of dark brown things, approximately the size of Yodels, that I was curious about.

"They're my version of the pig-in-blanket. Soy sausage wrapped in a crust of sprouted barley and spelt. They're yummy!"

"I make these, too," I said. "I use mini Hebrew National hot dogs and crescent rolls from a can for the dough. Mine are yummy, too."

"Let me tell you something. It's very important, so I hope you'll remember it: The whiter the bread, the quicker you're dead. Stick with barley and spelt." With that, Brad once again left us to greet other guests.

I have to admit, the fake pigs-in-blankets were good. The crust had a somewhat nutty quality that paired nicely with the fennel flavoring of the imitation sausage. Adam and I were about to have seconds when Gail arrived with a woman I assumed was Liz. I was guessing that Gail had come as a French woman—she was wearing a beret. Liz was dressed like Joan Crawford—she certainly had the right personality to play the part.

Adam nudged me to put my mask back on so they could fully experience our costumes. I obliged and after exchanging greetings, which was a bit awkward because Liz refused to say her name or acknowledge that we'd ever spoken before, we tried to guess each other's costumes.

"Yours are easy," I said. "Gail, you're French and, um…" I waited until Liz was looking at me so I didn't have to utter her name. "You're Joan Crawford," I finally said when I saw Liz make eye contact.

"Wrong!" Gail shouted triumphantly. "I am Faye Dunaway in *Bonnie and Clyde*, and Liz is Faye Dunaway *as* Joan Crawford in *Mommie Dearest*."

Liz raised her already ridiculously arched eyebrows and whispered, "No names."

I felt I should get credit for guessing "no names's" costume, but I didn't make a big thing out of it.

"Who are you two supposed to be?" Gail asked.

Adam took my hand. "Go ahead, sweetie, you can tell them," he said.

"We're two sad gay guys who can't get married."

Gail laughed her big Gail laugh. "That's what you get for being anti-drag. You could have been Faye in *Network*."

I couldn't think of a funny response that wouldn't be hurtful to Adam and the "statement" he was trying to make, so I said nothing. As a silence came over us that was seconds away from becoming awkward, Brad began shouting near the coat rack.

"This is not a costume! I'm not wearing a costume!"

Life in the city can get very busy, and in spite of the best intentions it's not uncommon to go weeks and even months without seeing people who you consider close friends. Such was the case with Brad. Between the extra time demands of his new relationship with Charlie and the extra hours spent at the paper now that circulation was up, and he actually had things to do, Brad had seen very few of his friends recently. And very few of his friends had seen his new look.

All evening long, Brad had been hearing that his was the best costume in the room. Diplomatically, he'd laughed each comment off. However, when Diana Ross, who was actually male and large enough to be Miss Ross and both Supremes, asked him if he was going to have to shave his head to get rid of the ghastly dye job—he snapped.

Brad had launched into a full-blown tirade, forcing Miss Ross to raise her arm in self-defense. This gave the impression that she was performing "Ain't No Mountain High Enough." I noticed Charlie watching the scene. He had the oddest expression on his face—a mix of satisfaction and shame. His lips were parted in a thin smile, but his eyes were glassy and filled with sorrow. I remembered Brad saying that it was Charlie who told him to go without a costume. Perhaps Charlie suspected this would happen—was even hoping that it would. I can't say that I'd blame Charlie if that were the case; still, it seemed a cruel set-up.

In grand diva style, Miss Ross exited the party. I wanted to leave, too, but knew that I shouldn't. Gail quickly pointed out that as the closest friend, it was up to me to make sure Brad was all right.

I didn't want to.

I stood, hesitating, suffering Gail and Liz's disapproving glances. I imagined that Adam was also giving me a disapproving glance. But of course, with his mask on, I could not actually see his face.

I took baby steps in Brad's direction, but thankfully Charlie reached him first. I was close enough to hear Charlie say, "We need to talk."

We need to talk is never a good way to open a conversation. For one thing the *we* always means *I* and the *talk* always means *vent*, unless, of course, it means something even worse.

I could see from the expression on Brad's face that he knew that's what Charlie meant. I watched as they slipped into the bedroom.

In the forty-five seconds that it took me to walk back to Adam and the girls at the food table, all the other guests (who I guess also knew the meaning of *we need to talk*) had fled the party.

"What should we do?" Adam asked.

"I'll stay," I volunteered.

"We'll all stay. We'll help clean up." Gail said.

And then I saw why Liz had chosen *Mommie Dearest* over *Chinatown* or *The Thomas Crown Affair*. From out of her pocket, she pulled a pair of rubber gloves. And she removed a bottle of ammonia from her handbag. She proceeded to reenact one of Faye as Joan's breakdown floor-scrubbing scenes—it was so convincing that I prayed Liz didn't notice all the wire hangers on the now empty coat-rack. I thought we were just going to put some Saran Wrap over the food and call it a day, but Liz was taking this cleanup task to a whole other level.

Just as we were ridding the apartment of the last signs of the party, Charlie walked into the living room. He was dressed now and carrying a suitcase. He started toward the door, but then seemed to change his mind. He abruptly stopped, dropped his bag, and ran over to us. He gave us all warm hugs—even Liz, whom he had never met. "Let's not be strangers, guys. I'll see you at the rally." To me, he added, "Take care of Brad," as he gave me an extra hug.

Poor Brad. I wasn't sure that he'd ever had his heart broken. Brad didn't have much experience getting dumped. He usually didn't let people close enough to him, so getting dumped was not a concern. On the rare occasion when he did let someone get close to him, he usually dumped him first—this I know from firsthand experience.

Adam and I said our good-byes to Gail and Liz. Perhaps Charlie's hug had inspired Liz. She was warm and gentle, she even allowed me to speak her name. She held me in a tight hug, and the toxic smell of ammonia, still on her skin, made me warm and tingly and reminded me of the hugs my mother gave me after a Saturday morning of cleaning. I liked Liz. She was not conventional. But then, who is?

Alone with Adam, he offered to go with me into the bedroom to check on Brad. I kissed him gently—mask to mask.

"What's that for?" he asked.

I wasn't exactly sure what it was for—not that there needed to be a reason. "Be right back," I said, not answering his question.

I walked into the bedroom. There wasn't a single light on in the room. No sign of Brad. It was completely quiet. I was overtaken with dread as I fumbled about for a light switch. I felt just like Jamie Lee Curtis in *Halloween*. This thought reminded me that I was still wearing my mask and I quickly removed it. Across the bedroom, I noticed the bathroom door was ajar. I wished that I'd had Adam accompany me, but I was not going to go back to get him. There was no psycho on the loose (except maybe me) so I summoned up my courage and called out Brad's name.

There was no response.

My heart was pounding. I have never once thought of Brad as the type, but now I was convinced that he'd committed suicide.

A little louder I called, "Brad."

Still nothing.

I walked into the darkened bathroom, flipped the light switch and saw him. He was naked. I was immediately embarrassed. Not because he was naked—we go to the same gym and I've seen him in the locker room hundreds of times. And years ago we'd dated. This was very different, though. It was kind of weird and felt a little creepy. I averted my glance and said, "Sorry."

He didn't seem to notice me.

Then I realized that he hadn't just been standing naked in the dark. He was standing naked in the dark *on his scale.*

Okay, this was very weird and more than a little creepy.

"What are you doing?" I tried adopting a casual tone, as if everyone cracks up while throwing a party, gets dumped, and then strips naked and stands frozen in the dark on his or her scale. "Brad? It's Steven."

He turned and looked at me. I was still gazing at the floor. "Am I so hideous looking that you feel compelled to avert your glance?"

I thought perhaps he would add "I am not an animal. I am a human being" to complete the *Elephant Man* motif, but he did not.

I looked at him. "I was trying to be polite, Brad," I said. "Why don't you come down off that scale?"

I took a step toward him but he gripped the sink with both hands. "Stand back!" he shouted.

I was finding this incredibly nerve-wracking. At least it was his scale and not a ledge, I thought. And the image of Brad playing out this stand-off two inches above the ground elicited in me the most unfortunate bout of nervous laughter. "Stand back or what?" I said, desperately trying to stifle my inappropriate giggles. "You'll jump?"

"Maybe," he said, still clutching the sink.

"Give me your hand, Brad," I said, regaining my composure.

For a moment he refused, but then he just seemed to give up and let go of the sink. I moved in to grab him before he plummeted to his—not death, of course, but to whatever happens when you fall off a scale.

I held his limp muscular body in my arms. "Charlie left me," he said.

I pulled him into me a little tighter. "I know. I'm sorry," I said.

"You know why he left me?"

I had plenty of theories, but I didn't know for sure. "No," I said.

We separated from our embrace. Brad took a seat on the john; I sat on the marble counter surrounding the sink. And for the next forty-five minutes or so, Brad proceeded to tell me his story. After a long period of Brad saying things like, "I look pretty good for my age, don't I?"

And after an equally long period of me assuring him that he did. Brad said, "Do you remember the night I met Charlie, and I called you? It was very late."

"Of course I remember."

"I called because I was really upset about something that happened when I was having sex with Charlie."

I now felt certain that my #1 theory was true. I was about to say, "Lots of men experience erectile dysfunction. It's nothing to be ashamed of," when Brad continued.

"Anyway," Brad said. "We were doing it and it was hot and sweet. And Charlie reached out and took my face in his hands. He pulled my face right into his and he said 'Fuck me. Fuck me...*Daddy.*'"

Brad pronounced "Daddy" with the same hushed voice that my mother reserves for times when she's forced to say "cancer." "Steven, he called me 'Daddy' like ten times. I just couldn't continue."

That had not been one of my theories.

"And then when I pulled out and was just lying quietly next to him, he started stroking my hair and he said, 'What's the matter, Daddy?' His voice was so sweet sounding. But I found the words profoundly disturbing."

Why, I wondered, if Brad was so upset by Charlie's father fixation, would he choose to color his hair white blond? It seemed a mixed message.

"I decided right then to start dressing younger to prove to him I wasn't old enough to be his daddy. But the clothes, the hair, the way I was speaking—God, I referred to you and Gail as my posse. What was I thinking? Everything backfired on me, Steven. Charlie doesn't want young. If he did, he certainly could get it."

I gave Brad another long hug. There was nothing at all erotic about it, but I could not help but be aware of the flawlessness of the body in my arms. I couldn't grasp Brad's insecurities. He's got more body issues than I do.

And I was fat for the first eighteen years of my life.

"What do *you* think, Adam?" Brad asked as he stepped back from my embrace.

I turned and saw Adam standing in the door frame.

"I think you're a very handsome man, Brad. You're very sexy."

"You think?" Brad asked.

Adam's words seemed to have a calming effect on Brad. He reached for the robe that was hanging from a hook next to the shower. As he tied the sash around his waist, ending the free show that I must confess I'd started enjoying, he said, "Thank you."

I assumed we'd leave him and head home, but Adam said, "You know what would make you look even sexier, Brad? Your old hair." While I had been talking Brad down from his scale, Adam had gone to the drugstore and bought a box of Just For Men. He removed the package from the bag he was holding and began reading the instructions.

Brad smiled, but didn't speak. He removed his robe and got into the shower. He seemed more beautiful to me now than he ever had before. Even more than in those long-ago days when I thought I'd loved him. Never before had I seen him display this level of vulnerability and trust. It was refreshing and real, and I felt so fortunate that he was my friend. After Peter, he was my oldest—as in, "known the longest"—friend.

I saw Adam looking at the bottle of dye and then back at the tuxedo he was wearing.

"I'm afraid I'll ruin this," Adam whispered to me. "What should I do?"

"Take it off," I said.

Adam proceeded to get out of his clothes, including his socks and underwear. Then he stepped into the shower and joined Brad.

That is *so* not what I meant when I said take it off.

I thought he was going to strip to his shorts and color Brad's hair at the sink. I didn't think he was going to take a shower with him. An enormous wave of jealousy washed over me. I went and sat on the toilet and tried, without success, not to watch my partner washing the blond dye out of my first boyfriend's hair. I thought of the drunken night when Adam got into the shower and washed me—such a selfless act.

Or was this just his thing, getting naked and hoping into showers with hot guys?

The color-process seemed to take Adam forever. When he was finally finished Brad turned to him and hugged him. *A naked hug!* And not a let's-stick-our-butts-out-so-that-nothing-touches hug. There was no personal space between these boys. I considered climbing onto the scale and leaping to my death—I would have, too, if either one of them had shown evidence of arousal when they separated from the embrace. They did not. Instead, as they pulled apart and the water was turned off, I heard and saw Brad's sobs.

Adam helped him from the tub. Brad reached his arms out to me and I held him. My envy and jealousy dissolved. This was one time that my inability to deal with conflict had helped me—it would have been so unfortunate if I'd made a scene.

Adam dressed and we tucked Brad into bed. My tux was damp from my embrace with Brad, but I didn't complain. As I was about to turn out his bedroom light, Brad said, "I wish you would make up with Peter and Amanda."

The statement seemed to come from nowhere. "Don't you worry about that, Brad." I said it a bit too condescendingly, like I was talking to a precocious child.

"I didn't realize that you aren't speaking to each other," he said.

Adam nodded at him as if to say, "Yes, that's right, we don't speak."

It seems that when Brad called to invite Peter and Amanda to his party, they declined because we would be in attendance—they had told Brad we were no longer talking to each other.

Based on Adam's nod, he was aware of this fact.

I was the only one not publicly acknowledging this change in our relationship.

Words are so powerful. Now the three devastating words—*we're not talking*—had been said aloud. I could no longer pretend otherwise. This problem was not just going to magically resolve itself. I couldn't send an e-mail and write, *Gosh been busy. What about you? What are you up to?* I couldn't continue acting like the only reason we'd been out of touch was our hectic schedules.

I replayed my mother's most recent voice message in my head. She was doing a dramatic reenactment of the way my Maia used to talk about her sister, Reta: *After what she's done to me! I'll see her in hell before I'll ever talk to her again!* Onda had imitated her mother, accent and all, on my machine.

I was contemplating history repeating itself when I heard Brad say, "I hope you don't mind, but I'm making an exception for them and going to their wedding. I'm one of Peter's ushers."

I quickly flipped the lights out. Keeping Adam from seeing the tears in my eyes.

Just before the lights went out I took another look at Brad's hair. It looked good. It wasn't perfect, but so few things are.

❖

Adam and I walked home. The party had fizzled at such an early hour that even with all the time we spent with Brad, it was only 10:30.

"I can't believe they told Brad we're not talking. Why would they say that?" I said.

"I can't believe he's going to the wedding." Then, as an afterthought, Adam added, "We're *not* talking."

"Well…" I started.

"After what they've done to us, why should we?"

Because it's right. It's honorable. Because I am not prepared to have us spend the rest of our lives alienated from our siblings. That's why we should be talking to them!

If you look very closely you'll notice there are no quotation marks around the above sentences. That's because I didn't actually say any of that.

Once again, my anger had rendered me silent. I said nothing. Pathetically, all I did was try to focus on the positive—at least Adam wasn't being as extreme as my grandmother. He hadn't made any allusion to seeing Peter and Amanda in hell.

CHAPTER EIGHTEEN:
A RECIPE FOR DISASTER

Several weeks before Thanksgiving, I was home making dinner, awaiting a call from Adam, who was at his office, making signs for the rally with a group of volunteers. Adam was going to ring me when they were finished so I'd know when to put the chicken in the oven.

Just at the moment I expected his call, the phone rang.

I put down the fresh rosemary and garlic I was macerating in lemon juice and answered the call. "Hi."

"Finally you pick up the phone."

This was not Adam.

"Hi, Mom." I was instantly sweating.

My hands blazed so hot that the scent of rosemary and garlic came pouring out of my palms. I was like the stress version of a Glade PlugIns air freshener.

"What are you doing for Thanksgiving?" she asked.

I always go to my mother's for Thanksgiving. I usually go the night before—so I can get up early, stuff the bird, and get it in the oven by 6:00 A.M. My mother makes the Romanian dishes—my favorite being *pita di curcubeta*, a pie filled with butternut squash. It's divine.

"Let me tell you what I'm doing for Thanksgiving," my mother continued. "I'm going to my son's house. Amanda is making her first Thanksgiving."

With all the over-the-top phone messages my mother had been leaving me, that simple statement hit the hardest. I wasn't really bothered by the phrase "my son's house." Onda had a long history of owning and disowning Peter and me based on which one of us was in favor at the moment. There had been plenty of times in the past when I was the only acknowledged child.

What hurt so much was that a new family holiday tradition was starting, and Adam and I weren't part of it. I didn't know what to say. I felt pressure behind my eyes and I rubbed them with my free hand. Lamentably, I'd forgotten about the residue of garlic on my fingers. My eyes burned from the contact.

"Steven? Why don't you and Adam come to my house for Christmas?"

"Really?" I sighed with relief. She wasn't disowning me; she was just dividing her attentions.

"Of course I want you to come for Christmas," my mother said. "Otherwise I'll be alone. Peter and Amanda won't be here. They'll be on their honeymoon."

Oh.

Unable to think of anything else, I said, "Where are they going on their honeymoon?"

"If you want to know where your brother is going on his honeymoon, call him and ask him!"

I guess I set myself up for that.

❖

By the time Adam called to say he was on his way home, I had cried, recovered, cried again, stopped, and was midway through my third jag.

That night over a dinner that consisted of roasted chicken and nothing else (I'd planned to sauté broccoli rabe and make some brown rice, but after my mother's call, I was undone), Adam suggested that we host our own Thanksgiving. At first I rejected the idea as being a sorry substitute for spending the day with family. Then I began thinking about some of the plusses.

For one thing, we wouldn't be spending the day with family.

I thought that a Thanksgiving without our families would be a Thanksgiving without conflict. That is, in fact, not correct. I now know the trick to a successful Thanksgiving is to have a mix of family and friends—that way everyone's likely to be on their best behavior. If you don't have any family in attendance, you let down your guard. You think everything will be fine so you get careless and sloppy, and you end up playing out those dysfunctional familial games with your friends.

We invited Jack and Malcolm. We hadn't seen them since their commitment ceremony. To our surprise, they accepted the invitation.

Apparently, they were having their own family issues, and they were happy to come to our house and avoid an angst-filled holiday.

Gail and Liz gave an immediate yes, when we asked them. I was thrilled. This was a way to thank Liz for making the rally happen. And Liz's presence meant the post-dinner cleanup would be a breeze.

Brad, who had also gotten an invitation from Peter, was joining us. I believe Brad was feeling like the child of divorced parents—torn and unsure where his loyalties lay. I was a little hurt by this. He wouldn't even know my brother if it weren't for me. I had spent years working for Brad for very little money. Toiling, selflessly, for his free gay paper. There was no question where his loyalties should lie. I managed to make this clear to him when he started squawking, nonsensically, about how Peter and Amanda had invited him to their place first.

Adam invited Vanessa, who had a girlfriend but was coming without her. It seems the girlfriend was only "a little out." That's how Vanessa put it. I'm not sure what that means, but I guess when you're only "a little out," you don't bring your girlfriend of three years—no matter how lipstick she may be—home to meet the folks.

While I stuffed and basted and sautéed and stirred, Adam worked on the seating arrangement—it's a job he takes very seriously. I know that it matters, but I never give it any thought.

The first argument we ever had took place after a dinner party when I'd made the huge faux pas of saying "Sit wherever you like" as the guests approached the table. Adam looked at me like I'd served the meal on paper plates or made that green bean casserole with fried onions on the top.

"Letting people sit where they want," he said sternly, "is a recipe for disaster." Adam said this to me at 6:10 in the morning as I was pulling the organs out of the turkey in preparation for making stock. He started diagramming possible seating arrangements on the back of an envelope. I wondered if he was aware that I had not yet had any coffee. Adam's big stumbling block: Gail and Liz. The problem was that I was not entirely certain how long they had been together. I was thinking ten months, but it might have been twelve. "Think," Adam asked with exasperated desperation. "Could it be twelve?"

At ten months, Adam was forced to keep Gail and Liz next to each other at the table. If they'd been together a year he could place Brad between them. We decided to play it safe and keep them together, which wreaked havoc on the already-off balance boy-girl alternation.

"What about Jack and Malcolm?" I asked.

"What about them?"

"Well, I realize they've been together for a hundred years, but they've only been married for a couple of months."

"They aren't married," he said.

At 6:15 in the morning, with no coffee, and the smell of the turkey's liver and heart on my hands, I found Adam's words hysterically funny. "You're right, they're not. They sit apart!"

"Okay, Jack. If I can have you sit here," Adam said, pointing to the chair next to his. "Malcolm, you're there," he said, pointing to a seat diagonally across from Jack.

Everyone was aware of the importance Adam placed on seating arrangements and knew that he followed all of the rules. When he was in doubt, which he rarely was, he referred to Emily Post.

Malcolm grinned, thinking he'd caught Adam in an etiquette misstep. "You know Adam, Jack and I should be next to each other because we've been married less than a year."

"I hate to break it to you, but you're not married." Adam said this like a Borscht Belt comic—I could actually sense that he was holding for the laughter. It didn't come. I guess because I had laughed so heartily at the line, he thought it was going to be a surefire crowd pleaser.

"Excuse me?" Jack asked rhetorically.

Adam said nothing—he was still waiting for the guffaws.

Desperate to get past this unfortunate moment, I began chattering away. "Oh, you should have seen their wedding!" I said to no one in particular. "It was just beautiful. Jack, how's Joop?"

"Which one?"

I'd forgotten that there had been multiple Joops in attendance. "The best man, who gave the toast."

"We're not talking," said Jack.

"Why should we?" Added, Malcolm.

"After what he said at our wedding, I'll see him in hell before I'll ever speak to him again!" Jack said.

I hadn't even finished carving the turkey yet.

At some point between carving the breast and removing the legs from the bird, I noticed Liz furiously polishing silver with her napkin. She seemed to be in a bit of a rage. This was a response to the wild flirtation that had been going on between Vanessa and Gail from the moment they'd been introduced to each other. Gail's big alto laugh had elevated into a lyric-soprano giggle. She let this foreign sound loose every time Vanessa said anything. Vanessa, for her part, seemed delighted to be talking to a woman who was more than "a little out." "I came out to my parents when I was fourteen," Gail said. "I couldn't be with someone who wasn't out. It must be so hard for you."

I put my carving knife down for a moment, but I noticed Liz reaching for it so I grabbed it again. I had resigned myself to the fact that this day was going to be a disaster, but I could not handle an actual homicide.

I think that's too much to ask of any host.

The meal was served. Turkey, gravy, stuffing, mashed potatoes, sweet potatoes, spinach casserole, fennel and leek gratin, and a salad (to be healthy). I had slept no more than seven of the last seventy-two hours.

Brad had clearly not yet recovered from his breakup with Charlie. In terms of hair and fashion, he had been restored to his old self. However, his emotions were another matter. He sat at the table, sullen and withdrawn. He spoke now for the first time. "Gravy contains white flour, correct?"

"It's just one day a year, Brad," I said gently as I watched him pass the gravy boat without taking any for himself.

Fortunately, the other guests seemed to succumb to the indulgence of the holiday. And, as we began eating, there were actually several minutes of pleasant conversation, mostly about the food. Great amounts of praise were heaped upon my gravy—but of course, not from Brad.

Jack and Malcolm seemed to have recovered from the wedding remark, in spite of the fact that Adam had made no attempt to apologize.

"We have big news," Malcolm said. "We're pregnant!"

Thank goodness, I thought, *a happy topic.* Thanksgiving was back on track!

Cheers and congratulations were offered from everyone but Gail. "How are you feeling?" she asked icily, between sips of Pinot Noir.

"Fine," Jack said. I could see that he was a little confused by the question.

"Gosh, I thought you were both men. But since you said you're pregnant, I guess you're *women*."

I picked up the carving knife and considered using it on myself.

Gail wasn't finished. "From everything I have read, it seems only *women* can get pregnant and only *women* can bear children. Now perhaps you are paying some *woman* to have this kid for you, and then you will raise the child. But make no mistake, only the *woman* is pregnant! And I'm sorry, but for you to suggest otherwise is completely offensive and dismissive of *women*."

I love Gail, but I really could have lived without this particular I-am-woman-hear-me-roar moment. I could see that I was going to end up with twenty-seven pounds of uneaten turkey.

Jack and Malcolm were silent.

Liz placed a hand gently on Malcolm's shoulder, "When are you due?" she asked warmly as she stared pointedly at Gail.

"May tenth."

"Wonderful. You must be so happy," Liz said before bursting into tears. "Excuse me," she said, running to the bathroom.

"Maybe you should—"

"She'll be fine," Gail said, cutting me off.

"That's one of the reasons we got married," Jack said, turning to speak to the less hostile guests. "We wanted kids but we didn't want them to be born out of wedlock." He said this without a trace of irony.

Do you remember on *The Carol Burnett Show*, how Carol and Harvey and Tim would try to make each other "break" during a sketch? One of them would ad lib something, and the others would find it so funny that tears would roll down their cheeks. They would bite their lips and finally turn up stage and laugh. This was how Adam responded to Jack's "out of wedlock" statement.

To be fair to Adam, he tried really hard not to laugh. He pulled his napkin to his mouth and he turned away. Later, he told me that he'd stuck the tines of his fork into his thigh—nothing helped. He rolled out of his chair in gales of laughter.

By the time Adam had gotten up from the floor, Jack and Malcolm were already gone.

That left Gail and Vanessa, who had moved to sit next to each other, and Brad, who had said nothing the whole day aside from his gravy inquiry. Fortunately, no one needed the bathroom because Liz was still in it and had given no sign of ever coming out.

I surveyed the table. I had made too much food and no one was eating, except for Adam—who seemed not to care that he, along with Gail, had destroyed the day. Gail and Vanessa were moments away from needing to get a hotel room. Brad, obviously off carbs again, was removing the skin from a small slice of turkey. He hadn't put anything else on his plate. He was still silent.

"We're going to leave now," Vanessa said brightly as if she'd spent hours lingering over a wonderful meal instead of the twenty minutes she'd spent pawing Gail and ignoring the food it had taken me three days to prepare.

I waited for them to offer to clear the table, or apologize for not eating anything, or to give me any sign of civil behavior, but got nothing of the kind. I was sleep deprived and certain the tears would be coming very soon. *It's my fault*, I thought; I had told Gail to leave Liz a hundred times—although I'd never told her to do it in my home on a major holiday. The worst part of it was that now I really cared for Liz, which was a good thing since she was probably never leaving my bathroom.

When the new lovebirds left, Adam said, "They make a sweet couple, don't they?"

"I think they're morally bankrupt," I said.

"You need a nap," Adam said.

"Why did I bother to cook this meal?"

"Because you like to cook and you said it would be fun."

I hate when Adam throws my own words back at me. Yes, I had said that—meant it, at the time. But he should have known it was folly and talked me out of it.

"You were excited. You kept surfing the web for new recipes," Brad said.

Now Brad decides to speak? Great. One naked shower and he and Adam are a team—united in attacking Steven. (I know I'm overwrought when I start referring to myself in the third person.)

"The food was great," Brad added.

"You ate nothing." I could feel my voice closing up.

"I just want to save a little room."

Did he think there were other courses coming after the ten I'd already served? "For what?" I asked.

"I'm going to..." He stopped himself, but I knew what he was going to say.

"You're going to my brother's."

"He did ask me first. I'm just stopping by."

I made a deliberate decision to shake my head disapprovingly. I had seen my grandmother do it to my mother on many occasions—and my mother always took the bait.

Brad didn't. "Thanks for a lovely afternoon. The food was great."

You didn't eat; no one ate, I wanted to scream. He gave us each a hug and left.

The guests had arrived at 2:00. I served the meal at 3:05; it was now 3:48.

"Are you mad at me?" Adam asked.

I was furious at him. "No, I'm not mad," I uttered barely above a whisper.

"You sure?"

"You think we'll ever see Malcolm and Jack again?" I asked, imagining that we wouldn't, and not exactly sure how I felt about it.

"I'll apologize. We'll send a lot of baby presents."

We sat there, surrounded by so much food. I felt so guilty. I knew that I would wrap it up, put it in the refrigerator, and in a week I'd throw it all out. So much waste.

"Hey," Liz whispered. She had come back to the table. I'd forgotten she was still here.

"Are you hungry?" Adam asked her.

She was.

I warmed the gravy for them and poured it over their plates. I was glad at least some of the food would be eaten. Not by me, though. I couldn't face any of it. For perhaps the first time ever, I'd lost my appetite. I sat at the table and pushed the food around on my plate, pretending to eat.

Adam and Liz thanked me and praised me and went back for seconds.

Adam ate with gusto as I looked on curiously. Usually I love the sight of Adam eating my cooking. It gives me great pleasure knowing that what I make for him brings him such joy.

Today, however, witnessing Adam blithely gorging really bothered me. With each bite he took, I was becoming more and more disturbed. How could he eat like that? Was he not at all reflecting upon the fact that we were separated from our family on Thanksgiving? Why wasn't he more troubled? Why weren't we talking about this?

He caught my eye and took a huge forkful of the fennel and leek gratin. He grinned, licked his lips, and gave me one of our special, private winks.

I winked back. But for the first time while doing so, all I felt was resentment.

CHAPTER NINETEEN:
THERE IS NOTHING ZEN ABOUT YOU, STEVEN

My mother has only vague memories of her life in the six-family house. She remembers standing in the bathroom on Saturday nights huddled around the pipes, singing church songs. In the bathroom, because of the way the pipes were installed, sound traveled easily between the six apartments. My mother would sing alto while her cousins, each in their own bathrooms, would sing their parts—turning the old house into an Orthodox church, minus the incense and candles. Standing by her side, on those long-ago Saturday nights, was her uncle Dean singing tenor.

By the time Onda was nine, her parents had saved enough money to buy a two-family house on Elmwood Avenue, in the West End of Bridgeport. My grandfather, my Papu, was not the first member of the Macedonian-Romanian community to become a homeowner, but he was among the first—and certainly he was the first to accomplish the feat on a waiter's salary.

Papu was like an immigrant Donald Trump, only with better hair and worse English. His hard work and frugality made possible the purchase of several homes that he, along with his brother Dean, ran as rooming houses. Soon, he elevated the family solidly into the world of the middle class. Unfortunately his frugality was often mistakenly confused with cheapness. He wasn't cheap; he was just a little eccentric where money was concerned.

As young children, my brother and I always received a twenty-five-dollar bond from my grandparents for our birthdays, Christmas, and on our name days (the day corresponding with our namesake saint's feast day). One Christmas, instead of the usual bonds, my brother and I were given checks in the amount of $18.75. We thought this rather bizarre. Onda explained to us that $18.75 was the amount of money that a twenty-five-dollar bond cost. Papu had gotten frailer and was no longer able to get out to the bank, so he gave us the money to buy the bonds ourselves. It never occurred to him to just give us a check for $25.00, which he could by then easily afford.

My grandfather's dynasty was managed by Uncle Dean, who acted as the super for the six buildings. I never knew Uncle Dean. He had a massive heart attack the year I was born. I remember Maia saying, "He was too quiet. Never wanted to make trouble. It killed him." She also once said, "Your grandfather was too stubborn. Never wanted to listen to anybody. It killed him." I didn't point out that my grandfather was eighty-six when he died.

My mother confirmed that Dean was quiet, "and very gentle," she said, remembering her favorite uncle. She had given me his name for my middle name—Constantine—which Romanians pronounce *Coast-On-Dean*.

Dean was my grandfather's baby brother. Although not born in the States, he was far more American than Papu. His English was impeccable. He was an avid reader, a natty dresser, and a champion jitterbugger. By 1941 he'd become a U.S. citizen and he immediately joined the army.

Maia called him a hero but the exact details of his war experiences are sketchy. "He never talked to begin with," Maia said. "When he came back, he talked even less." He worked hard, read his books, and stayed close to home. He never married.

"He wasn't the marrying kind," my mother once said in describing him.

"You mean he was gay?" I asked. This was several years before I'd come out to Onda.

"Of course not!" she said. I remember how outraged she was at the suggestion. He was a war hero, there was no possible way he could be gay. I thought of saying: "I'm gay, and you always say I remind you of him—so maybe he was gay." Instead I said, "I'm sorry." I was furious with myself for this—for feeling the need to apologize for asking if someone was gay.

"He just never met the right girl. It happens."

That afternoon, talking with my mother, was the last time I ever heard her refer to someone as "not the marrying kind." In fact, I can't recall the last time I heard anyone use that expression. I think that as gays and lesbians started to become more visible, people realized that most of their spinster aunts and mama's-boy-uncles weren't unlucky in love; they were unlucky because they were in love with people they couldn't tell anyone about.

❖

When I finally came out to my mother, after the tears and the questions about what she'd done to cause this, she said, "I think Uncle Dean was gay."

I didn't bring up our earlier conversation when she so adamantly rejected that possibility.

"I remember at his wake, I was pregnant with you and everyone said I shouldn't go because it would be bad luck. Everyone loved Uncle Dean and the place was packed. Anyway, the crowd was mostly Romanian but there were some Irish and Hungarian people there, too—tenants from the rooming houses."

My mother paused here and then launched into a description of the rooming houses. How much she hated them because she had to wash sheets and clean all the bathrooms, and couldn't go to the movies until all her chores were done. "Your childhood was so much easier than mine. You have no idea."

I tried to get her back on track. "How does this make Uncle Dean gay?"

"There was an Italian man sitting at the back of the funeral home. He was about six feet tall; in those days very few men were six feet tall, certainly not any of the Romanians. But what was really odd was we didn't know Italians. I mean, I did, but not Maia and Papu—they kept to their own kind."

"So how does this make Uncle Dean gay?"

"I'm trying to tell you!" Onda said, determined to weave her tale at her own pace. "I walked up to the Italian, his name was Franco, and I thanked him for coming. He hugged me and wept." Here she stopped and shook her head knowingly.

"I know Italians are emotional," she continued. "But this was very extreme. He would not stop hugging me, and then he said to me, 'Your uncle was my best friend.' He knew my name—knew all about me." She sat back, satisfied, resting her case.

"That's it? That doesn't make him gay. Straight people have best friends."

Onda shook her head, astonished by my naïveté. "Honey, straight people don't have best friends that they never mention and have never introduced to anyone."

Over the years, I've thought a lot about Constantine and Franco—Dean and Frank. Did they ever hook up with guys named Sammy and Peter and create their own little Rat Pack? If so, did they all go see *Ocean's Eleven* together? I wonder if Frank and Dean ever spent a whole night together or if they always rushed back to their separate straight lives. Working hard, going to church, denying themselves, and atoning for their sins. Was there ever a moment when they weren't on guard, when they just allowed themselves to relish the sweet, tender bliss of their relationship?

❖

It had been a while since I'd relished the sweet, tender bliss of *my* relationship. With the rally now days away, there was so much to do that I found it, if not exactly easy, at least possible to ignore my anger at having felt the need to choose between Adam and the rest of my family. Aside from my column, I'd begun writing additional news pieces focused on the marriage issue. When I wasn't at the paper, I was making phone calls, posting flyers, and rounding up volunteers.

Adam was doing as much—more, probably—to ensure the event would be a success. He'd personally reached out to other wedding planners and florists that he knew, and several of them had decided to stand with him in solidarity. Also around this time, he became obsessed with seeing if word of the movement had spread beyond New York. As a means of tracking the movement, each evening before going to bed Adam would Google "Adam More" and "marriage" to see what he'd find. The night after Thanksgiving, Adam hit pay dirt when he found himself featured on a blog called *QueerUSA*.

I was not mentioned.

Adam began corresponding with the blog's creator. They spent hours IM'ing each other. Adam said they were just strategizing, but frankly I didn't buy it—especially when I discovered that the blogger's screen name was Hung Fat. I calmed down a bit when Adam told me Hung Fat was the blogger's real name. He's Asian.

What cruel parents! You're in America now; it's time to retire Hung from the list of potential baby names. My heart broke for poor little Hung, thinking of his first grammar school locker room experience and the taunts and jeers of his pubescent classmates.

Hung offered to fly out from his home in San Francisco to help with the rapidly approaching rally. I, of course, thought it was a bad idea. Adam immediately accepted the offer.

"Where's he staying?" I asked when Adam signed off at 2:00 A.M. after another marathon chat session with Hung Fat.

"With us. You don't mind, do you?"

I did mind. I minded very much. "Of course I don't mind. I can't wait to meet him." I felt the familiar scratch at the back of my throat.

"Great," Adam said. "I didn't want him to have to go to a hotel. Not on a blogger's salary."

I'm not exactly sure how blogs work, but I'm fairly certain that the phrase *blogger's salary* is an oxymoron.

Hung got on the red-eye and was in our apartment by 7:30 the next morning. Seeing him, I realized how often I make stereotyped assumptions. In my mind I'd pictured 5′6″ and waif-like. Hung was 6′2″ and mostly muscle. "I used to dance, but not in years," he said as we sat at the kitchen table having breakfast. Great, a dancer—Adam had failed to mention that portion of Hung's résumé.

I made a caramelized onion frittata and popovers with homemade cranberry preserves. If Adam was planning on falling for Hung's long-legged charms, I was going to remind him just how good he had it at home.

"If you don't mind," Hung said after finishing a second helping of frittata, "I'm going to take a nap. I couldn't sleep on the plane. Then maybe I'll try and find a yoga class. That always helps me reset my clock."

"Steven takes yoga," Adam offered.

"You do?" Hung asked.

I couldn't tell what he meant by the "You do?" *You do? You don't look like you do yoga, you're a little doughy, and you're very high-strung. There is nothing Zen about you, Steven.*

As I pondered what dark things Hung meant but didn't say, he asked if he could go to class with me.

"Sure," Adam said, when I didn't immediately answer.

"I'd love that," I added. It bothered me that I was becoming one of those people who constantly say the opposite of what they're actually feeling.

❖

I'd hoped Hung would decide to pass when he learned that it was a naked yoga class, but he was intrigued. He'd read all about Hot Nude Yoga and was very excited to join me. "It'll be a great addition to my blog."

On the subway ride downtown, he went on and on about how great Adam and I were. How we were going to be remembered always as important activists. He said, "Steven, I know it's hard. This must be a lot of pressure on you. It's always hard to be the first. But soon you'll see. Many others will follow."

I was unnerved by his words. He wasn't just looking at me; he was looking right inside me, and seeing every one of my doubts.

We climbed the four flights of stairs in the industrial warehouse. I was breathing a bit hard; Hung was taking the steps two at a time and still chattering away. I wondered, if this was tired, jet-lagged Hung, what was he going to be like after a good night's rest?

I was grateful for the silence that accompanied our entrance to the yoga studio. The space was illuminated by candles, one of which was scented a very mild lemon—a fragrance that I always associate fondly with cleaning. We removed our shoes in the hallway and, as is the custom at Hot Nude Yoga, we undressed, rolled out our mats, and waited for class to begin.

When I tell people that I take a naked yoga class, invariably there are smirks and crass comments about checking out the other guys. I have been asked if the session ends orgiastically. It does not. And the last thing on my mind as I move into Warrior Two is what the guy next to me looks like. For me, this class has been about overcoming the lifetime of body shame that comes from having been a fat boy. When I stand, naked on my mat, exposing myself, sweating, working hard, I feel powerful and proud. I am aware that there are others in the room, but they are there taking their own journey, supporting me in mine. They see me but they don't judge me.

Oh, and it's great not having any gym laundry.

I felt differently being in class with Hung. I had decided he was my rival. I needed to see up close just how stiff the competition was. Hung stretched out on his back and closed his eyes, thus affording me my first real opportunity to size him up.

I placed my hand to my mouth. I needed to be sure that the scream I was hearing was only going on in my head.

Apparently Hung's parents were not being cruel or giving him an undue burden when naming him. Not at all—his parents were just being painfully literal. I thought of how Hung's grammar school taunters must have been silenced when he disrobed in the locker room. How those humiliating jeers must have morphed into hushed respect with a single glance. The power, regardless of sexual orientation, that comes with being Hung.

There were eleven of us in class that day, twelve counting Aaron, our teacher and Hot Nude Yoga founder. In addition to Hung, there were several new students. So Aaron had us set up our mats in a circle and one by one we went around saying our names.

"I'm Brian."

"I'm John."

"I'm Kevin."

"I'm Robert."

"I'm Hank."

"I'm Thomas."

"I'm Marcus."

"I'm John."

"I'm Bill."

"I'm Steven."

"I'm Hung."

Around the room, eyes widened. Aaron gave Hung a welcoming smile.

❖

Just before ending class in Savasana (corpse pose), Aaron had us do a partner exercise. I was trying to get the attention of one of the two Johns when I felt a large warm hand on my shoulder. It was Hung's. He was smiling and positioning himself right in front of me. I had little choice but to do the exercise with him. Aaron asked us to sit face to face, cross-legged in front of each other, maintain eye contact, place a hand on each other's hearts, and breathe together.

We only had to do it for a minute. It would be no problem—simple, I thought. A minute can be an excruciatingly long period of time. I hadn't really looked at Hung's eyes before. I'd been too busy looking elsewhere. They were black and large and perfectly almond shaped. The lashes were long but not so long as to ever be considered feminine. When he blinked they gently brushed along the lower lid. But mostly, he didn't blink—he held my gaze. And what shone from those eyes was kind, righteous, and generous.

His heartbeat was calm and quiet beneath my hand. I pressed more firmly against his chest, hoping that my own racing heart would slow to match his. When it did, he smiled at me. I smiled back and felt the taste of tears in my mouth. Not my usual kind of tears. I'm more of a keener than a cryer, but now they were falling silently. And even as the water flowed out of me, Hung held my glance, unembarrassed by my spectacle.

When Aaron finally called time, Hung wiped the tears from my face and thanked me for being so open. I should have been thanking him. I didn't know what to say, so I gave him another smile and moved into corpse pose.

❖

"Do you mind if I ask what made you cry in class?" Hung asked as we were walking back to the subway at Twenty-third and Seventh.

"No, I don't mind," I said. I didn't mind, but I didn't really know how to answer the question either. My impulse was to say that I'm insecure and deeply flawed and constantly jealous without reason, and as I was trying to figure out a way to say all that while still making myself seem like a great guy, something entirely different came out of my mouth. "I really miss my brother." I was crying again.

Going to yoga was something I did with Peter. Okay, not naked yoga—but add some women and some clothes and it's the same thing. Sitting in class with Hung had triggered a longing for times spent with Peter. Having a common history is powerful—a shorthand language shared only by siblings. I had lost that.

"Adam and I come from a long line of people who have stopped speaking to their families. I thought we'd be different."

"Everyone comes from a long line of people who've stopped speaking to their families. It's like a rule, I think."

Maybe Hung was right.

"My father did not talk to his brother for nine years because my uncle did not think *The Empire Strikes Back* was a good *Star Wars* sequel."

"You're kidding," I said.

"I'm very serious. My father was George Lucas's dry cleaner for a time. It colored his personality."

"After nine years of not speaking, what brought your father and your uncle back together?"

"Cancer."

❖

Hung offered to make pot stickers for the pre-rally organizational meeting we were having at the apartment. It was his mother's recipe, which she'd brought with her when she emigrated from Hong Kong. They sounded amazing. I didn't want him to go to all that trouble—he was a guest. Also, since they're fried and contain white flour, I was afraid only the lesbians and I would eat them. With all the Thanksgiving leftovers I still had in the refrigerator, I didn't feel the need to add fried dough filled with pork to the list of simple carbs I was mainlining.

So, instead, Hung helped me cut vegetables for crudités and we made one of Brad's yogurt dips—not nearly as tasty as the dumplings would have been, but I felt good about the decision.

The rally was set for a Saturday during the holiday season—a huge mistake in terms of getting people to show up. There are so many scheduling conflicts in the weeks before Christmas. But Adam took a tip from that old shampoo commercial and called all his friends and asked them each to tell ten friends about the rally. And I had been writing about little else in the paper.

So it seemed, even with the event being so ill-timed, there might actually be a crowd.

With only fourteen hours to go before the throngs were scheduled to descend upon the Javits Center, our apartment was filled with friends and friends of friends who'd volunteered to be group leaders and organizers for the protest. It was kind of like a pep rally, and Adam was senior class president. He'd spent the whole day working on a speech to motivate the troops and was anxiously checking his watch to see when he should call the room to order.

I was serving drinks, saying hellos and in general playing host. We'd had an amazing turnout—everyone but Malcolm and Jack showed up. Their absence was no surprise; Adam had still made no attempt at apology after the Thanksgiving fiasco, even though he had assured me he would. Gail and Liz and Vanessa were all there, which I feared might be awkward, but the three of them were standing together and laughing about something Gail had said. Gail laughing and having a grand time with her ex-girlfriend and her brand-new girlfriend was a sight I found unfathomable. I love lesbians. But I don't really understand how they can do that break up and be instant best friends thing.

Brad and Charlie were also in attendance, but they were not talking to each other. Brad was going out of his way to make sure they were always on opposite sides of the very crowded room. Brad had latched on to Ginger Beer, the extremely tall woman who owns Man Land, and was using her as a human shield whenever Charlie was less than twelve feet away. *That's* the kind of behavior that makes sense to me after a breakup.

Just as Adam was shouting to get everyone's attention, I noticed Barney coming in the front door. I hadn't seen him since before my brother fired him. I'd thought about calling him and asking him to come but I'd been too embarrassed. Also, with his nonstop "Quando Quando Quando" routine, phone conversations were a bit of a challenge. Adam must have invited him. I realized I felt in some way responsible for Peter's actions. I approached Barney just as Adam had gotten the room silenced and was delivering his rallying cry.

"There are a few things I want to say. First, thank you for all the hard work. All the phone calls you've made. I couldn't have done it without you."

The mood in the room was so upbeat and festive that I, too, got swept into it. I cheered and toasted Adam. I felt Barney's arms as he reached out to hug me. I hugged him back, waiting for an awkward moment. It didn't arrive. Barney's eyes were bright and he wore a large toothy grin. I don't recall ever having seen him smile before—it's very difficult to sing and smile at the same time. And then I realized that he wasn't singing. I was debating whether or not to mention the smile and the lack of song when Adam resumed his speech.

"I'm sure you all know this already, but as a reminder, this will be a totally non-violent event tomorrow. Nobody touches a hair on Vera Wang's head! You got me?"

At this, the crowd broke into gale-force laughter. Hung, who had just at that moment taken a large sip of Chardonnay, did a spit take, which only added to the level of hilarity. As Adam waited out the laughter, I grabbed Barney and pulled him into the bedroom to apologize and catch up with him.

"How are you?" I asked when we reached the relative calm of the bedroom. I could still hear the faint sounds of Adam's pleas for silence.

"I haven't sung a note since I read your article."

I wasn't following.

"I take that back. I've sung, but not obsessively. Now I have other things—important things—to think about." He was smiling at me.

I still wasn't following. "Are you *sure* you're okay?" I asked, feeling guilty and responsible for his unemployment.

"I'm good, thanks."

Barney looked good. There was no reason to doubt him, but the Romanian in me made me think that perhaps he was just acting—putting on a brave face after being destroyed by my brother (and indirectly, me).

"I'm so glad you came," I said with a note of earnest concern.

"I wouldn't miss it. Great cause, right?" he said, still acting as if he hadn't a care in the world.

I had to be a grown-up and bring up the subject. "I felt a little weird seeing you after…" Then instead of saying *Peter fired you*, I turned my head away, did a sort of vague half nod, and muttered, "Um."

"What?" Barney asked, pretending not to know what I was talking about.

"You know," I said. He really didn't need to be so coy with me.

"I really don't know what you're talking about," he said, rather convincingly.

"My brother." I paused here for effect, staring knowingly at Barney. All I got back in return was his blank stare. "He fired you. Didn't he?"

"Oh, that." Barney chortled. "Technically, he did. Although most employers don't sob uncontrollably when they're letting you go. Your brother makes wedding cakes. I couldn't expect him to pay me just to watch him work, right?"

"Right," I said, realizing that point hadn't occurred to me before.

"I'll never have another boss like Peter. What an amazing guy, right?"

"Right," I said again, hoping this was not some new annoying linguistic quirk that Barney had replaced his constant singing with.

"We should get back out there, right?"

"Right." I stopped myself and said, "I mean, yes."

"I really want to catch up with you, though. I guess we'll have plenty of time at the wedding, right?"

My knees buckled. I reached for the post of my bed for support. Gay activist Barney was making an exception and going to my brother's wedding and I was not. I felt ill. I realized he was staring at me, waiting for a response. I couldn't think of anything to say. "Right," I muttered, and we walked back into the living room just in time to hear Hung comparing Adam and me to Rosa Parks.

At that moment, I felt like a lot of things: a fraud, a coward, a hypocrite—these all sprang quickly to mind. What I most assuredly did not feel like was the extremely courageous Rosa Parks.

CHAPTER TWENTY:
NEED A SIGN?

When I was eleven, I performed in a play called *Horse Sense*. I played Paul Revere's horse. It was one of the few moments of my childhood when my extra weight worked to my advantage. The great thing about playing the horse was it was the biggest part, and the character of the horse was really smart. Paul Revere, on the other hand, was portrayed as kind of a lay-about loser. In this version the horse was the real go-getter. He talked to Paul the way that Mr. Ed could talk to Wilbur. Anyway, the horse was the one who got Paul off his lazy ass and forced him to climb on him and shout, "The British are coming, the British are coming." This horse was a visionary. Were it not for the horse, Paul wouldn't even be a footnote in the history books.

Adam may be the one who's prone to bad dreams, but in the early hours of this morning, just before I was to get up and go to the protest, I dreamt about *Horse Sense*. I was back in rehearsal for it. Everything started out great. I was the age that I am now and thin, but everyone else was eleven or twelve. And the production was still being directed by Mr. Gilroy, who was, and in the dream continued to be, my thirty-five-year-old sixth-grade homeroom teacher. He was blond with a handlebar mustache, which was out of style even then, but looked great on him. In the sixth grade I was in love with him. And I expressed my affection for him by volunteering to be in charge of cleaning his blackboard and erasers. My love for him, in spite of the way I made his boards sparkle, went unrequited.

The dream started going sour when Mr. Gilroy announced that he was going to recast the show. I ran for the papier-mâché horse's head. If I had it, I reasoned, he couldn't take the part from me. Just as I was about to grab it by the mane, someone else snatched it away—Adam. It was Adam, looking gorgeous in his gray Prada suit. He pranced around the stage wearing the horse's head while Mr. Gilroy cheered and told him how great he looked. It appeared to me that Mr. Gilroy was cruising Adam. I was not happy about it. Then Mr. Gilroy looked at me and said, "I think you're better suited to play Paul Revere, don't you?"

I pleaded with Mr. Gilroy, but he wouldn't listen. "Actors call it sense memory," he said. "You must think about all the times you've been lazy, unmotivated, and uncommitted and incorporate those memories into your portrayal of Paul Revere. I'm sure it will be very easy for you!"

Then Adam and Mr. Gilroy took a shower together and they made me watch. I was crying so hard it was difficult to tell where my tears ended and their steamy water began. At some point, it seemed like they felt sorry for me because Adam threw the horse's head to me and said, "If it's that important to you, you play the horse."

I put the head on. This really cheered me up until I realized that the play had changed. Suddenly, we were doing *Equus*. I was one of the horses in the stable. The other horses were being played by Peter, Amanda, Hung, Nate Berkus, and Anderson Cooper.

Fortunately for me, I woke up before Adam could gouge my eyes out.

❖

Hung had gotten up early and made steel-cut oats. He wanted us to have a nutritious and hearty breakfast before we went to the rally. I was still shaken from the dream and did not really have much of an appetite, but I ate a bowl to be polite. Aside from offering Hung a few words of thanks for the porridge, I sat in silence at the table. I occasionally let my hands move to my eyes to confirm that they were in fact still in their sockets and had not been plucked out during my all-too-vivid dream. My strange hand movements did not go unnoticed.

"Are you okay?" Adam asked.

"Why?" I asked gravely.

"I thought maybe something was wrong with your eyes."

"No," I said.

"You keep rubbing them."

There was a tension between us that I was hardly even aware of, but I could see that Hung had registered it. He got up from the table and started nervously cleaning the breakfast dishes. I was concerned that Hung thought whatever was going on between Adam and me was the result of his presence in our home.

I tried to lighten the mood by changing the subject. Foolishly, instead of choosing something safe like the weather, I said, "We need to send the response card in for Peter and Amanda's wedding." I said it very matter-of-factly. I wasn't trying to get into a fight, but whatever our response was going to be, we needed to make one. I knew that with Adam's strong sense of etiquette he would agree.

"I sent that back the day after it arrived with our regrets. Didn't I tell you?"

He had not.

"Thanks for breakfast, Hung. I'm going to shower and then we should go," Adam said as he raced from the kitchen.

I glanced over at our invitation-free refrigerator. I felt tears running down my face. Again, I was crying in front of Hung—most unfortunate. I was really putting way too much pressure on a houseguest. No wonder he was anxious and making special breakfasts for us. Hung seemed to take my hysterics in stride. He came over to me and placed his hands on my shoulders. "I know," he said, gently kissing the top of my head. "It's an historic day. Very emotional." Hung was crying, too.

He really didn't get it.

❖

I'm not sure if they were actually members of the Gay Men's Chorus, but when I arrived at the Javits Center there were about fifteen guys singing an a cappella version of "The Times They Are A-Changin'" in four-part harmony. They were certainly very talented, but to my taste the sound was a tad too pretty. I would have preferred something a little more earthy and raw for this occasion. They did, at least, refrain from adding any synchronized hand choreography to the routine.

Aside from the chorus of fifteen, there were hundreds, perhaps thousands, of other sign-carrying and rainbow flag–waving people in attendance. I was having a low-level anxiety attack. It was different from my usual low-level anxiety attacks. There is a very specific race my heart runs, accompanied by a disturbing tingling at my temples, that I reserve exclusively for times when I'm standing in the midst of big crowds. I was experiencing the sensation that morning, so I know the event was a success.

We were positioned behind police barricades, so as not to block the convention center's main entrance. Max, who of course had started his own firm after leaving Adam's, was trying to sneak in without being noticed. But it's very difficult for a 6'3" 230-pound man with crossed eyes to be inconspicuous.

Max didn't have a chance. Adam spied Max skulking with his eagle-eyed glare. Adam started screaming, "That guy's gay and he plans weddings!" I thought it was a little harsh, especially since only a few months before Adam was happily planning them himself—but the protesters certainly responded to his jeer. Max blocked his face with his hands, the way indicted criminals do when they're entering a courthouse. He ran into the Javits Center as the crowd shrieked, "Traitor, traitor, traitor!"

There were very few other incidents, as most of the vendors had been tipped off about the protest and had arrived very early, thus avoiding any confrontation with us. A rumor was going around that Vera Wang was in the building. But I don't think that could have been true. I can't believe that at this point in her career Vera is working the trade shows hawking her own gowns. She must have reps doing that. Still, the thought of it had the crowd extremely energized.

After the Vera buzz died down, things got a little quiet for a while. The expo didn't open until 10:00, so no future brides and grooms had arrived. The protestors were just hanging out, talking, drinking coffee, and in general having a grand time, united as they were in their common cause.

I was getting antsy.

Perhaps Adam could tell. He grabbed me between my bouts of fidgeting, grinned an enormous, Cheshire cat grin, and kissed me on the mouth. I remembered the day we met—making out in the middle of that crowd in front of St. Patrick's Cathedral—the rest of the world disappearing the instant he had me in his arms. For a moment everything was wonderful. And then I felt the crowds, which were pressed all around us, and I needed air.

I pulled from the kiss quicker than I would have liked to. "Sorry," I said. "It's just a little close."

Adam knew I wasn't great in crowds. It was a problem that had grown worse over the years, and he gave me a reassuring nod.

I was sweating profusely despite the cold December air and it crossed my mind that perhaps it wasn't an anxiety attack but something far more serious.

I'm having a stroke!

"Stay calm, Steven," I whispered to myself.

I didn't want to make a scene or spoil the rally, so I decided not to say anything unless my arms started to tingle.

I did have a little pain in my shoulders, but it was most likely caused by the sign I was carrying. It read *Justice for All*—kind of dull. I would have much preferred something zingier. But since I had not made a sign for myself, I could hardly complain about carrying what I was given. The "All" was three times the size of the other words. The "artist" responsible for this creation had used celadon paint on mauve poster board, which in my opinion defused the intended impact of the words. Everything about the sign was wrong, including the very short post it was attached to, which meant that I had to hold my arm straight up to avoid blocking my face. By contrast, I thought Gail's sign was perfect in every way. It was written in big, black block letters that read: HERE COME THE BRIDES!

I had not complained about my sign because the alternative had been to wear my Halloween sad-gay-guy-who-can't-get-married mask. And even in the context of this rally, I didn't think anyone would get it and I really didn't want to spend the entire day saying, "No. No, that's not it. I'm a sad gay guy who can't get married."

I might have made it through the entire event with nothing more than a slight case of sign-carrying-induced tendonitis in my shoulder were it not for two things happening that I found truly upsetting: First, Adam started jumping up and down and craning his head around. (Not the upsetting part.) Then he said, "I can't see any reporters. I hope somebody from the press shows up today." (The upsetting part.)

Because, you see, I consider myself to be a member of the press. I had, after all, been covering this story for the last three months. I was a big part of the reason this crowd of three hundred, or a thousand, or five thousand, had gathered here this morning. They hadn't read about it in *The* (real) *New York Times*.

"Don't get sensitive," he said somewhat dismissively when I called him on his comment. "You know what I mean."

I knew *exactly* what he meant.

I was recovering from this indignity when the straight couples began arriving—which leads to upsetting part two. The protesters started hissing and jeering them, and shouting, "Don't go in. Go home!"

To me, it seemed like one of those awful scenes in front of a Planned Parenthood office. Poor, distressed teenage girls try to enter the building—only to be verbally attacked by the "Christians."

Whatever one's personal beliefs, people have rights. That must always be respected. Infringing upon another's civil liberties is intolerable.

Standing here right now, I felt no better being a part of this group. Well, that's not true. I'm exaggerating. This was not in the same league with blocking the doors of Planned Parenthood. Still, all the harassing screams weren't exactly filling me with pride. I started shouting, too. Only I was chanting, "Leave the brides alone." My cries could not be heard.

Adam smiled at me, seeing my mouth moving but not hearing my heretic's wail.

As the taunts intensified in volume, I noticed Peter and Amanda approaching the entrance to the Javits Center. Their backs were to me, but it was unmistakable—it was them. I tried getting Adam's attention. He was shouting so loudly that he could not hear me. And he was waving his sign so athletically that I was afraid to try and tap his arm—for fear I'd get clobbered by his flailing placard.

I decided to break out of the crowd and talk to Peter and Amanda. So, as I had done all those years earlier, the day I met Adam, I began shouting, "Excuse me. Pardon me"—now loud enough to be heard. The crowds parted for me and I made it out of the crush and up to Peter and Amanda.

"Hey," I shouted as I placed a hand on her shoulder.

She turned around, screaming hysterically.

Her fiancé shouted, "What the fuck?"

Oops—not my brother and future-sister-in-law. The resemblance was so striking from behind—not even close from the front.

"Sorry, sorry. I'm so sorry," I said, still touching the apoplectic bride-to-be.

"Get your hands off her."

For the record, I had only one hand on her—I moved it.

The two of them fled into the safety of the Javits Center just as I noticed a few police officers running toward me.

Best to flee, I thought.

I headed back toward the protesters, thinking the cops would be unable to distinguish one queer guy from another. But the thought of pushing myself back into that mob again was overwhelming. Even if I did muster the courage, I couldn't see Adam, or Gail or Hung, or anyone that I knew. The police officers (who I realize were just doing their job—often difficult, often criticized) were hot on my tail. I dashed for the street. They didn't catch me, or perhaps they never followed me. I was too terrified to slow down and find out if they were still in pursuit.

As I approached Ninth Avenue, and began to feel safe again, I noticed Daniel, our waiter from Lucca's. Had it not been for him, we might never have started a movement. Now that I was on the lam, I wasn't sure how I felt about seeing him again.

"Hi," he shouted to me.

"Hey," I said, allowing myself to stop running. "Need a sign?"

I didn't give him the chance to answer. I thrust the sign into his hands and continued running.

I ran for at least twenty minutes, heading east with no real destination in mind. I reasoned that since I was able to run this long, most likely I had been having an anxiety attack at the protest and not, as I feared and self-diagnosed, a stroke.

I felt great. Alive. I was experiencing a little pain in my left arch brought on by the brown suede John Varvatos boots I was wearing. (This is in no way meant to disparage Mr. Varvatos's shoes—I find them exceedingly comfortable and chic—but this particular model was not really designed with marathon running in mind.)

I stopped to examine the condition of my footwear and realized I was standing right in front of Great Cakes, my brother's shop. I wondered what Dr. Freud would think about that—not the Dr. Freud Adam and I met at the wedding, I mean the famous one.

I could be brave and go into the bakery, or I could go home and soak my feet in Epsom salts. I figured that thirty minutes one way or the other wouldn't really affect my blisters—so I went in. Actually, I thought that the guilt that was already devouring me would completely finish me off if I didn't make things right with Peter—so I went in.

Walking into the shop, feeling the warmth pouring out of the ovens in the back, smelling the blend of sugar, cocoa, and vanilla, I realized Peter would let me make things right. My brother spends his life baking things that bring people joy and happiness. Every time someone leaves his shop they're smiling. It's not just because of the cakes. It's Peter. The sweetness I smelled in the bakery was the essence of its owner.

I remembered my most difficult conversation with Peter—coming out to him. I was nineteen, nearly twenty, and he was seventeen. It was his birthday. I'd come home from school for the occasion and Onda had taken us out for Greek food. She would have preferred Romanian food, but there were no Romanian restaurants near us, and in her opinion Greek was a close second. As far as my brother and I were concerned, there was really only one significant difference between the two cuisines—the spinach pies. Our *pita di spinak* is subtle, airy, and considering it contains a pound of butter, surprisingly light. By contrast, the Greek's spanikopita is like a fast food imitation of the gourmet original. It's heavy, greasy, and way too thick. I'll eat it in a pinch. But every time I do, I find myself thinking longingly about my mother's extraordinary versions of the dish.

After gorging on souvlaki and watching and listening to our mother weep and wail for an hour that "My babies are all grown up," we came home. My brother and I immediately went to our room for a respite from Onda's laments.

We'd had our own rooms when we were kids, but the moment I went to college my mother turned my room into an office. However, she continued to use the kitchen table to pay her bills—never once using the new desk she had placed in my old room. My theory is that she turned my room into an office because she found it heartbreaking to look at my empty bed every evening. My absence was particularly hard on her because I had become her surrogate husband after my father left.

Onda was prepared for Peter to leave—in a sense he'd left the day he went to his first Cub Scouts meeting. I was the one who'd always been by her side. I was the one she thought would go to community college, stay at home, and never marry (well, it seems, at least for the moment, she got that part right). I was supposed to stay with her forever.

In the weeks before going home for Peter's birthday, I had planned how I would tell him I was gay. I would be open; I would answer all his questions, but I prayed he wouldn't ask any. The entirety of my experience was my very brief relationship with Brad—but there were other clues to let me know I was definitely gay: I watched *Knight Rider* reruns constantly, and it had nothing to do with the car.

Not surprisingly, when I tried to tell Peter I was gay, I couldn't. I started strong, "I have to tell you something—important."

"Yeah?"

I was silent. Then after my long dramatic pause, I said, "Happy birthday."

"Thanks."

I climbed up into the top bunk. I was a failure.

Peter turned out the lights and spoke to me in the dark. "Hey, Steven?"

"Yeah?"

"I know you're gay. It's cool."

I didn't say anything—I tried but couldn't. I was out of the closet—kind of. Peter knew I was queer. It was a start.

❖

I didn't imagine Peter would make things quite so easy for me now. I stood at the counter. A girl named Sally was finishing with a customer. I'd never seen her; she was Barney's replacement, I assumed.

"Hey, how you?" she twanged in a voice that suggested she'd arrived in Manhattan by way of Dallas.

"Good, thanks."

"How can I help you?"

"I'm Steven. I just want to speak to my brother."

"Peter? I didn't know he had a brother."

Of course she didn't.

She led me back into the kitchen area. Peter was pouring a fifty-pound bag of flour into an industrial mixer. I hadn't thought before how hard he worked. Making cakes always seemed so easy, but as I looked around and surveyed the massive boxes, sacks, and machines he used, I realized what strength it took to create his delicate confections.

"Hi," I said over the din of the mixer.

Peter nodded at me. I thought perhaps he also smiled, but I wasn't sure. I might have been projecting.

"I had to come see you." I was drenched in sweat; the combination of anxiety and my sprint across the city had done me in.

Peter was watching me, waiting for me to continue.

"I'm coming to the wedding." Finally, I said it—it only took me three months.

"I know," Peter said.

"What do you mean you know?" What did he mean—he knew?

"I know you're coming. I always knew you'd come. Adam, probably not."

I had the urge to pick a fight—but that seemed silly. "You're right," I said. "But you didn't know I was coming because I didn't know I was coming."

"Well," he said, like only a needling brother can. "Maybe you didn't know you were coming, but I knew. If I didn't know you were coming, then why haven't I asked anyone to be my best man?"

I was not expecting that at all.

I ran to him and moved to hug him just the way our mother taught us.

Peter put up an arm to stop me.

I ignored it. I held him tightly and told him I'd be honored.

As we separated, I realized why Peter had tried to keep me from embracing him—I was covered, head to toe, in flour.

CHAPTER TWENTY-ONE:
LET'S NOT ASK FOR THE MOON

I stood in my shower, under the water's massaging pulse, watching the last of the flour swirl down the drain. I had gotten home before Adam and was taking this time to think of a way to tell him that I would be attending the wedding.

My skin had begun to prune and I still had no idea what I was going to say. The only approach that made any sense was honesty. And that seemed so hard.

"Honey, I'm home," Adam called from the other side of the bathroom door.

I had no choice now but to come out of the shower. Actually, I might have stayed in there longer, but I'd run out of hot water several minutes before.

"I lost you today," Adam said, sounding concerned. "Where were you? Hung looked for you before he left for the airport. He sends his good-bye."

I was dressed now and had somewhat less wrinkled skin. Adam was on the couch. I joined him. "I…"

"Hold that thought. I want to check the local news."

Adam clicked on *Eyewitness News*, and after a couple of stories about the last of the three celebutantes still on the lam, the anchorman introduced the story of gay rights activists protesting the wedding expo at the Javits Center.

Looking at the images, I was impressed by the crowd. It was huge, and the faces of the men and women were passionate and committed. Adam appeared on screen. We both cheered. I noticed Daniel the waiter standing next to him holding the "Justice For All" sign above his head.

Unfortunately, that short handle must have begun to cause Daniel pain, and just as Adam was about to open his mouth to speak. Daniel let his arm drop, and the sign blocked Adam.

"Darn!" Adam shouted. He finds even the word "damn" offensive.

I was worried Adam would connect me to the offending placard, but before he had the chance to say anything the anchorman was back segueing into a related story.

"And now we go to Tiffany Feldspar, live on the Upper West Side, with the story of the wedding reception that wasn't."

Tiffany had an obscene amount of L'Oreal blond hair. Her scarf was blowing in the brisk December winds, yet her hair managed to remain completely frozen in a *That Girl* flip. She stood, ignoring the weather, directly in front of the entrance to Lucca's.

Beside her a young man and woman, who were barely twenty-five, stood arm in arm. He had shoulder length hair parted straight down the middle and wore a pea coat with a *Live Green* pin on the lapel. She was in braids, granny glasses, and one of those oversized bulky sweaters made to look like a coat.

"Think you had trouble with your wedding?" Tiffany began. "For one couple, their heavenly day turned into a day from hell." She nodded pitiably at the young couple.

"I'm standing in front of Lucca's Italian Restaurant with newlyweds John and Mary Goode. They're the couple believed to be the first casualties of the marriage boycott. You planned to hold your reception at Lucca's, which is a family-style restaurant. Is that correct?" She jabbed at Mary with her microphone.

"Yes." Even with amplification, Mary was barely audible.

"Lucca's? I must say, it doesn't seem an obvious spot. Tell me," Tiffany exhaled a visible stream of cold breath, "*why* Lucca's?" She thrust the microphone into John's face.

"Well..." John hesitated.

"Go ahead, John. *Tell them.* Tell them what you told me." Tiffany pressed.

"Well...to be honest with you, we were trying to economize a little bit."

"*Why*, John?" Tiffany prodded as she nodded encouragingly.

"Because I've just gotten back from two years in the Peace Corps. And I'm still interviewing for jobs in my chosen profession."

"And what profession is that, John? Tell the viewers!" Tiffany had worked herself into an *Elmer Gantry* fervor. She seemed moments away from speaking in tongues.

"I'm a counselor whose specialty is working with inner-city kids trying to free themselves from the scourge of gangs and drugs."

"God bless you." Tiffany choked back a tear. Then, with the satisfied smirk of a newscaster who'd just found her ticket out of local and onto network, Tiffany Feldspar moved onto Mary, shamelessly grilling her for her story.

"I teach autistic children in the South Bronx," Mary Goode said, cracking. "I also read to the blind. But that's just volunteer."

Adam and I looked at each other.

"We did that." We spoke simultaneously, but with extremely different vocal inflections. My words were laced with culpability and shame, Adam's with amazement and pride.

"That poor couple," I said.

"Don't feel sorry for them," Adam commanded, using a tone that I really didn't appreciate. "Remember, no matter what happened at their reception, they were still able to get married."

As I looked at Adam, I could hear Tiffany coercing the Goodes into spilling the last gory and tragic details of their aborted wedding reception. I heard John saying, "Luckily I worked as a bartender in college, so I jumped in and made cosmopolitans. Of course, with no food to eat, the drinks made everyone horribly drunk. My poor mother got so sick."

I turned off the TV to spare myself having to hear another word.

"Why did you do that?" Adam asked, grabbing the remote from my hand.

"I saw Peter today."

"He was at the rally?"

"I left the rally early and I went to the bakery."

"Oh? And why did you do that?" Adam's shoulders rose several inches. His hands clenched so tightly, I feared the remote might snap in two.

"I'm going to the wedding."

"No." Adam dropped the remote and clutched his heart. He never would have clutched his heart like that before we met. I guess couples really do morph into each other. Adam had picked up so many of my overly dramatic gestures. And while it seems completely natural when I do them, seeing them performed by him seemed very childish and put on.

"You can't go to the wedding. We're finally getting all this press. You can't do this to me," he said, his left hand still at his bosom.

"It's not all about you, Adam. It's about my brother."

"If you go to that wedding, nothing will ever change for us." I could tell by the way he said the word "us" that he did not just mean the two of us. We were now personally responsible for obtaining civil rights for every homosexual in America.

"Tell me, Steven, what happened to the guy who wrote: 'What does it say about a man if he refuses to acknowledge injustice? Who would rather be nice than righteous? Who chooses complacency over change?'" Adam was quoting my first marriage article and throwing the words back in my face. "Didn't you mean any of that?"

"Of course I did. But when I wrote that I didn't know our siblings were about to get married."

"The fact that they're getting married shouldn't make any difference. If anything, their wedding is the one we really have to skip."

I didn't actually say: "What are you talking about? That's ridiculous!" But Adam must have intuited that from the hands on my hips, the tilt of my head, the purse of my lips, and the bulge of my eyes.

"Steven! That's an event where our absence will really be noticed. It doesn't matter if we skip the weddings of people we barely know. Who cares about that? Missing Peter and Amanda's will have an impact. It's going to get people talking about the issue. How can you not see that?" He stopped, sighed heavily, and then snarled, "You are so selfish."

Twenty years earlier, I would have said: *I know you are, but what am I?* Actually, I still had the impulse. But instead I removed the hands from my hips and responded, "You're going to destroy your relationship with your sister."

"That won't happen."

"It might."

"What I'm trying to accomplish is more important than my sister."

That seemed harsh to me. They had always been extremely close. I couldn't believe how cavalier he was being with their relationship. And then it occurred to me that if he'd sacrifice his sister for this cause, perhaps he'd do the same thing with me.

I didn't really want to know the answer, but I asked the question. "Is this cause more important to you than I am?" I didn't ask it the

way my mother would have. Or the way I would have usually asked—
pleading, begging, desperate for reassurance that I was the center of his
universe. I asked the question quietly and simply. And then I waited for
a response.

I looked at Adam and saw disappointment, frustration, anger, and
sorrow marked on his face. I imagine my countenance mirrored his.

Time passed. Still, Adam did not speak. After nearly a minute
of silence, spent wishing I'd not asked Adam to pick between the
movement and me, I realized that he'd given me an answer. It wasn't
the one I was hoping for.

I had no experience, no frame of reference, for what was
going on now. Adam and I never fought—and not just because I'm
temperamentally incapable of it. We were a month shy of our seventh
anniversary, and until this issue, we had rarely disagreed on anything
significant. After all these years of merrily enjoying the good times,
I didn't know what I was supposed to do now that things were bad.
When things went wrong for my parents they did not engage in a
healthy debate of their problems. Instead, my father fled and my mother
pretended he was dead.

After a lifetime of modeling my mother's behavior, I chose this
moment to act like my father.

I fled.

I'm not exactly sure what the sequence of intervening events was,
but the next moment that I remember clearly was me standing at the
door, calmly telling Adam that I was leaving him. Vincent and Theo
were rubbing their heads against my ankles—their sign that they want
to be held. I was ignoring them. I carried my overnight bag, crammed
with some necessities. I clutched the bag against my chest like armor.
It was the only thing shielding me from the scary world that awaited
me. A world I was about to venture out into alone for the first time in
over six years.

On good days, when I'm feeling focused and I'm not bloated, I'm
still aware of some very low level of panic lurking at my core. On this
very bad day, I was overwhelmed with terror. Somehow, though, I was
holding it at bay—determined not to let Adam see it.

Perhaps I was able to keep it in check because I really didn't think
our split would be forever. We loved each other; we were best friends,
we'd just hit a rough spot—all couples did.

But another nagging part of me kept reminding me that it *might*
be forever. It was possible we wouldn't survive this. My parents'

relationship evaporated right in front of my eyes. My Maia never spoke to her sister again after the WWII letter slight. Margaret went for years without speaking to her sisters, and even now things weren't really right. And there was Hung's father—only cancer reunited him and his brother.

"I have to go." I said this because I didn't know what else to say or what else to do. And I was channeling my favorite role models. That's how I imagined Susan Hayward or Lana Turner or Bette Davis would have played the moment. While I was speaking, I didn't even really feel present in my body. It was as if I was hovering above the scene, watching this melodrama play out like an audience member. I saw myself turning dramatically on my heels. I headed for the door. My exit line had been delivered.

Adam refused to let me have the last word. "How is it that you lose your voice when we try to decide what television show to watch, but you have no difficulty telling me that you're leaving me?"

For the record, that only happened once—Adam didn't want to watch the final episode of *Sex and the City*. We watched the entire series and suddenly he's not interested. Of course I was upset. It's not like I went ballistic because he refused to watch a *Who's the Boss* rerun on Nick at Nite. "I'm not angry, Adam," I said, with tears welling in my eyes. "I'm just really hurt." As you can see, I was still clinging to my '40s B-movie script.

I scooped up Vincent and Theo, who were still circling my ankles, and gave them one last hug. I held them like a mother about to abandon her children—which is of course exactly what I was. When I finally let them go, I turned once more and walked out the door. This time, Adam didn't stop me.

I stood in the hallway muttering the words, "I'm just really hurt." At some point I started thinking, *Not only am I hurt, but I'm the only one of us who's hurt. I am the only one who's injured. The only one who's suffering.* I had suddenly placed all blame on Adam and exonerated myself of all wrongdoing. I had no culpability.

That's the mighty power of delusion.

The truth is, I was not the injured party. I had left Adam for having principles and conviction, which are the reasons one should stay with a partner. (They're right up there with funny and good in bed.) I would never have said, "Oh, he's an amazing lover and he makes me laugh, I'm leaving." Actually, given the state I was in, I might have. But hopefully one of my friends would have pointed out what a really bad idea that was.

I was in the hallway and I was single. How did that happen?

I wasn't exactly sure, but I think it has something to do with the fact that I've seen *Now, Voyager* seventeen times.

The first time I saw the film, I was with my mother. It was forty-one days after my father had walked out. I know this because for the first forty days we had been forced to endure my mother's mock-grieving ritual and, consequently, we were not allowed to watch television.

On day forty-one, after my brother escaped to the relative safety of the outside world, Onda and I watched the 4:30 Movie on channel 7.

"You're going to love this movie," she said when Bette Davis's and Paul Henreid's names appeared on screen. "What a tear-jerker."

For a woman who cried six or seven times every single day, my mother still had plenty of tears left in reserve for a good melodrama.

Those of you who have not seen *Now, Voyager*, I do hope you'll add it to your Netflix queue. Bette Davis plays a depressed spinster who lives with her overbearing and verbally abusive mother. I think one reason my mother loves this movie so much is that she always feels so good about her own parenting skills after watching the number this old lady pulls on poor Bette Davis. And indeed, I, too, always greatly appreciate Onda for several days after a screening of *Now, Voyager*.

Anyway, through a series of difficulties, Bette sort of cracks up and gets sent to a mental hospital run by the kind and earnest Claude Rains. It's not really a mental hospital, though; it's a lot more like Canyon Ranch. There is some therapy going on. But really Bette just has her very unruly eyebrows waxed, gets some new dresses, and plays a lot of tennis. And like magic—she's cured.

This makes perfect sense to me. As a Romanian, I know firsthand what a curse it can be to have one giant eyebrow extending right across both eyes. Personally, I prefer sugaring to waxing or plucking (longer lasting, less pain, and far less skin irritation), but whatever method you use the end result is still transformational.

Once Bette has completed her therapy and has pencil-thin brows, a snazzy wardrobe, and a killer backhand, she sets off on a cruise. This is where she meets the dashing Paul Henreid. Their love is intense and instant, but alas, destined to go nowhere because Paul is married.

Since Paul's married they can't have sex—but they can smoke.

And, in the greatest moment of tobacco industry propaganda the world has ever seen, Paul takes two cigarettes, places them between his lips, lights them, takes a giant drag, and then places one of the cigarettes between Bette's lips. Together they smoke and gaze lustfully into each other's eyes. I detest smoking, but their passionate inhaling is the sexiest thing I have ever seen.

Their relationship is based on nicotine, not on communication and shared experience—except of course for smoking. Yet somehow their relationship survives and flourishes. The reason their love flourishes is clear: Bette was horribly abused by her mother, she had her spirit broken, so she doesn't believe that she deserves happiness or a truly available life partner—she's content to settle for second best. It's not much, but it's a lot more than she ever had before.

That is, of course, my opinion and is perhaps not the opinion of the screenwriter and filmmaker.

After the cruise, Bette goes back to the mental hospital, but now she's working there. She's helping other young women overcome crippling emotional disorders with the help of herbal body wraps and mud masks. One evening, after an exhausting day of playing tennis, reading Jane Austen, and receiving Swedish massage, when all Bette wants to do is retire to her room, a little girl is admitted who desperately needs her help.

The little girl has all the classic signs of mental instability (including the unibrow). Bette's heart breaks for the little urchin, who tells Bette all about her terrible and despicable mother and her amazing and dashing father. She explains that her father has abandoned her only because he needed to save himself. The child seems to bear no ill will toward the man who left her to suffer alone with a witch of a mother.

Bette plucks the girl's eyebrows, buys her an ice cream cone, puts her in a super-cute dress, and offers to be her foster mother. The girl is cured!

Then Bette meets the little girl's father—it's Paul Henreid. They cry, they long for each other, they smoke.

Bette takes the girl home with her, raises her, pines for Paul, and most likely, although it's not shown on screen, begins taking her life frustrations out on her foster child in a thousand little ways, thus repeating the abusive cycle begun by her mother.

At the film's end, Paul comes for a visit, but doesn't really spend any time with his daughter; he's far more interested in seeing Bette.

He tries to apologize for his part in the miserable, lonely life Bette's leading.

She stops him. They have a smoke and she says, "Jerry"—that's the name of Paul's character—"Jerry, let's not ask for the moon. We have the stars."

The scary thing is for the first thirteen or fourteen times I saw this movie, I thought it was the most perfect romance I'd ever seen. Theirs was a relationship I aspired to have. I only saw the positive in it—they had burning love.

What else do you need?

I didn't think that maybe they needed equality, respect, communication, and honesty. It didn't occur to me that they should spend more time together than one Lucky Strike–fueled cruise. Or that a lasting love was built day in and day out through really hard work paired with thoughtfulness and care.

In the movie, the score told me what to feel, and so every time Paul lit a match, I reached for a Kleenex and began to weep.

❖

I was standing in the hall. Adam and the kids were on the other side of the door. Silence. There was no film score playing. I was alone—no dashing man was lighting a match, and yet, still I found myself reaching for a Kleenex.

CHAPTER TWENTY-TWO:
WE DON'T KNOW ANYONE NAMED ADAM OR STEVEN!

I showed up at Brad's with my one bag and my two red eyes, just as he was about to go out. He got me settled and offered to stay with me, but I wanted to be alone and was glad that he had plans. He handed me a set of keys, promised he wouldn't be home late, and then left me in his grand apartment. I had no idea what to do with myself, but decided that listening to music might have a calming effect.

And it might have, had I not opted to listen to Melissa Etheridge's rendition of "Breathe" thirty-six times in a row. I sang along with Melissa in a key bearing little relationship to the one she was singing in.

At some point during the thirty-fifth repetition of the song I stopped thinking about my problems and started thinking about Melissa, whom I don't actually know.

Melissa has integrity. She's a celebrity who's living a completely out life at a time when so many chose not to. She's not coy about who she is; she doesn't have some agreement with the press to not talk about her personal life so that she can appeal to a wider, homophobic audience. Oh, and let's not forget, she's a cancer survivor. The only thing I've survived is the slight discomfort associated with a day of full-body sugaring.

In lieu of more "Breathe," I decided to write. I pulled out a pad and began making a list of the pros and cons of being separated from Adam. I filled five pages with cons. I had three pros—not pages, lines.

I tried to focus on the pros.

1) Swear whenever I want.
2) Eat foods known to cause bloating whenever I want.

3) Find a guy with a pierced tongue and kiss him whenever
   I want.

As I stared at my paltry list, I realized I had to strike out item number two immediately. I don't enjoy being bloated. Aside from the unsightly appearance, it's uncomfortable. And so it's with very good reason that I avoid the trigger foods that cause this problem as often as possible.

That left two items on my list of pros. I had to admit, I had come to agree with Adam—swearing is uncivilized. With such a rich language at one's disposal what is the point of relying upon vulgarity?

That left one item on the list. I had to comfort myself with the knowledge that now I could make out with someone with a pierced tongue. I have always been curious to find out what that feels like. But if I really wanted to have that experience, I was pretty sure Adam would let me. Not whenever I want to—but certainly once in the interest of science. And just how often did I really want to be kissing some patchouli-scented slacker?

Great, I had five pages of cons and not a single pro.

Brad returned home and found me huddled over my notebook, contemplating a life without Adam—it was not a pretty sight.

"Are you writing?" Brad asked.

"Yes." I thought he'd be thrilled.

"Your column?" His tone was fraught.

I nodded. I had not intended this to be a column, but I guessed that I could turn it into one.

"That's a very bad idea. You need time. I want you to take a few weeks off."

How thoughtful and considerate Brad was. And then I realized his true motivation. Brad didn't want me writing a column because, as he said: "I don't want anyone to find out that the poster couple for gay marriage is on the rocks."

How absurd. Poster couple? We're not heartthrob movie stars with the paparazzi hounding us. I've never thought of myself as poster couple material.

Poster child, maybe.

❖

With three weeks off from the paper, I decided to volunteer my services to Peter and Amanda. I was sure they needed help with their super-rushed ceremony. This would be a way for me to make amends for all the heartache I'd caused them.

I met Amanda at the Columbus Bakery and we sat eating cranberry scones and drinking cappuccinos. It was awkward, not because Adam and I weren't together or because I had originally said I wouldn't be attending the wedding. I realized, as we sat making small talk, we'd almost never been alone together before. I spent so much time with her, but only as part of the familial group. She was my brother's girlfriend, my boyfriend's sister. The four of us were always so busy traveling in a pack that Amanda and I never really established our own relationship.

I felt like I was on a first date. I wanted to make a good impression. I wanted to be charming and please her. I wanted to do whatever it took to make her wedding preparations easier. All she had to do was ask, and her request would be granted.

"That's so sweet," she said. "Come with me to Queens."

For those of you who don't live in Manhattan, let me explain something. Queens, one of the other five boroughs of New York City, is not a place that Manhattanites travel to. Manhattanites stay in Manhattan unless they are traveling to their weekend homes, the West Coast, or Europe. The occasional trip home to one's place of birth is also acceptable.

I, however, was not born in Queens.

"Queens?" I asked so lightly you would have thought I'd been there yesterday. "What's in Queens?"

❖

I found myself on Ditmars Boulevard in Astoria, Queens, walking into Bernice's Bridal Shoppe (Bernice's spelling, not mine) to get a tux that matched Peter's—a waste in my opinion, black is black, but Amanda wanted an exact match. More importantly, we came to the Shoppe because Amanda was having the final fitting of her gown.

Bernice was short-staffed; actually she was alone in the store, so we occupied ourselves looking at dresses. Despite my personal no-drag rule, it was a lot of fun.

"This is what I've chosen for the bridesmaids," Amanda said, holding a gown at arm's length.

How best to describe this gown?

It was DayGlo orange. I'm guessing that's all the information you need to form an opinion as to its merits, but I'll say a little more. The only non-orange parts were the white Peter Pan collar and the white sash at the waist. As for the fabric—I was stumped; I had no idea what it was. All I can say about the material is that I hoped none of Amanda's cousins were smokers, because I'm sure the dress was highly flammable.

"What do you think?" Amanda asked.

She had to be teasing me—this *couldn't* be the dress. But a nagging little voice kept whispering in my head, "What if she isn't kidding?"

Amanda had asked way too loaded a question for a first date. If she was joking and I said that I loved the gown, she'd think that I was a liar—or worse—that I had no taste. But if this was really the dress she'd purchased, how could I tell her it was revolting? I needed to say something. Something truthful, yet inoffensive. Honest, but vague. I went with: "Orange. I've never seen *that* before." Big, wide smile plastered on face.

Amanda shook her head knowingly and whispered, "I had to travel all the way to Queens to find it. There wasn't anything half as ugly as this in Manhattan."

She laughed. It was the first totally relaxed moment of our outing.

I laughed, too. I felt confident that we'd be having a second date.

"You deliberately bought an ugly gown for your bridesmaids?" I thought it was funny, but I didn't really understand why she'd do such a thing.

"Steven, you have borne witness to each and every bridesmaid atrocity that my cousins have inflicted on me. Do you not recall the Marge Simpson powdered wig that I was wearing just three months ago? It's payback time! I can't wait to see my cousins dressed up like Creamsicles."

I wonder if that's the reason that bridesmaid dresses are all so awful. Perhaps there is a vicious cycle of retribution, each bride punishing their maids for the sartorial wrongs that they've suffered. It would explain so much that is otherwise so inexplicable.

Finally, Bernice came over to help us. She was wider than she was tall and she was frazzled. "Sorry to keep you waiting," she sighed. "I've had some staffing issues. How can I help you?"

"I'm Amanda More." Amanda seemed surprised that Bernice

didn't recognize her. I was, too, especially since Amanda was holding the orange dress. How many of those could Bernice be selling? "I have a fitting," Amanda prompted.

"Oh, of course you do. I'll get your wedding gown from the back."

"Thank you," Amanda said. "While you're back there, I believe you're holding a tuxedo in the name Steven Worth."

"That's me!" I said, using a ridiculous and inexplicable note of exclaim.

Bernice paused, then turned and looked at me. "Are you the writer?"

I barely think of myself as *a* writer, let alone *the* writer. "Yes, I am," I said like I was being asked the question for the tenth time today, instead of for the first time in my life. I smiled graciously at Bernice and felt around in my pocket for a pen, preparing myself to sign my first autograph.

Bernice walked over to Amanda and quickly snatched the synthetic, pumpkin-hued frock from her arms.

"Get out of my shoppe right now!"

"What?" Amanda tried to snatch the gown back, but she was no match for Bernice.

Bernice charged at me.

I closed my eyes. What did I do?

"Three of my best salespeople quit because of this nonsense you've started."

If I wasn't so busy thinking about the headline of my obituary—MANHATTANITE MURDERED AFTER FOOLISHLY VENTURING INTO QUEENS—I would have been really excited. Maybe Adam was right. It was kind of a thrill to discover I had become a minor celebrity. Of course, it would have been more thrilling, if I had had a little more time to enjoy my new-found celebrity status before I was killed by an obsessed stalker.

Bernice was right in my face. I have no idea how she accomplished that since she was about 4'6". But there we were, face-to-face.

"Get out! Get out! Get out!" she screamed.

I didn't need to be told three times; I got out. I made a dash for the door.

Amanda held firm for a moment, but when Bernice lunged, Amanda fled. At the door, Amanda stopped. "Hey, *sister*," she shouted, but it lacked any feeling of sorority. "What are you going to do with those seven orange dresses now? You think you'll ever sell them? You better start praying for a bride with a Halloween wedding date *and* a sense of humor!"

I clasped Amanda's hand and we ran as fast as our super-fit legs would carry us. We didn't stop running until we made it to the N train's platform. I didn't really take a breath until we were safely inside the subway and heading back to Manhattan.

These kind of horrible, tragic moments either bring a couple together, stronger than they were before, or they completely tear them apart. I glanced over at Amanda as we traveled home, and what I saw coming back at me was her glacial stare. Yikes. I guess we were destined for the completely-torn-apart camp.

After twenty minutes of silence, with Amanda frostily glaring and me pathetically smiling, Amanda spoke. "It's not the bridesmaid's dresses that I care about so much. I can always find an ugly dress. But I have no wedding gown now. What am I going to do? What will I wear?" she sobbed.

I wrapped an arm around her and she cried into my shoulder. "I will do anything I can to help you," I said just as the conductor was announcing that we'd arrived at Lexington and Fifty-ninth Street.

"Get up. We're getting off here," Amanda cried, although there wasn't a hint of tears. She bolted for the open subway doors. "Move it!" she barked at me.

❖

I found myself standing on the main floor of Bloomingdale's, dodging perfume spritzes and listening to Amanda's demands.

"First," she said, "Since this is all your fault, I want to thank you for offering to, and I quote, 'do *anything* I can to help you,' end quote. Here's your assignment."

Something was telling me that I should have left well enough alone and let our relationship get completely torn apart.

"My fear," Amanda said, "is that the bridal department is going to be staffed with wedding protesters who won't let me buy a dress."

"Amanda, that doesn't make any sense."

"It's my *fear.* It doesn't have to make sense! So you should go up there and tell those militant sales clerks you're a drag queen and you need a gown for your new show."

"*But—*"

Her icy stare returned. "Pretend that you are buying a dress for *yourself*. And when you accomplish this assignment, I will forgive you. Get me something elegant. You have excellent taste, I trust you. Oh, I'm a perfect size six."

"But I'm an eight!"

"Tell them you're doing Jenny Craig. And meet me in bridal registry in fifteen minutes. I need to add a couple of things to my list."

There had been no anti-wedding demonstration in Bridal. There had, however, been strong encouragement from the saleswoman that I might be happier in a fuller cut dress. I ignored her advice and snatched a cinched-waist, strapless number that I thought *I*—I mean, Amanda— would look great in. I was standing next to her in the bridal registry department exactly fifteen minutes later, with the gown in hand.

"I still haven't been waited on," Amanda said, taking the gown from me. "While we're waiting, let me show you the crystal I registered."

"Don't you and Peter already have crystal?"

"As much as I love the Pottery Barn, that's not crystal." She dragged me over to the French stemware.

Amanda and I had spent quite a long time admiring the pattern she'd chosen when we realized that while the store was swarming with customers, there was only one salesperson working.

The salesperson's forehead was as wrinkled as a shar-pei's and his eyes were sealed in a squint. He was either being blinded by an intense sun that no one else could see, *or* he was on the verge of having a nervous breakdown.

"Listen up!" he shouted to the mass of shoppers as he compulsively clicked the top of a ballpoint pen. "Here's what's going to happen. I am going to hand you each one of these forms. It is the bridal registry sheet. You will then be given pens, like the one I'm holding." He clicked three times. "I need the pens back, people! I will teach you how to identify the SKU number of the merchandise you want. You write down the SKU, the quantity and the price on the *CORRECT LINE*." Here, he stopped and eyed the shoppers. He didn't want any mistakes. "When you're through, hand it back to me. Any questions?" It was surprising that a man so obviously suited for a career in the military had ended up in housewares.

Anxious couples grabbed the forms. A few of the couples had questions but they made the very wise decision to ask their fellow shoppers and not *The Great Santini*, who was doing a menacing pace behind the main cash register. One brave-looking woman—only her shaking hands betrayed her—approached him with a question about Lenox China.

"It's a plate. You eat off of it," was his less-than-helpful response.

Amanda was finishing up adding the few essentials she'd failed to register previously. You know, essentials like a set of pearl-handled fruit knives and a sterling silver table crumber. With the final addition of shrimp cocktail forks, she was done. This was great news because it meant that we got to leave the store, but it was terrible news because it meant that we had to face the wrath of the salesman.

"I'm not usually like this." The salesman was falling apart. "There should be six other people here. I'm only one man, for God's sake!"

I thought about offering to call someone to help him but it really wasn't my responsibility. We all have troubles—I myself, not twenty minutes earlier, had squished myself into a perfect size six. Enduring a plethora of snide comments from the "helpful" saleswoman in Bridal.

The Great Santini started clicking his pen against his temple.

"So anyway," Amanda said, ignoring the pen, "here's my completed form." She held out the form and waited for him to take it. When he did, we both instinctively started backing away, slowly. The way one might when face-to-face with a rabid dog or grizzly bear.

"Just a second there, not so fast."

Amanda and I froze.

The salesman smiled warmly. Perhaps some medication had kicked in. "Let's go over the form and make sure you got everything right."

His tone was so pleasant that we were thrown. We let down our guard and approached him.

Santini examined the list of merchandise Amanda had selected and fortunately found no errors. He then moved onto the personal information: "Same address for you and your fiancé, I see, more and more common now. Who can blame you? Rents are through the roof, hard to pay one, let alone two." He glanced up to the names. "More and Worth. Any relation to Adam and Steven?" All pleasantries had ended. The salesman had returned to his sinister ways.

I felt as if I had somehow stumbled into the long and excruciating second act of an After School Special; I really didn't feel like sticking around for the dénouement.

Amanda froze. I could see the vein at her temple begin to pulse. Beads of sweat were forming above her upper lip. She stammered.

Before Amanda could say anything damning, I jumped in: "We have never heard of anyone named Adam or Steven!" I said in my most indignant, outraged-consumer voice.

We marched to the elevators with our heads held high.

We were back on the ground floor. I felt like we had gone to war, and I had proved victorious in the battle against our crazed clerk. I was a soldier on the front lines—a soldier who was in desperate need of a jar of moisturizer, so we headed over to the Origins counter.

I love their products. I'm especially fond of Have a Nice Day with added SPF 15. It's not too greasy, not too smelly—it's perfect.

As long as I was buying, I grabbed a tube of the shaving cream they call Blade Runner and their yummy facial scrub, Never A Dull Moment. "I would kill to be the guy who makes up the names of their products," I said to Amanda. "That's gotta be a fun job."

"Oh, Christ!" Amanda wailed, apropos of nothing.

"What's wrong?"

"My caterer is a lesbian!"

"I'm sure it will be *fine*," I said, certain that it was going to be many things, but *fine* was not one of them. I envisioned myself preparing surf and turf for two hundred.

As my purchases were being rung up, I noticed another Origins product that I was in desperate need of, a product guaranteed to calm. I added the tiny bottle labeled Peace of Mind to my pile. I was really hoping it would deliver some.

CHAPTER TWENTY-THREE:
A DAY OF BEAUTY?

Isn't there an adage that goes something like: If you want a different outcome you must change your behavior? Or, create a different strategy? Or something like that? I don't really know the exact words. Which might explain why the very next morning, I met Peter at the Columbus Bakery. We sat at the very same table that I'd sat at with Amanda the day before, eating cranberry scones. And as we chatted, paying no heed to recent history, I uttered the same foolish words that I'd previously uttered to Amanda. "I'll do anything you want me to. Just ask."

"Anything?" Peter asked.

"Sure," I said, suddenly regretting that I hadn't included any qualifiers. But I tried to calm myself; whatever it was that he was going to ask of me couldn't be more painful than modeling a too-tight wedding gown on the fifth floor of Bloomingdale's.

However, there was something in the way my brother looked at me that let me know, whatever my assignment would be, it would not be fun.

I should have realized that my mother would be a key player in this *Mission Impossible* he was assigning me—but I didn't.

❖

Peter and I sat at our mother's kitchen table eating a magnificent lunch—leg of lamb with garlic and rosemary, roasted potatoes, sautéed spinach and, since I'd missed it on Thanksgiving, *pita di curcubeta*. She had provided bowls of feta cheese and kalamata olives and had even bought a good (in other words, *not* Romanian) bottle of wine. She'd laid her finest linens, including the runner my Maia had crocheted for Onda's hope chest.

It would have been a wonderful afternoon were it not for the fact that my mother was on all fours on her spotless kitchen floor with her head planted firmly inside the oven.

I could see the sweat running from Peter's brow, the anxious twitch in his left eye. He'd never witnessed this drama before. When we were kids, he'd always been out playing when Onda tried to "kill herself." I had had the privilege of discovering her on three different occasions. Although the first time I didn't realize what she was doing. I just assumed she was in the oven along with a can of Easy-Off.

I was determined to enjoy the meal, so I did my best to ignore my mother's theatrics. I stared pointedly at Peter every time he began to plead with her to come out.

As I started on seconds of the lamb, I lost all patience with Onda. "Can I get you a pillow, Mom? You'll be more comfortable."

I hope you don't think me insensitive, but considering her oven is electric I was not actually concerned about her welfare. She wasn't even in danger of burning herself—the oven was off, and had been for quite some time before she entered it.

It was the revelation that my father would be attending the wedding that had provoked my mother's oven ritual. Telling her was the task that Peter had assigned me. I had somehow thought that it would not be a big deal—how could she think that our father would not make it onto the guest list? I had, however, insisted that Peter make the trip to Bridgeport with me just in case I needed backup.

When my mother finally pulled herself out of the oven, she looked at us the way Medea must have looked at her children just moments before she slaughtered them.

"Did you really think Peter wouldn't invite Daddy?" I asked.

"Do you have any idea what your father has done to me? What he continues to do to me?"

I took this as a positive response. Her use of the phrase "continues to do" suggested to me, that at least for the moment, she was acknowledging that he was still among the living.

"So," she said, joining us at the table at last. "Is he bringing the Secretary?"

"Mom," I said, desperate to end this conversation.

"Is he?" I was thrilled that she directed the question to Peter—it was his wedding, after all. I was just the messenger.

As Peter stammered a response to Onda, I thought about how many times we'd played out this particular scene in the twenty years since Daddy had married Roz (a.k.a. the Secretary.)

I had planned on spending the night at Mom's. It would give Brad a break from having me as a roommate. More importantly, I needed the extra time with Onda because, having done such a great job choosing Amanda's wedding gown, I had been enlisted to help our mother buy dresses for both the rehearsal dinner and the wedding. "If she insists on wearing black," my brother begged, "please don't let it be refugee black."

I cannot find the words to describe the level of regret I was feeling at the prospect of spending fifteen hours alone with my mother.

❖

She drove Peter back to the station. We waited for the arrival of his train. Peter was sitting up front with Onda. I was slumped in the back. We had arrived extremely early—"Let's go. God forbid we hit traffic," my mother said, forcing us to leave the house twenty-five minutes earlier than necessary.

As we sat in the parking lot of the Fairfield, Connecticut, train station, Onda took the opportunity to fill us in on the details of the rehearsal dinner—I have to admit I was very impressed by the extent of her efforts. My mother loves to drive. She had been commuting into Manhattan almost daily for the past month, first in search of a restaurant to hold the event, and more recently to hire florists, a photographer, musicians, and a printer to create place cards and menus to place on the gold leafed chargers she had chosen to use on the tables. I could tell my brother was thrilled at the lengths Onda was going to in order to ensure that the night would be a success. My mother also seemed to have lucked out in terms of avoiding wedding protesters. While the actual wedding celebration was proving to be rife with difficulties and sabotage by zealous anti-wedding activists, the rehearsal dinner seemed to slip through a well-it's-not-the-actual-wedding loophole and had been planned without a single staffing incident.

When my mother had finished relaying every grand detail of the party, she looked into her rearview mirror and spoke directly to me: "Where are you holding the stag, Steven?"

The stag? I had not given it a thought. I'd never been a best man before—I'd never even been an usher. I'd completely forgotten about that part of my responsibility.

"I don't want a stag party," Peter said instantly. I suspected he said that to save me being embarrassed and also to spare me Onda's wrath.

"Of course you want a stag," Onda said, dismissing Peter. I could see her eyes darting back to me in the rearview mirror. "Steven, where are you having it?"

"I thought I would take Peter to a spa for a day of beauty," I said, joking. No one laughed. Before anyone could respond, the train whistle blared as the 3:24 came rolling into the station. Peter and I jumped out of the car; he kissed me hard on the cheek and thanked me—for what, I'm not exactly sure. I watched him board the train. He was on his way to the freedom land. I was on my way to the front seat of the car for a further adventure with Onda.

"A day of beauty?" my mother asked as I buckled myself in for the trip to the mall.

❖

I pulled out a dozen dresses for my mother. All were rejected. "Too garish, too expensive, too short, too synthetic, too trendy, too old-fashioned, too bright, too blah, too beige, too flashy, too flimsy, and too conservative," she announced as she modeled each garment.

As we were about to leave the store empty-handed, my mother grabbed the dress she had described as too expensive. It was black, but chic and sexy, and fit her like it had been designed for her. It was nothing like her usual black dresses. She took one more look at the staggering price tag as we approached the counter. "Why not spend the money?" she asked, rhetorically. "It's the only wedding party I'll ever be throwing."

I was stung and I was silent. I'm not sure if the hurt showed on my face, but I don't know how it couldn't have.

"I'm sorry. That was a horrible thing to say."

"It's okay," I said, wishing I'd screamed, shouted, or done any of the myriad scene-inducing things that come so naturally to other Romanians.

"It's not okay. I can't imagine how hard this is for you." My mother was crying now.

The tears I recognized; the words were unfamiliar.

"Things will work out for you," she said, holding the costly evening dress at arm's length to avoid staining it with her tears. "I see it in the glass."

"What?"

"I do *di ocui* for you every morning. Your readings are good." She kissed me. "You have no worries."

Was she kidding? I had nothing but worries. Still, I found my mother's words comforting.

❖

Onda rented *Now, Voyager* and we sat together, curled on the couch under one of the ancient afghans Maia had knitted. We ate chocolate-dipped halvah that I'd picked up at Zabars. My mother gasped and sighed every time Paul lit a cigarette. She wept, as usual, but for the first time watching this film, I did not.

After the movie, I went up to bed. There was a knock on the door.

"Come in," I said.

"Are you too old to get tucked in?"

"No," I said, realizing, of course, that I was far too old for such a thing. The truth was I desperately needed to feel my mother's safeguarding, if somewhat smothering, touch. I had not had a single decent night's sleep since I'd been apart from Adam and the kids. When Onda was finished cocooning me in my comforter, she kissed each cheek and my forehead, too.

"I love you so much, Ma."

"Oh, my Stavri Constantine, I love you, too." Onda sat at the edge of the bed smiling at me. "So, about the stag," my mother said, still smiling at me. "A day of beauty?"

I smiled back at her.

I made a mental note to self: *Check Yellow Page listings for strip clubs.*

CHAPTER TWENTY-FOUR:
HOT TOPICS

I think all men are wired to really dig breasts. Breasts are sexy, magical, beautiful, and nurturing—all at the same time. This fascination with breasts is not limited to straight men. Why do so many gay men spend countless hours in the gym doing chest presses? Answer: to get big boobs. The man who doesn't want a woman still wants to be able to get his hands on an impressive rack. Use of the term "pecs" can't disguise the fact that it's all about breasts.

I hadn't really given this mammary theory of mine very much thought until the evening I took my brother Peter and his buddies to VIP for his stag. VIP is billed as a "gentlemen's club," but there are no leather wingback chairs, no Brits speaking in hushed tones, and no valets offering cigars and pouring brandies.

Peter and his friends were a little squeamish. They were acting as if they were too evolved and sensitive to spend a night out at a strip joint. Hogwash, I thought. So just to get the party going, I asked one of the young ladies to give me a lap dance.

I'd never had a lap dance before—not exactly. I did have a kind of lap dance experience at my thirteenth birthday party. Someone (definitely not me) organized a game of spin the bottle. Molly D'Onofrio spun the bottle of Blue Nun I'd taken from Onda's pantry, and it pointed at me. She waltzed across the circle and sat right in my lap. I was terrified.

My anxiety had nothing to do with the fact that she was a girl, as I was pretty oblivious to my sexual orientation at that point. I was a wreck because she, like me, had an entire mouth filled with wire braces. I was sure we'd lock and be unable to separate. As she leaned toward me I imagined my mother's screams. *If you think I'm calling Dr. Mendeloff and explaining this, you can forget it. I'll just have to get the pliers and separate the two of you myself!*

Molly's mouth moved against mine. I could feel her tongue try to break through my impenetrable lips—she did not succeed. After a minute of her failed attempts at French kissing, a dejected Molly returned to her place in the circle. On the school playground the following Monday, Dennis Fatsi called me a fag. It was the first time anybody ever called me that. It wasn't the last.

Now I was grinning and displaying my perfectly straight teeth. At first, I was just pretending to enjoy the lap dance, to set the tone for the other guys, but then something switched for me and I really got into it. Maybe the fact that I was newly single and reeling from that, had something to do with my delight. Or maybe I liked it so much because it was an enormous amount of attention focused solely on me. But I'm ashamed to admit, most likely the cause of my ecstasy was that I was "passing"—and it felt good. It was a huge rush to have this woman think I was a straight man. As far as she could tell, I was just another horny guy with nothing but girls, beer, and sports on my mind. I've never been that guy. Suddenly, I was the good old boy in charge, running the show. For once in my life, I felt like I had nothing to prove. I was powerful.

When Cherry—probably not her real name—finished with me, I stuffed a fifty into her G-string and said, in a voice so deep I did not recognize it as my own, "Take care of my brother, sweetheart. He's about to get married." I pointed toward Peter, who was doing his best to disappear into the Naugahyde banquette he and his pals were occupying.

Peter declined Cherry's advances—he felt it would be hurtful to Amanda.

I tried to point out that it was his stag party, his last chance for excitement. He was adamant. None of the other guys seemed very into it either, but Brad and Barney both offered to give it a go. This made me wonder: Are these places all filled with gay guys pretending to be straight? Perhaps actual straight guys aren't that into lap dances. It was an interesting theory I had, but one glance around the room at all of the beer guts and very unfortunate footwear made me realize that I was most assuredly surrounded by heterosexuals.

That is, of course, except for the boys at our banquette. I knew that Peter wasn't the only straight man at his stag, but all his buddies possessed that very erotically ambivalent quality, that leaves one asking: *European or metrosexual?* These guys were all neat, soft-spoken, and color coordinated. Based on the overpriced haircuts, bronzed, moisturized complexions, and chunky sterling rings, these were straight guys who'd been unduly influenced by the eye of some queer guy.

Their choice of careers only added to my confusion vis-à-vis their sexual orientations. There was an opera singer, a drama coach, an antiques dealer, a poet, and a reiki master. I sat there, a columnist for *The Gay New York Times*, realizing that, compared to the rest of these guys, I had the most macho profession at the table.

Actually, I had the second most macho profession. There was a fireman named Chad in attendance. Only Chad seemed like a "real" man to me. He wore well-worn Levi's and a corduroy shirt. His shoes were brown but his belt was black, suggesting to me that he was a heterosexual man—and obviously single. No woman would have let him out of the house dressed like that. His good looks more than made up for the attire. He was graying and chiseled. The jut of his jaw was so extreme that it cast a shadow on his corduroy shirt. He looked to be about forty.

Brad seemed very taken with him. So much so, that he almost tripped the reiki master as he darted into the spot next to Chad.

I was puzzled. Chad was so old by Brad's definition. It troubled me that Brad might be trading in his unhealthy obsession with young guys for an unhealthy obsession with straight ones.

I was stuck next to the reiki master, who was sipping Perrier because, as he shared with me while I was enjoying my martini, "alcohol is pure poison. You can't imagine the toxins I *feel* when I'm working with someone who's even a moderate drinker."

After listening to an exhaustive description of his work—"Oh, no. I don't actually touch anyone. I just allow the Universe's energy to pass through me and I send it on to my clients"—I felt it was time to excuse myself. I turned so I could introduce myself to Chad, who was seated on my other side.

Unfortunately, Chad had his back to me and was completely engrossed in a conversation with Brad. I pretended I was talking to him anyway, so that I could avoid any further contact with the reiki master's mighty energy.

I sat there, feigning actual conversation and eavesdropping on Chad and Brad.

"I didn't catch your name. I'm Chad."

"I'm Brad." I thought I saw a little drool at the corner of Brad's mouth, but that might have been my imagination. "How do you know Peter?" Brad asked.

"The fire house where I'm stationed is right by his bakery. I come in to get muffins for the guys. Anyway, we hit it off. Started taking kickboxing together."

I guess Peter moved on to kickboxing when I abandoned him for Hot Nude Yoga. Maybe I should take up kickboxing. Be a little more aggressive—I enjoyed the lap dance, after all. I was weighing the merits of this switch in cardiovascular activity and forgot about my eavesdropping. When I brought my attention back to Brad and Chad they had moved on to the other safe topic for strangers at a party: They were talking about their jobs.

"I'm the editor of *The Gay New York Times*," Brad said, more proudly than I'd ever heard him say it before.

"Wow. Cool. I read it all the time."

"No. Not that one," Brad said, sheepishly. "*The* Gay *New York Times*."

"Right. Great paper."

I couldn't believe it. Chad? Gay? How could that be? He was physically coordinated and sartorially uncoordinated. I was becoming as clueless at detecting homosexuals as Adam.

"Hey, Brad," I heard Chad say as I returned to listening in. "This might sound crazy, but don't you find it hard having such a hot name? It's a lot of pressure, isn't it? I mean if you're a Walter or a Norman..."

There really *is* someone out there for everyone.

Brandi, who according to her nametag dotted the "i" in her name with a heart, asked if we wanted another round. I was about to say yes when Peter jumped in. "What do you think guys, getting late?"

In the time it took me to blink, the poet and the antiques dealer had vanished. I just managed to catch a glimpse of the opera singer's back as he walked out the door. The reiki master had the courtesy to thank me and shake my hand before he departed. I admit I felt a little tingle when our hands touched—energy, I guess.

Brad and Chad left together. As they were exiting, I heard Chad saying something about meeting for kickboxing and then grabbing a muffin and coffee. "Sounds great," said Brad.

I looked at my watch. It had been a forty-minute stag. I used to believe that I knew how to entertain—but with Thanksgiving, and now this bachelor party, the evidence was mounting against me. I guess living with a party planner had shielded me from my own shortcomings. Now that I was alone, what would I do? I would become known as the guy with the inappropriate party themes and/or combative guests. "Oh, it's one of Steven's parties? Let's be sure and come late and leave early."

"Thanks for the great party," Peter said reassuringly, apparently reading my mind.

"It was an awful party. Let me buy you another drink."

I could see that Peter didn't want to spend another minute in this grim, fairly depressing, and not really erotic club. I threw this party because I thought it was the way things were done. I didn't give any real consideration to what my brother might actually like. And then I thought of something that I knew he'd love—that we would both love. "I'm going to take you someplace else," I said.

"Really?"

My little brother excitedly headed for the exit. Cherry caught my eye and blew me a kiss. I gave a self-conscious smile in response and followed Peter out on to the sidewalk.

"Peter," I said when we arrived at Nickel, the Chelsea spa for men, "I'm telling you right now if you let them paint your nails, I'm going to pretend I don't know you."

That evening, after leaving Peter and finding myself once again alone in Brad's guest room, I felt the bleak grip of desolation take hold. Even the sight of my freshly pedicured feet did little to offset my sorrow. Nights had become astoundingly difficult. I managed to get through most days without completely falling apart, but after dark, when I had fewer distractions, I wasn't so successful. I missed Adam and the kids terribly. My longing for them decimated my already tenuous relationship with sleeping. How naïve I'd been, for all those years, considering myself an insomniac. I had no idea what insomnia was before my breakup with Adam. Whatever my past claims, I'd been a rank amateur.

Sleep was the dream I no longer remembered.

Now I spent my nights watching television. My thoughts raced so that I couldn't focus on reading. I couldn't even focus on *Us* magazine. Instead I Tivoed shows that reminded me of Adam, and while the rest of the city slept, I watched them.

I always started with *The View*. It didn't matter that most of the hosts had changed since Adam's one appearance on the program. It was the show itself that I connected so strongly with him.

I sat on the foot of the bed and turned on the TV. But tonight, even television seemed too complex and challenging for me to absorb.

On *The View*, the women sat at their table and argued. I couldn't listen to them. I'd spent too much time lately listening to people fight. I didn't want arguing. I wanted harmony from the hosts.

I'm not sure how long the bickering lasted. I checked out soon after hearing their tirade begin. As my mind wandered, the hosts' voices were replaced by the voices of my family. I heard my mother yelling and Margaret and Amanda. Peter was shouting, and Adam, too.

And then I heard a voice I didn't recognize: "Do you really mean to sit there and tell me that if your gay brother failed to show up to your wedding, you wouldn't mind? You'd support him?"

"Yes, I would. That's exactly what I'm saying!"

"I don't buy it!"

I wasn't listening to my family scream. Suddenly I realized it was the ladies of *The View*. This was Hot Topics.

Oh my God! The movement was a Hot Topic! I jumped up from the bed. My first thought was to call Adam. He mustn't know about the show. If he did, surely he would have called me. Wouldn't he have?

I believe I spent the next hour or so pondering whether or not Adam knew about *The View*. I worried about what it meant if he did know but had neglected to call me. By the time I decided that he couldn't know and that I should call and tell him, I realized it was far too late to be using the phone. I'd have to wait until morning.

CHAPTER TWENTY-FIVE:
MY HEART STOPPED

By morning, it occurred to me that perhaps seeing Adam was a better strategy than calling him.

I had doubts, though, so I phoned Gail for advice.

"Vanessa and I had our first fight last night," she blurted before I'd managed a hello. "And it's all your fault."

I attempted no self-defense; I offered no resistance. I allowed Gail to harangue me.

"Vanessa thinks you're doing the right thing."

"I see. And you?"

"Obviously Adam's right," said Gail, with the assurance of a woman who's never seen a shade of gray in her entire life.

"I'd love to help you and Vanessa work things out, but since I can't work things out for myself—"

"Oh, you *can*. If you want to."

"Actually, that's why I called. I need your advice."

"Skip the wedding."

"No. But with regard to Adam, I've been thinking of going to the apartment." I stopped; I was trying to formulate a plan even as I spoke. "Then I was thinking I'd, I don't know…wait for him to come out of the building…and…I'm not sure exactly what. All I know is I miss him, Gail."

"Let me see if I can read between the lines, since you're always such a clear communicator. You're going to set up a stakeout on West End Avenue, perhaps behind a parked car or lamppost, in hopes of catching a glimpse of Adam as he leaves the apartment. Is that it?"

Gail made it sound so tawdry.

"I'm worried about him. I just want to *see* him," I cried.

"Again, and I'm asking just as clarification, so I'm certain I'm getting this straight. When you say 'I just want to see him,' do you think there is any chance that the authorities could interpret that as 'I just want to stalk him'?"

"I have to say, I expected a little more sympathy, Gail."

"You want sympathy? Call Vanessa."

I did not call Vanessa. Instead I took a cab to our—or I guess I should say Adam's—apartment. Not to stalk him. Not even to see him, as I knew he'd be at the office. I just wanted to be in the space. And I wanted to spend some time with the kids.

As difficult as the decision had been for me, we'd decided that Adam should have sole custody of the kids. Brad had made it clear that while I was welcome to stay in his apartment as long as I needed, the kids were not. Even if Brad would allow it, Vincent and Theo are not exactly expert travelers.

That's the problem with housecats; you can't really take them out of the house. They don't enjoy it. They might enjoy sitting in the windowsill all afternoon, vainly trying to attract birds, with their beguiling meows—Theo is particularly deft at making hers sound like a chirp—but put them outside, up in a tree with the actual birds and they are terrified.

I had been visiting the kids infrequently, and only when I knew that Adam would be at work. I had become a completely indulgent, guilt-ridden father. To compensate for the lack of time I spent with them, I doled out the catnip, let them race across the furniture, and gave them actual turkey, chicken, and on one occasion, wild Alaskan salmon. They adored the salmon; but eighteen dollars a pound—what was I thinking?

When I walked into the apartment today, my bribe of choice was a brand-new Rosie-the-rat-on-a-stick, still in its plastic package. It's the kids' favorite toy. I opened her up, unwound the long string attaching Rosie to the end of the stick, and shook as hard as I could, making Rosie-the-rat race across the floor.

Back and forth I whipped the stick. Yet oddly, there was no sign of the kids. They were nowhere to be found. Usually they were at the front door the instant they heard the key in the lock. To entice them out of their hiding place, I began running a frenzied race around the living room, hoping they'd come out to play with Rosie and me.

Finally, they skulked out from wherever they'd been sequestered and joined me in the living room. Then the most distressing thing happened. Right in front of my eyes, the kids transformed themselves into cats. Theo turned her back on me, began shedding profusely, and darted under the sofa. Vincent, my sweet little boy, hissed and bared his claws. I dropped the stick, leaving Rosie's lifeless body lying motionless on the floor.

"Please, Vincent. It's Pop. What's wrong, angel?" I took one step toward Vincent, instantaneously recoiling at the sight of his arching back.

I was terrified. The arching and the hissing continued. Vincent's blue-eyes turned an ungodly red. I looked like a less anemic Rosemary upon introduction to her newborn.

Unlike Rosemary, I did not embrace the baby.

Instead, I ran for the door.

❖

By late afternoon, I decided that perhaps exercise would help calm my still-jangled nerves. Lifting weights, I reasoned, might help me deal with some of the frustration of being spurned by my children. I walked over to Equinox at Columbus Circle. Still more than a block from the gym, I was already losing interest in physical fitness. I began bargaining with myself. *Just do chest and then you can leave. You don't have to do the whole body. Maybe the biceps, nothing more.*

As I awaited the light change, so I could cross the street to Equinox and complete the workout that had now been negotiated down to ten minutes, I saw Adam exit the gym.

My heart stopped. That's just an expression, but I did have a moment when I thought I might actually die.

Adam didn't see me. He walked along the sidewalk and stepped into the main entrance of the Time-Warner Center.

I followed.

I did not have a clear plan. Just like the first time we met, I thought maybe I could get myself into a position to be standing next to him and pretend our meeting was pure chance.

Adam took the escalator down to Whole Foods. I snuck behind at a distance.

I wasn't certain that Adam had ever been in the store before—I always did the grocery shopping. He pushed his cart through the produce section. I grabbed a cart and a giant poinsettia, which I thought might block my face if he turned around, and I tailed him from a safe distance. I saw him reach for a box of pesticide-laden, non-organic strawberries, and I gasped. Who eats a strawberry in December? How was he surviving without me?

Down four aisles, I watched him make one bad choice after another—I had no idea it was possible to make so many bad choices at Whole Foods. When we wheeled into the frozen section and I saw him filling up his cart with boxes of sodium-rich TV dinners, I decided it was time to intervene. I was just about to "casually bump into him" when I noticed her.

Amanda was entering the aisle at the opposite end! My pulse quickened. For some reason, the sight of Amanda coming toward us made me acknowledge the nefariousness of my activity. Gail was right. I was stalking Adam. I could not allow myself to be caught and humiliated.

What to do?

My first thought was to grab one of the large frozen turkeys that I was conveniently standing next to, add it to my cart along with the poinsettia, crouch down, and hide behind it. On second thought, I would be a man. Atone for my sins. Go up and speak to him.

On third thought, I grabbed the biggest turkey I could find. I peered over its wings and watched as Adam and Amanda bumped into each other at the far end of the aisle.

"Hi," he said, sounding rattled. He wheeled his cart closer to hers.

"Hello," she said, her shoulders inching toward her ears.

It seemed like they might not say anything else to each other. Five or six seconds—which felt like five or six hours, past. Then they both began speaking at once.

After several starts and stops: "Sorry. You go," they said in unison.

Again, silence.

"Sorry to hear about you and Steven."

"Thanks."

They had another awkward silence, which corresponded perfectly with their rather awkward conversation and their even more awkward relationship.

"I should get going. I have an appointment." Adam sounded formal, cautious.

"Of course, I wouldn't want you to be late for your *appointment*." She gave him an icy smile as Adam began pushing his cart past.

"Before you go," Amanda continued, "I have something else to say. I can't believe you broke up with Steven because he's coming to my wedding. You bastard!" She was screaming now.

It was a very *Knots Landing* moment.

I noticed that a woman who was grabbing a bag of frozen shrimp had stopped to listen to the fight. Her cart provided me with an excellent row of additional camouflage, allowing me to inch my frostbitten face slightly farther back from the frigid turkey.

"Listen, not that it's any of your business, but that's not exactly what happened with me and Steven. Look, I'm sorry for you. But what about me? This is not just about your wedding. This is about a cause!" He matched both Amanda's tenor and passion.

"Whatever you say," she screeched, sarcastically.

"What's that supposed to mean?"

I was shocked by their conduct; I exchanged glances with the woman hiding behind the bag of frozen shrimp who appeared shocked as well.

This didn't seem like Adam and Amanda's sort of behavior at all, but I guess that's what happens to Anglicans when they become intimately involved with Romanians. We rub off on them and they start acting *ethnic*. And the next thing you know, they're screaming at the top of their lungs as they stand in front of the hormone-free, antibiotic-free, organic, free-range, frozen chicken tenders.

They were both shaking and clutching their carts for support. "What do you mean, whatever I say?" Adam shouted.

"This *isn't* about the cause. It's about your obsession with celebrity and your need to always be the center of attention."

Before Adam could respond, Amanda continued: "The entire time I have known Steven, he's been working for the cause. He works for *The Gay New York Times,* for Christ's sake. What exactly have you done? Donated the occasional bunch of balloons to a benefit?"

Adam was furious. His whole body shook with rage. "Listen to me," he screamed. "I have never, in my life, worked with balloons!" He started to push his cart away but Amanda blocked him in.

"Look at me, Adam. Remember me? I thought I was your sister. Am I really the face of the enemy? Am I? You don't think I support the cause? Of course I do. Just explain to me how missing my wedding is going to help you achieve your goal?"

Adam opened his mouth to speak, but Amanda continued. "Please let me finish. Have you ever wondered who I was going to have walk me down the aisle?"

I could see Adam's back stiffen. He slowly shook his head.

Amanda was crying now. "Every single time I look at you, I see our father. I can't even bear to look at your eyes right now. All I see is him. Do you know how it breaks my heart that he won't be there? He *can't* give me away."

"Amanda," Adam started.

"I miss him. I think about him every day."

"Me, too."

"Yeah? At least Father's got a good excuse for skipping my wedding: He's dead! What's your excuse?"

Adam dropped his head, muttered something. I didn't catch it.

"So, Adam, on what is supposed to be the happiest day of my life, I now get to grieve the loss of both the men in my family. I'm getting married in two days. I'll be completely alone. My father will not be there. And you, my only brother, will not be by my side. Thank you!"

"I'm sorry." Adam was shaking.

"If you were really sorry you'd be at my wedding."

Amanda abandoned her cart right there in the aisle, running off before Adam could say a word.

With the show now over, the shrimp lady made a hard right turn with her cart and raced away, leaving me alone with Adam. He was leaning against his cart, crying. I could have easily left the aisle undetected. But even I was not that big a coward.

As I approached him, slowly pushing my cart, I heard him gasping. He seemed short of breath.

"Adam," I said. "Are you all right?"

For a minute, he just looked at me, thrown by my sudden appearance. When he finally spoke it was with effort. "Did you hear all that?"

I nodded.

He wheezed again, his breathing still labored.

"Are you all right?" I asked again.

"Great. My boyfriend left me, my father is dead, and my sister hates me."

"Your sister doesn't hate you," I said, since it was impossible to refute the veracity of his first two statements.

"I need to go home now," Adam muttered wearily. At least his breathing had begun returning to normal. "I should go."

I didn't want him to go yet.

"I'm finished shopping, too," I said too brightly for the occasion. "I'll walk with you to the checkout."

Adam grunted unintelligibly. But I decided to interpret it as *Terrific. I miss you so much. Walk with me.*

We walked, but we didn't say anything. Even though we weren't talking, I was thrilled to discover there was a long line at the cashiers, twisting back and forth and winding its way all the way back into the cheese department. We were going to be together a while.

It seemed we might not say another word to each other. I had to do something about that. "Adam, I couldn't help noticing those strawberries aren't organic."

"Oh? I didn't realize." He removed them from his cart and set them atop the mountain of aged Gouda he was standing beside.

"Steven?" Adam asked, after several long minutes of awkward silence. "I have to ask you something?"

"Yes?" I asked, betraying all of my hope, desperation and longing.

"Why are you buying a poinsettia and a thirty-six-pound frozen turkey?"

Now it was my turn to grunt unintelligibly.

CHAPTER TWENTY-SIX:
TOMORROW WE BECOME ONE FAMILY

A ll the next day, as I took care of a few last-minute errands for the rehearsal dinner, I worried about Adam. I vowed to get through today's party and tomorrow's wedding, and then go right home and work things out with him. My mother was on her way into the city and was planning to come over to Brad's to dress before we traveled together to the rehearsal dinner. She wasn't due for an hour.

I called Vanessa. She was, as I'd learned from Gail, on my side with regard to the wedding issue. Spending so much time with Adam, Vanessa would surely know how he was feeling. I was confident she'd be happy to give me a full report.

"More Wed—I mean, More Parties!" Vanessa said without a hint of exclamation.

"Can you talk?"

"Steven? Yes, I can talk. Adam's in his office. He won't come out unless I pry him out. He's not in great shape."

"I know. I saw him last night. He looked horrible. He was having trouble breathing. That's really why I'm calling. Is he any better today?"

"He's sitting in his office in the dark."

"What? Why?"

"He told me that since all he's trying to do is see into his soul, he has no need for light."

"Please tell me he didn't really say that."

"I'm afraid he did. I'm worried about him. I gather you know he had a run-in with his sister last night. I think it really shook him up. And I suppose I'm also to blame for his consternation," Vanessa confessed. "I've spent the last week telling him that he'll carry the regret of missing Amanda's wedding with him to the grave and beyond. Maybe I went a little too far."

I heard Vanessa's intercom buzz.

"Who are you talking to?" Adam's voice was shallow. I hardly recognized it.

"It was a wrong number, Adam."

"Why doesn't anyone call us anymore?"

"I've told you before, Adam. You're a wedding planner who doesn't plan weddings. That's a very specific target audience you're aiming for."

I heard her click off from Adam.

"Steven," she said. "I've got another four hours with him. I think you should give me the address of the rehearsal dinner. Just in case. I wouldn't bet my new Manolos that he'll show, but you never know."

❖

I looked at my mother as she stood in the foyer of Brad's apartment, and what struck me most was the dress—it was not the black one we'd chosen. It wasn't black at all. It wasn't even gray or beige or brown. It was a riot of color. It was a Pucci-esque floral print created by some designer who had obviously done a lot of psychedelic drugs. Which is not to say that it wasn't attractive. It was actually quite beautiful, and it looked sensational on Onda.

"You look amazing. What happened to the black one we bought?"

"Don't you think it's time I stopped wearing black? Besides, I decided not to give *him* the satisfaction."

Him was my father. And I guess the satisfaction would have been *him* seeing that *she* was still in mourning for *him*.

"Have you seen him yet?" She had dropped the italics on the "him" but she was still very upset.

"I haven't. He called when he got to the hotel, but I haven't seen him."

"I want you to know, Steven, that if you decide not to hug him, I will understand."

My mother has delivered some variation on the "you don't have to hug him" speech every time I've seen my father in the last twenty years. I always hug my father. For so many reasons, I find it very hard to blame him for leaving Onda. I used to wish that he'd taken me with him, but I can't really picture myself in Palm Springs—way too much sunlight for me. The sun is why my father moved there. He worships the sun. He is the blackest white man on earth. He makes George Hamilton look a little pasty. He has no patience for that destroyed-ozone-layer theory. He slathers on the baby oil and he's good to go.

❖

Every time the front door to the restaurant opened, I looked to see if it was Adam.

I noticed my mother marching up to me with a big fake smile plastered on her face. She grabbed my arm and began speaking in a stage whisper. "What are you thinking?" My mother was clearly annoyed with me.

I had no idea what she was talking about; I was standing in the corner of the restaurant minding my own business. I wasn't bothering anyone. I wasn't even talking to anyone.

"You're not talking to them!" My mother motioned across the room to where Margaret was standing with several of her nieces, the bridesmaids, I assumed. "Tomorrow they become a part of our family."

"*Tomorrow* they do?" I asked, not really expecting an answer. As I usually do, I obeyed my mother and glanced over at Margaret. She caught my eye, offered me a large, gleaming white warm smile, and held out her arms to me. Never before had she greeted me in such a fashion.

I approached her, matching her smile in intensity with mine. Just as I was about to hug her, I realized whom she was actually smiling at: my brother, Peter. She held him tightly as she kissed his cheeks.

I tried to inch away before she noticed my outstretched arms and giant grin. I almost got away but not quite. "Steven," she said. "You have a wonderful brother."

"I know," I said. What else was I going to say? I regretted having come over to talk to her and was plotting my escape. "I need to check on my father, excuse me."

"Of course," she said. "Oh, Steven. Have you started dating yet?"

I stood there praying something clever and cutting would pop into my head to say to her, but before I could think of anything the photographer summoned us for a group, family photo.

"Peter, stand next to me," she said, almost blushing.

What? Was she in love with him?

As the photographer adjusted the lighting and we were all kept on hold, I took a step or two away from the group. I felt utterly alone standing close to, but somehow separated from, everyone. My mother had wanted me next to her. But I just couldn't. Not because I wanted to be cruel or anything like that. I didn't. I love my mother. But, at the age of thirty-three, I could not once again step into the role of Onda's surrogate husband. I would be very happy to be a husband. Just not my mother's.

When the photographer was finally ready, I felt a strong arm wrap around my shoulder. Thank God. He'd come.

"Sorry I'm late."

I looked to my right. Saw Brad standing next to me. He smiled.

"You looked like you could use a friend," he said.

"Thanks," I managed.

❖

Dinner arrived. Adam did not.

We were seated at one, incredibly large, King Arthur–size round table, eating the salad course. Beside me was an empty chair intended for Adam. I thought it was a little callous that the chair had not been removed or at least not positioned directly next to me, considering Adam and I were separated.

I thought of Adam's cousin's wedding and that sad, drunk woman Vickie. Her presence had inspired Amanda to accept Peter's proposal. She'd had an effect on me also. I had pitied her, sitting alone, next to the empty chair meant for her adulterous husband. I remembered thinking how that would never be me—wrong! At least I wasn't drunk, although I had done a serious number on the breadbasket.

I was about to take another biscuit when my mother stood to speak. "I would like to welcome you all here tonight. Tomorrow we become one family."

What is with this "about to become one family" nonsense? What exactly have we been for the last six years? I was starting to feel like I should have boycotted the event—it was too late for that now.

My mother continued: "If my husband were alive..."

"I'm right here," my father said brightly, seemingly unfazed by Onda's suggestion that he was no longer breathing.

"If my husband were alive I know just how thrilled he'd be to have Amanda as a daughter-in-law." She had stopped wearing black but had obviously not completely changed her ways.

"I *am* thrilled," my father said as he stood to show the future-in-laws that he was still alive.

"I'm thrilled, too!" said Roz (a.k.a the Secretary).

My mother was about to say something else but my father started a very loud round of applause that thankfully spared us the rest of her speech.

I looked around the table at our one-big-happy-family. Margaret was sitting next to Peter. Actually, if she'd been any closer to him she would have been in his lap. Peter was loving the attention. They had such ease around each other. It didn't seem forced or affected. They were genuinely enjoying each other's company.

Peter leaned into Margaret to listen to a private joke—co-conspirators sharing secrets. Peter stifled a laugh and smiled. She touched his hand.

How much of this was I expected to endure? I had only one recourse—I reached right into the breadbasket and came out holding sourdough. I was reaching for the butter when I saw Margaret stand. Now what?

"May I say something?" Margaret said. She held her glass, something she does quite well. "Today is one of the happiest days of my life. Tomorrow will be a happier day still. Tomorrow I get another son. One that I love very much." She was crying. Not like my mother would cry, but considering her heritage, it was a rather dramatic display of emotion. "Onda, I hope you won't mind me saying this…Peter, I hope you'll start calling me Mom."

I was gagging. It wasn't the speech, exactly. I'd inhaled the roll in one bite.

No one noticed my distress. They were too busy cheering, drinking and congratulating each other on the glorious union.

How was it, with all the weddings I'd attended in my life, that I'd never fully grasped the intense power the institution of marriage has on society? The married are included in a group that the non-married can never be a part of. Without legal rights, we will always be relegated to the status of outsider.

I reached back into the breadbasket. Empty. How many rolls had I eaten? What would I do without more bread? I forced myself to breathe.

It wasn't until I noticed everyone looking at me that I realized I was standing.

"Amanda, you should know that you're about to marry a Romanian. Piriclui Tose Worth is a Romanian *gypsy.*" Technically, my people were not gypsies; I come from a long line of semi-nomadic herdsmen. But gypsy always gets a bigger laugh than semi-nomadic herdsman.

I had no idea what I was saying or where I was going with this speech. "Anyway we don't speak the mother tongue." Again, people laughed—I can't explain why—it must have been the delivery. I think perhaps I made "mother tongue" sound a bit risqué. As I waited the few seconds for the laughter to subside, I realized what I was about to do.

"I do know a couple of Romanian words. Most of them are dirty, but one of them isn't. *Daruta*: It's a pretty ugly-sounding word, isn't it? But it has a beautiful meaning. It means one whose heart is filled with love for their family."

My mother and father were in tears. I saw him reach across the table and gently touch Onda's hand. The WASPs were nodding respectfully as they acknowledged our colorful heritage.

"When I say family," I continued, "I mean it in the largest, most global sense." I became intensely aware of the empty chair next to me. I imagined Adam sitting there—my family, my friend, my love.

I looked at Margaret and raised my glass. "Margaret." That seemed too formal. "Meg." Still not right. Oh, what the heck, *"Mom,"* I said. "Your son, and by that I mean Adam, not Peter, your son is such a person. He is *daruta*. He is love and compassion and conviction. I toast to him."

Everyone raised a glass. I think because they were relieved I'd stopped speaking.

But I hadn't stopped speaking. I raised my glass one more time.

"Peter and Amanda, here's to the two of you. You are so very lucky. I wish you happiness…" I couldn't speak—it wasn't my affliction—I just didn't know what to say.

There was nothing to say. Adam was right. I was wrong. "I hope you accept this as my toast—a day early. Sorry, I won't be at the wedding tomorrow."

I exited to the sound of my mother's wailing.

On the sidewalk, I realized I'd have to go back in—not to apologize. I'd failed to stop at the coat check. I was freezing. I was trying to figure out how to get back in unnoticed, when I saw Adam running toward me. He was carrying a large bouquet of white roses.

He handed me the flowers. I accepted them, although I certainly didn't feel like I deserved them.

"I'm sorry," we said together.

"You were right," we said at the same moment.

"No you were," I said, quickly. "I'm not going."

"I am. I hope you don't mind."

"Adam, you can't go. You were right. I get it now. Nothing will change for us if we keep going to weddings."

"Maybe that's true. I don't know. I don't care." He stopped. Just like last night at the grocery store, Adam began gasping for air. "It's really cold," he said.

I noticed that despite the temperature, there was sweat beading on his forehead. "Adam, are you okay?"

He nodded unconvincingly. "I have to be there for my sister. For my father." His eyes were red-rimmed. "Steven, I think it's okay if we disagree. It's normal. I'm sorry."

I reached out to grab him.

He didn't grab me back.

Instead, he grabbed his chest. He winced with pain. For a second there was stillness and then he fell to the sidewalk.

I was standing on the sidewalk on the spot where Adam had been. My coat was around my shoulders—I've no idea how it got there. I was staring at the ambulance's swirling red lights. Our family was around me—Adam's and mine. There were other people, too—Brad and Chad paced anxiously on the sidewalk. I saw waiters, the coat check girl, and other people I didn't recognize—passersby, I guess.

I saw Adam on a stretcher being loaded into the back of the ambulance—that snapped me into the present. I ran over to join him—started climbing in. My hand was nearly on the stretcher.

The EMT stopped me: "Sir," he barked. "You can't ride with us. You have to follow behind."

I was about to protest but the doors swung shut. I stood in the street, watching the red of the taillights as the ambulance sped away.

CHAPTER TWENTY-SEVEN:
SING OUT, LOUISE!

I leaned up against a vending machine that contained the kind of dreadful coffee that people only drink while they're waiting helplessly in the purgatory of the ER—I was drinking mine black. There was palpable suffering all around me. It was registered on the face of every person in the room. Actually, that's not true—it was not registered on one woman's face.

She was across the room from me. A petite woman of about forty, she was performing "Rose's Turn" from *Gypsy*. She seemed completely oblivious to the fact that this was not exactly an appropriate setting for her one-woman show. She was a little too young for the role and she had a very distracting bandage on her forehead. (I prayed she hadn't been struck by a fuming florist's flying flowers.) But in every other way she was an ideal choice for the part.

Mama Rose sang with absolute conviction, and were it not for the bandage, the venue, and a few distressing facial tics, she could have been a star. I could sense that others in the ER were disturbed by her big number, but I was calmed by it. I found it comforting and encouraging that she was able to continue to create in spite of her obstacles. To me, she symbolized courage, hope, and the ability to survive. Things I needed desperately at the moment. I would have watched her all evening. But alas, five members of the security staff came and whisked her away.

They dragged her, kicking and singing, right past me. She looked at me—it was as if she knew me. And with the strength of Ethel Merman and Rosalind Russell and Angela Lansbury and Tyne Daly and Bernadette Peters and every other woman who has ever played Rose, she broke free from the guards and ran up to me. She clutched my shoulders and shouted, "Sing out, Louise!"

"Yes, Mama," I said as they tackled her, cuffed her, and carted her away.

Peter and Amanda ran over to me to make sure that I was all right. I was not, but it had nothing to do with Mama Rose. I looked at them, realizing that Margaret was not with them. "Where's your mother?" I asked Amanda.

"She's in with Adam."

What? How was that possible? I had tried to get in but had been stopped by security.

I excused myself and walked over to the guard who was keeping me separated from Adam. "Hi. My partner's back there," I said with a smile.

"Yes. You told me." The security guard was smiling, too.

"Right. And you said no one was allowed in."

"I remember," the security guard said.

"But his mother is back there with him."

"Okay."

Okay? The security guard and I did not seem to be communicating. "Do you understand my confusion?"

"I do."

He did. Thank God.

"I'm very sorry," he said. "We do sometimes make exceptions for the immediate family."

"And I am what?" I asked, but my voice was going.

"Look, I'm not a bad guy. It's my job."

"Okay," I said. It was not possible that he heard me. I had developed full-blown laryngitis.

I gave up. I walked away from the security guard. I was defeated.

I saw Peter and Amanda standing together. They were holding hands. She had her head on his shoulder. Amanda was standing in a public place with her head resting on the shoulder of the man she loved. I realized neither of them would ever find themselves in the situation I was facing. No arbitrary law about what it is that makes one person the family of another would ever separate them. If a tragedy struck, they would be at each other's sides. Even if something happened now, as an unmarried couple, they'd have more rights than me. They would just say they were married. They'd never be asked to prove it. They wouldn't have to show a license. Their opposite genders would always gain them access to each other.

And I knew then that I *would* gain access to Adam. No three-hundred-pound guard with a weapon was going to keep us apart. This was so scary. I couldn't believe I was choosing this potentially lethal moment to start living an authentic life. But of course it had to be this moment. My great love was mere feet away, most likely dying. I would not let him die alone. Or, more to the point, I would not be letting him die with Margaret by his side and me in the lobby waiting for Mama Rose to come back for an encore.

I walked back toward the guard. At first, I just felt a little tingle in my throat—it was a slight burn that eased into a pleasant warmth. It felt like I'd eaten honey or sucked on an entire bag of Ricola drops.

"You know what?" I was still a bit hoarse but I was audible. I cleared my throat, gave it another try, and when I spoke again my voice boomed out from me. "You know what? You're right. You are just doing your job. And I'm just doing mine. My partner is back there, dying, for all I know, and I am going to be with him."

"Sir." The security guard tried to interrupt me, but I had kept my mouth shut for far too long. I would not be silenced now.

"While I may not be his legal family," I said, "I assure you, I *am* his family. I am his immediate family!"

"I understand that you're—"

Now it was my turn to cut him off. "I don't need you to tell me what you understand. Let me tell you what you'd better understand: I am going back there right now to be with my partner. *Understand?*"

You could hear a pin drop in the emergency room.

"I can't let you back there," the security guard said.

"I see that you have a gun. So you can, if you choose, blow my head off."

"Sir, I'm not going to—"

"But if you blow my head off, every fag in America will be at the doors of this hospital!"

You know that scene in *Terms of Endearment* when Debra Winger is dying and she's overdue for her medication, but the nurses don't bring it to her so Shirley MacLaine marches down to the nurses' station and just totally goes off on them? That's just how I was. I was screaming and I wasn't scared a bit.

The security guard was begging me to calm down.

I paid him no mind. "Do you hear me?" I was screaming. And then, I somehow managed to shout it even louder. "Do you?" I was certain I'd lose my voice now, but at least it would result from actual vocal strain and not be brought on by some psychosomatically induced aversion to conflict.

Then I heard a meek, frail, little voice whisper, "Steven?"

"What?" I growled.

I turned to look at the owner of this weak voice; it belonged to Adam. He looked pasty and tired but he was dressed and standing. Margaret was by his side.

I looked back to the security guard. Perhaps I had slightly overreacted. "Will you excuse me, please?"

I ran over to Adam. "Didn't you have a heart attack?" My tone suggested disappointment, but I assure you that was not my feeling. I was deeply relieved to see him standing in front of me.

"I had a panic attack," Adam said.

This information took me a moment to process: I'd almost been shot in the head for a panic attack.

"Sweetheart, I'm so sorry." Having had a couple of them during my high school years, I knew how scary they could be. "I thought I was the one who couldn't express emotions," I said lightly.

"Apparently not," Adam said, as he scrutinized the now visibly distraught security guard.

Amanda and Peter ran over to join us. Peter had his arm around me and Amanda was crying and hugging Adam. Everyone was saying, "I'm sorry." "No, I'm sorry." "No. No, *I'm* sorry."

When that stopped, Adam looked at his sister and said, "I hope you'll let me give you away tomorrow, because nothing would bring me more honor. I'll be at your wedding."

"You are absolutely forbidden from attending my wedding," she said.

"Amanda, please don't be hasty. Let's all put this behind us. Your brother wants to come to the wedding," said Margaret.

"He can't," said Amanda.

"Why did I bother to have children?" Margaret wailed.

"I am trying to do the right thing," Adam said to his sister. He was too weak to argue with her.

"I am, too," Amanda said. "And tomorrow when two hundred of our closest friends and family members ask us why the two of you aren't here, I'm going to tell them why. I'm going to tell them how proud I am of you and your decision to stop going to weddings. I'm going to tell all two hundred guests exactly what happened here tonight."

"Could you do me a favor and not mention the panic attack part?" Adam asked, hoping he'd be able to hang on to some small bit of his dignity.

Amanda continued: "Adam, what you and Steven are doing is really important. And I'm sorry that I didn't get it before. What would have happened if Rosa Parks had just gotten off that bus and hailed a cab?"

What is it with everybody and the Rosa Parks comparisons? We're not Rosa Parks. I didn't say anything to Amanda, but as a black woman, in Alabama, in 1955, if Mrs. Parks had tried to hail a cab she would have waited a really, really long time for someone to pick her up.

As we made our way out of the ER and approached the exit to Seventh Avenue South, Peter made an announcement. "I'm changing the name of my shop. What do you think of Great Cakes for Every Occasion Except Weddings?"

We all loved the sentiment but agreed that the name might be a wee bit wordy for an awning.

The cab arrived and Margaret smiled in my direction. I looked behind me to see who she was gazing at—there was no one there. Her tender glance was directed at me. "Thank you, darling, for always taking such good care of my son," she whispered to me.

That was a surprise.

Adam and I got into the back of the cab. I felt the full weight of him as he leaned against me. I wrapped his arm around my shoulder. Adam was shaky and scared, but he'd be fine. His strength would return. Until it did, I was confident that I was strong enough to support him.

Chapter Twenty-eight:
There's No Law against That

If it had just been one or two degrees colder, Amanda and Peter would have had a glorious snow-covered wedding day. Snow falling in Manhattan is always spectacular. It makes the city still and quiet. I'm not sure if that's because people are actually speaking in more reverent, hushed tones or if it's because the drifting snow acts as a blanket, muting the constant blare of the city.

Aside from the odd taxi, streets are free of traffic, but thanks to our amazing subway system, no one is housebound. Residents meet at their local bars and restaurants and celebrate and marvel at the wondrous beauty of nature. Cares melt away from usually harried New Yorkers—everyone looks a little younger, brighter, and well rested. That's what happens here in winter, when precipitation is paired with a thirty-two-degree temperature.

Alas, it was thirty-four degrees. A nasty, pelting, frigid rain was coming down.

I was wearing sweats and I'd laid out a pair for Adam to lounge in. Sweats are a clothing category that neither Adam nor I really approve of. Adam takes issue because their shapeless cut is not chic enough. My chief objection is the drawstring waist. I am terrified of wearing any pair of pants that will continue to fit me comfortably even if I put on forty-seven pounds.

We had made an exception to our no-sweats rule due to the extraordinary circumstances surrounding this day—Adam was recovering, I was nursing him, and we were both hiding away from the world during a near typhoon as our siblings were being married across town, without us in attendance.

That was a lot to deal with; we deserved to be comfy.

I made a big pot of lentil soup. Lentil soup is to Romanians what chicken soup is to Jews. We believe that it has the ability to heal any and all ailments. My mother had called and told me to make the soup for Adam. This was her prescribed course of treatment based on the *di ocui* reading she had just done for him. I was delighted to make the soup; it was so much easier than spitting on him or telling him he was ugly.

After we each finished a bowl, we curled up together on the couch. The kids were on Adam's lap. Thankfully, they were no longer menacing me. But I was being ignored for having abandoned them. I couldn't really blame them; it's always hardest on the children. I wanted Adam to nap but he wasn't tired. He asked me to find an old movie on TV.

As much as Adam and I love old films, we are not experts. We both have huge, glaring holes in our cinema history knowledge. I've never seen *High Noon*, for example. So I started flipping channels. *White Christmas* was playing on two different stations. We watched it long enough to hear Bing Crosby sing "Count Your Blessings." But truthfully, neither of us was really in the mood for a Christmas movie. *The Birds* was on TNT. Adam wanted to watch it but I put my foot down. I was not going to let him see something that scary the day after a major panic attack—I didn't want a relapse.

I continued flipping until I came to AMC. We were just in time for the start of something. They were having a Barbara Stanwyck festival—perfect! We love her. My personal love affair with Ms. Stanwyck began when I was nine years old and saw *The Thorn Birds*. The scene where she's checking out a naked Richard Chamberlain made a lasting impression on me.

"Barbara Stanwyck makes a mother's ultimate sacrifice in *Stella Dallas*," the announcer said.

That sounded great. Neither of us had seen it before. I grabbed a box of Kleenex just in case we needed them (who am I kidding?—of course we did).

Have you seen this movie? There is nothing that Barbara Stanwyck (Stella Dallas) will not do for her daughter. The ultimate sacrifice referred to by the announcer is…

SPOILER ALERT!
You have been warned.

…she gives up her daughter. She sends her daughter—her only child—away so that the girl can have a better life. Stella's from the wrong side of the tracks—she's a good-time girl. She meets and falls in love with the wealthy, educated industrialist Steven Dallas. Despite objections from his family, they wed. They have a daughter named Laurel.

Things are good—for a while.

But Stella can't change her ways. She's no society dame. She's a broad, and proud of it.

Steven and Stella divorce. Stella has custody of Laurel. She loves Laurel and wants Laurel to be classy. Stella doesn't want Laurel to become a hard-drinking partyer like she is. But in spite of her best intentions, Stella is making a complete mess out of motherhood. And so Stella gives up custody and vows to never see her daughter again. She sends Laurel back to her ex-husband, Steven, to live a life of quiet sophistication. And Stella returns to a life of saloons and pool halls.

This would have been more than enough heartbreak for one film—but there's still more.

Laurel grows up. She meets a man. They fall in love and decide to wed. Stella may not be in society, but she does read the society pages. She sees the column about her daughter's wedding—a wedding she will not be attending.

At this point, I thought about turning the movie off. Under the circumstances I thought it would be too stressful for Adam. It was certainly borderline for me. I reached for the remote. Adam snatched it away from me. We were seeing this tale through to its conclusion.

Just as it was pouring rain on this, Peter and Amanda's wedding day, there was a freezing, driving rain the day Laurel's getting married in the movie. We see that Laurel is getting married at home.

She is devastated; she'd sent an invitation to Stella but Stella isn't coming.

Laurel's stepmother, one of those I'm-an-American-but-I-speak-with-a-British-accent types, is comforting Laurel and getting her ready for the ceremony. She tells her stepdaughter that everything Stella has ever done has been for Laurel. Laurel dries her eyes. We hear the wedding march.

Laurel is getting married in her living room standing in front of an enormous bay window. The scene is shot from the street. We see rain hitting the window and we see the beautiful bride within. And then the angle of the camera turns and we see the sidewalk outside of the house *And* we see: STELLA!

She's trudging through the pouring rain in her tattered coat and shabby hat, which are waterlogged and ridiculously out of fashion. But she is there. She is watching her daughter wed. She has kept her word. She has managed to be a part of the day, even if no one else knows.

A huge clap of thunder struck right outside our window just as the end credits rolled. The kids ran and hid. I turned off the TV. Adam was staring at me. "You know, we could..." He didn't have to finish the sentence. I knew exactly what he meant.

We leaped from the couch and headed toward the door.

"Wait," Adam shouted.

"Adam, we have to hurry."

"Fine. But we are not leaving this house in sweats."

He had a point.

Presto change-o! We were looking dapper, and out the door we ran.

❖

Adam and I had been unable to find a cab, so we ran across town, which I didn't think was a good idea in light of Adam's delicate state, but Adam insisted. And you know how men are—there's no talking to them when they have their mind made up. We found ourselves standing in front of a pair of massive, solid oak doors that we definitely could not see through. On the other side of these massive, solid oak doors our siblings were getting married. Terrific. Why had it not occurred to either of us that churches do not have bay windows?

The only good news was the rain had slowed and was now little more than an annoying drizzle. We were not sure what to do. We knew we had to leave before the wedding ended, but our best guess told us that we had at least twenty minutes before they'd be emerging through those massive, solid oak doors (that we could not see through!).

I didn't want Adam spending any more time in the cold—not in his condition. "Let's go back home," I said.

Adam moved to one knee.

Oh, God help me if he is having a heart attack—or even another panic attack, I thought. "Adam, what's the matter?" I didn't sound nearly as hysterical as I actually was.

"Nothing's the matter. I just want to ask you something."

"Adam get up. It's wet."

"Steven, stop talking."

I intended to keep talking until he got up. It was cold, wet and I did not want him getting sick. He interrupted me:

"I'm trying to ask you to marry me," he said on one wet knee.

I started to cry but I didn't know how I was going to tell him I wasn't interested in a fake ceremony. If we ever do it I want a real, legal marriage.

"Adam," I said. I didn't say anything else.

He was still on his knee, his pants now in certain need of a trip to the dry cleaners. "Please. Answer me," he said.

"If we could, I would."

"Is that a yes?"

"Honey, yes. But I—"

Adam stopped me. "Please no buts. I know what you're going to say. I know we can't get married now. I know that. But no one can stop us from getting engaged. Unless I'm mistaken, there's no law against that."

Adam stood. And once again, we were kissing passionately in front of a church. "Someday, the laws will change and we'll get married," Adam said when our lips finally parted. "In the meantime—"

"In the meantime, you can throw us a huge engagement party," I said as we walked down the worn stone steps of the church.

"Great idea," he said. "We can register for Baccarat! I have a feeling you'd like that."

Adam took my hand, holding it as we walked the last of the steps. The drizzle had stopped and things were beginning to dry out. Suddenly it occurred to me that if we were able to marry, I'd become Steven Worth-More.

It has a nice ring to it, I think.

Just then, I noticed an elderly couple on the sidewalk—they were watching us. I became a little self-conscious that we were holding hands, but I resisted the urge to separate from Adam. I held him tightly. Besides, they were eighty if they were a day. I could definitely handle them if they turned ugly.

They did not turn ugly. They smiled. The old man gave us a slight nod.

We smiled, too. I mean, we had been smiling all along, but now we directed our smiles toward them.

"This is my fiancé," I said with pride to the old man and wife. Perhaps I really was saying good-bye to my old, timorous nature.

"We just got engaged!" Adam was jumping up and down.

"Congratulations!" the old man said.

His wife took a step toward us. I noticed the way her husband looked at her—like he was noticing some glorious, enchanted creature that he'd never seen before. His eyes twinkled. He was captivated by her beauty. She put her hand on top of our two joined hands. "So," she said. "When are you getting married?" She was grinning. She was hungry for every detail.

"Well..." Adam said. "We haven't set the date yet."

She cast a glance to her husband—she was just checking in, making sure he was all right. She returned her focus to Adam and me. "Listen to me," she said. "Don't wait too long." She glanced back to her husband.

We watched, as they flirted and laughed and walked away together.

We walked away, too, still holding hands. Adam and I began planning our engagement party. I decided to leave most of the details to him—it was time he got back to work. As we chatted and strolled, and I listened to Adam's rapturous descriptions of finger food and flowers, I was struck by how lucky I was to have Adam in my life. He's my joy. I leaned in, kissed him again, and felt the sun on the back of my neck.

For today, the storm had passed. The clouds lifted. Adam and I broke from our embrace and turned around so we could feel the warmth of the sun on our faces. Adam saw it first. I didn't believe it, but there it was—barely visible, almost obscured by the skyline, but there was no denying it was there—a rainbow. You never see a rainbow in New York City.

And it wasn't just any rainbow. The colors weren't pale, and it lacked the typical, ephemeral quality of rainbows I'd seen before. This thing was painted across the sky with a bright Crayola primary palette. In fact, this rainbow looked exactly like one of those silly gay flags.

My mother would have taken that as a sign—a good omen.

Maybe. We'll see.

APPENDIX

Inspired by Adam and Steven and interested in becoming part of the movement? Please visit the websites of these worthwhile organizations and get involved:

1n10
www.1n10.org

American Foundation for Equal Rights
www.afer.org

Broadway Impact
www.broadwayimpact.com

Catholics for Equality
www.Catholicsforequality.org

Connecting Rainbows
www.connectingrainbows.ning.com

Couples for Equality
www.couplesforequality.org

Courage Campaign
www.couragecampaign.org

Empowering Spirits Foundation
www.empoweringspirits.org

Equality Across America
www.equalityacrossamerica.org

eQualityGiving
www.equalitygiving.org

Equality Matters
www.equalitymatters.org

Equal Rights Washington
www.equalrightswashington.org

Family Equality Council
www.familyequality.org

Fierce
www.fiercenyc.org

Fight Out Loud
www.fightoutloud.org

Freedom to Marry
www.freedomtomarry.org

Gay and Lesbian Victory Fund
www.victoryfund.org

GetEQUAL
www.getequal.org

Human Rights Campaign
www.hrc.org

Immigration Equality
www.immigrationequality.org

Join the Impact
www.jointheimpact.com

Know Thy Neighbor
www.knowthyneighbor.org

Marriage Equality USA
www.marriageequality.org

Minnesotans United for All Families
www.munited.org

National LGBT Museum
www.nationallgbtmuseum.org

National Marriage Boycott
www.marriageboycott.ning.com

National Stonewall Democrats
www.stonewalldemocrats.org

PFLAG: Parents, Families & Friends of Lesbians and Gays
www.pflag.org

People for the American Way
www.pfaw.org

Queer Rising
www.queerrising.org

Save Dade
www.savedade.org

Standing on the Side of Love
www.standingonthesideoflove.org

The Ali Forney Center
www.aliforneycenter.org

Truth Wins Out
www.truthwinsout.org

White Knot for Equality
www.whiteknot.org

About the Author

Ken O'Neill was born in Bridgeport, Connecticut, to an Irish Catholic father and a Romanian Orthodox mother, which means that most years he had the good fortune to receive Easter candy not just once but twice.

Ken lives in New York City with his partner and their two cats. When he's not checking his Amazon rating to see if anyone is buying his book, he enjoys reading, dancing (though usually when no one is watching), and eating dark chocolate, purely for medicinal reasons.

The Marrying Kind is his first novel.

Visit Ken at: www.themarryingkind.org

Books Available From Bold Strokes Books

The Marrying Kind by Ken O'Neill. Just when successful wedding planner Adam More decides to protest inequality by quitting the business and boycotting marriage entirely, his only sibling announces her engagement. (978-1-60282-670-0)

Sweat: Gay Jock Erotica by Todd Gregory. Sizzling tales of smoking-hot sex with the athletic studs everyone fantasizes about. (978-1-60282-669-4)

Missing by P.J. Trebelhorn. FBI agent Olivia Andrews knows exactly what she wants out of life, but then she's forced to rethink everything when she meets fellow agent Sophie Kane while investigating a child abduction. (978-1-60282-668-7)

Touch Me Gently by D. Jackson Leigh. Secrets have always meant heartbreak and banishment to Salem Lacey—until she meets the beautiful and mysterious Knox Bolander and learns some secrets are necessary. (978-1-60282-667-0)

Slingshot by Carsen Taite. Bounty hunter Luca Bennett takes on a seemingly simple job for defense attorney Ronnie Moreno, but the job quickly turns complicated and dangerous, as does her attraction to the elusive Ronnie Moreno. (978-1-60282-666-3)

Dark Wings Descending by Lesley Davis. What if the demons you face in life are real? Chicago detective Rafe Douglas is about to find out. (978-1-60282-660-1)

sunfall by Nell Stark and Trinity Tam. The final installment of the everafter series. Valentine Darrow and Alexa Newland work to rebuild their relationship even as they find themselves at the heart of the struggle that will determine a new world order for vampires and wereshifters. (978-1-60282-661-8)

Mission of Desire by Terri Richards. Nicole Kennedy finds herself in Africa at the center of an international conspiracy and is rescued by the beautiful but arrogant government agent Kira Anthony—but can Nicole trust Kira, or is she blinded by desire? (978-1-60282-662-5)

Boys of Summer, edited by Steve Berman. Stories of young love and adventure, when the sky's ceiling is a bright blue marvel, when another boy's laughter at the beach can distract from dull summer jobs. (978-1-60282-663-2)

The Locket and the Flintlock by Rebecca S. Buck. When Regency gentlewoman Lucia Foxe is robbed on the highway, will the masked outlaw who stole Lucia's precious locket also claim her heart? (978-1-60282-664-9)

Calendar Boys by Logan Zachary. A man a month will keep you excited year-round. (978-1-60282-665-6)

Burgundy Betrayal by Sheri Lewis Wohl. Park Ranger Kara Lynch has no idea she's a witch until dead bodies begin to pile up in her park, forcing her to turn to beautiful and sexy shape-shifter Camille Black Wolf for help in stopping a rogue werewolf. (978-1-60282-654-0)

The Fling by Rebekah Weatherspoon. When the ultimate fantasy of a one-night stand with her trainer, Oksana Gorinkov, suddenly turns into more, reality show producer Annie Collins opens her life to a new type of love she's never imagined. (978-1-60282-656-4)

Ill Will by J.M. Redmann. New Orleans PI Micky Knight must untangle a twisted web of healthcare fraud that leads to murder—and puts those closest to her most at risk. (978-1-60282-657-1)

Buccaneer Island by J.P. Beausejour. In the rough world of Caribbean piracy, a man is what he makes of himself—or what a stronger man makes of him. (978-1-60282-658-8)

Twelve O'Clock Tales by Felice Picano. The fourth collection of short fiction by legendary novelist and memoirist Felice Picano. Thirteen dark tales that will thrill and disturb, discomfort and titillate, enthrall and leave you wondering. (978-1-60282-659-5)

Words to Die By by William Holden. Sixteen answers to the question: What causes a mind to curdle? (978-1-60282-653-3)